And I Serve the Fairy Queen

Book Three
of
The Return of the Tribes

By Alice Taylor

First Edition

The Rum Lot Publishing
Lowestoft, Suffolk, UK
2025

ISBN- 978-1-918079-07-4
Paperback Edition

Books of this series are available for download on

Amazon Kindle
or
The Rum Lot Publishing
www.rumlot.com

"Over hill, over dale,
Thorough bush, thorough brier,
Over park, over pale,
Thorough flood, thorough fire,
I do wander everywhere,
Swifter than the moon's sphere;
And I serve the fairy queen,
To dew her orbs upon the green.

– Puck, Midsummer's Night Dream

Prologue

Caddy sat in the international terminal of Los Angeles International Airport, waiting to board her flight to Bangkok. She was alone.

Ricky sat back in Texas, insisting that he couldn't take even a day off work and doggedly sticking to his routine. Lizzie came back home to take care of him while Caddy was gone. She was a daddy's girl anyway, and he would listen to her. At least he would be fed, and Lizzie would make sure he didn't do anything stupid.

Resenting her husband, she smouldered as she sat by the huge windows that overlooked her gate and worked on her fourth Fiendish Sudoku of the day.

Three months earlier, poor sweet John had died in a car wreck, hit head-on by a drunk driver speeding at two in the morning on the wrong side of the road down a dark godforsaken stretch of FM 483. It took three hours before anyone spotted the smouldering tangle of wrecked cars when a pick-up load of Mexican ranch hands drove by on their way to repair some fence. The three hours later didn't matter; no one in either car had a chance in hell anyway.

Caddy was the one who identified the body. She was the one who called Lizzie and broke her heart with the news. And, gods help her, she was the one who stood in the echoing atrium of the government office building where Ricky worked and told her husband he had to come home because John was in a car crash. And John didn't make it out.

Ricky fell apart.

Caddy was the one who made the funeral arrangements, and she was the one who went, alone, to clean out her boy's apartment in Austin. And months later, she was the one still settling the affairs of a bright young man who had no will but who did have a good job with life insurance, bank accounts, a pension he would never use, and all the bits and chattels of a modern life.

Ricky spent the first month sitting in his dark home office and staring at the blank screen of his computer. He wouldn't talk to anyone about John. Then he went back to work and the routine of his old life, but only on the surface. John had died, but Ricky was the ghost.

He moved out of their bedroom and, for the first time in thirty-five years, slept in the spare room. He said the bed was better for his back. He would take his dinner, such as it was, to his office, where he studied his Russian and kept up with the news coming out of the Soviet Union. Changes were coming, he said, and he needed to be on top of them.

There were days when Caddy went to work, and she didn't see Ricky at all. He would drive off to Lackland before she was up, and he would come home late and go straight to his office at home. She knew he hadn't moved out because there was a light under the door of his office, and she found his dirty clothes in the hamper for her to wash. But he didn't want to talk to her because if he did, she might say something about John.

John was their first. According to the nurse's notes, Caddy was an "elderly prima gravida" when she found she was pregnant at twenty-seven. She and Ricky had been married for four years and had an active and unprotected sex life, but no babies. They were just starting to think something might be wrong when Caddy fell pregnant. Everything went smoothly, and nine months later, they were a real family. Ricky was over the moon. Lizzie arrived two years later, and Conary was a thirty-fifth birthday surprise for Caddy. Ricky doted on his three beautiful, red-haired children.

Conary was difficult. He was slow walking and slow talking and slow at everything. Just when Caddy and Ricky would have arguments over whether to take him to a specialist or not, he'd just do whatever milestone needed to be done. He would barely move, and the next day he was walking. He never said a word, and then the next day he was speaking in full sentences and giving baby lectures on dinosaurs.

When he was seventeen, he was an unhappy, brooding loner holed up in his bedroom listening to Aerosmith and the Dead. Then he was invited to a party, and eighteen hellish months later, he was out of the house, a heroin addict living in a squat somewhere in Austin, Texas, totally cut off from his family. The police were no help at all; they said he was over eighteen and free to go anywhere if he wanted to. So Caddy filed a missing person's report and did what she could to find him, but he vanished as if he never existed.

Then, four years after Conary disappeared without a trace, John died, and when Caddy was cleaning out his flat in Austin, she found a scrap of paper in his desk. It was Conary's address. John's brother was in Bangkok, and he had kept it a secret from his parents. Caddy had a pretty good idea why Bangkok was a draw for a drug addict – but maybe, just maybe, her baby boy was there. Maybe he could be saved.

She wrote to the address. Unsurprisingly, no answer. She asked Ricky to go with her to Bangkok and see if they could find Conary, and he was appalled, then furious. He was NOT going to take time off work to go on a wild goose chase to *Bangkok*. He absolutely forbade Caddy from going. It was too risky. Bangkok! Didn't she know what that city was like? No, it was too risky, too foolish, too – unplanned. The possible bad outcomes that would come from such a wild, half-cocked, wasteful, useless journey were more than he could process.

So she bought herself a single ticket, packed a bag, and told Ricky through his locked office door that she was going to Bangkok for three weeks to hunt for Conary, and Lizzie would be there in the morning. Then she got in the waiting taxi and left.

Of course, she never found Conary. Caddy went to every doss house, every bar, every hostel, every beach where drug-addled westerners hung out and partied, and found nothing. She filed missing persons reports at the American and British embassies, and while she got sympathetic looks, she didn't get any information. She felt in her bones he was there and that he hadn't moved on to some other place where lost souls gathered. Several times, she had that mother instinct, or maybe it was her sleeping abilities, but she was sure in her heart that she had just missed him. Once she *knew* he was watching her. But nothing.

When Ricky called her, sobbing on the phone and begging her to come back home, she readily agreed. She had done everything she could.

Three months later, the Thai police posted a small cardboard box to Texas. It was Conary's ashes. An unknown American with no ID had been found on a beach, dead from an overdose. Someone in a Bangkok morgue matched up the body with the missing person's report and made a positive ID. In between the time the body was found and the match made the body had been cremated. The box came with an invoice, and Caddy paid it and put the box on the top shelf of her bedroom closet.

Book Three Begins

Kyrylo

"I'm the lucky one; we're not married."

Months later, that still bothered Kyrylo. It was an offhand comment, a joke, but it was the truth. When that banquet guest had turned to Lord Kyrylo and complimented him on his luck with finding such a lovely wife, Caddy had made her joke, and everyone had a good laugh.

He loved her with all his heart, but he hadn't asked her to marry him. Did it matter? Do lords even marry?

He was pretty sure she loved him just as passionately, but –

– but she had had lovers before him who were still around. Neptune was still floating around doing his Lord of the Sea thing, and he was pretty stiff competition. Kieran was human, but a nice guy, and although he had moved on and married someone else, he was still out there. Kyrylo knew all she had to do was bat an eye, and both would come running back.

But there was also the possibility that more lords would pop out of the woodwork. A new female had shown up a couple of months ago. Alizah. She was still in rehab, and it looked like she was healing well, but what she represented was more important. Her existence showed that lords were out there, hiding amongst the humans. Most, like Kyrylo before he met Caddy, probably didn't even know they were lords.

Part of Caddy's master plan was to introduce the lord and elven tribes to the humans in a non-threatening way and use any publicity generated to offer a home to any lost lords. It had worked with Alizah. It would work again.

In a very short time, the world had gone from no elves and three lords (two of whom were stuck in their morph bodies) to six lords and hundreds of thousands of elves and merfolk, with more coming every day. It was Caddy's mission in her long life ahead to guide that transition, and Kyrylo's lifelong mission to support Caddy in any way he could.

Was it selfish to try to lock her down? To tie her formally to him? What if her Real True Love was sitting in Albuquerque or Pretoria, and he was standing in her way?

Kyrylo wasn't worried about missing out on any unknown female lord pining for him in the fjords like a Pythonesque Norwegian Blue Parrot. He was fully bonded to Lord Cadence Aeldor, and that would not change. According to Bram, the only way he could un-bond with her was to die.

And that was part of the problem.

She had never said she was bonded to him; she had never mentioned marriage. She said she loved him. She said it every day. But she said that to others, too. Shit, she said that to Ellen and every elf she met. She said it to her customers at The Rum Lot.

So Kyrylo nursed his insecurities and brooded about what to do and say, and Caddy wondered what the hell was wrong with him.

Ellen

Ellen pondered the invitation and talked it over with Norma. Of course, Caddy would make the final decision on whether to accept or not, but it was Ellen's job to think of the pros and cons and look at it from all sides, particularly from the public relations angle.

Lord Cadence Aeldor and Lord Kyrylo Melnyk were invited to visit the UN in New York as representatives of the Elf Nation. They wouldn't be asking for formal membership; this was just a toe-in-the-water visit. They'd just sit in a special gallery and watch some speeches as a non-member observer state, wave to the crowds, go to some cocktail parties and a banquet or two, and generally just have a good ol' schmooze.

Ellen was sure that if it were known Lord Cadence was in New York, she'd also get an invite to Washington and probably every other country in North and South America.

The problem was security. There were no awakened elves on the North American continent, so all security would have to be handled with local assets and their own human security force.

Caddy had already been kidnapped once. That wasn't going to happen again.

America was very far away.

Ellen and Norma started typing and soon had a brief exploring all possibilities, which was emailed to both lords.

Caddy

Caddy sat in her office and dandled Matt Hadid on her lap while she looked over his mother's brief. He gurgled and threw a dinosaur rattle on the floor. She mentally picked it up and levitated it back to him, which made him laugh, and he plucked the toy out of the air and threw it on the floor again.

They did this over and over and over. He never tired of throwing things on the floor and watching her bring them back.

Kyrylo walked in just as Matt threw the rattle on the floor for the 11,564th time.

"What are you doing?"

"Multi-tasking. Reading this UN paper, exercising my abilities with this damn rattle, watching Matt while Ellen is busy, and waiting for you so we can have lunch." Suddenly, she stood up and held the surprised baby at arm's length. He made a little o with this mouth and began to concentrate. Magic was happening.

"Norma! Somebody! SHITTY BABY!" An elf popped in, and Caddy handed off the baby, and they decided to eat elsewhere. The room smelled.

As Caddy reached for her hat, she said, "And there we see the benefit of having staff. I must have changed ten thousand diapers between three kids, and I don't need any more practice."

"I've never changed a diaper in my life. I wouldn't know where to start." Kyrylo sniffed the air, grateful that wasn't ever going to be a talent he'd have to develop.

"At the bottom, of course. Where do you want to eat?"

They decided, for a change, to go to the Hatfield, where they lucked on a nice sea-view table and a lovely portion of fish and chips. Caddy asked Kyrylo if he had had time to read Ellen's UN paper; he had, so they discussed it over lunch. Kyrylo, as always, zeroed in on security issues. They would have to fly in, and while heads of state from around the world flew into NYC almost every day and no one got shot down, that didn't make him feel a whole lot better about it. They would be pretty helpless in a jet flying into New York City, and it was one of the few places their individual abilities wouldn't do a whole lot of good if they were attacked. Anyone who was really out to get them would know that.

"Lester would certainly see that as a weak spot." Kyrylo dipped a chip into some ketchup and popped it in his mouth. He wasn't going full-on Brit yet, and he was not a salt and vinegar man.

"Yeah, he wouldn't be able to resist taking us both out at the same time."

"I will think –" Kyrylo smiled. "Or maybe I think too fast and should say, do you want to go at all? Maybe I don't need to worry if you're not keen on going."

"Oh, I think it would be a good thing to go. Ellen's paper lays out all the positives, and there are a lot. So I'm willing if everyone can work it out so you're happy."

He nodded and worked on his fish. As they got up to leave, Caddy pointed out the window and turned to smile at him.

"Look! A cruise ship! We don't see big ships like that this close to shore very often. I bet it's out of Harwich. Did I ever tell you about the one time I almost took a cruise?"

"No, you'll have to tell me."

They walked home up the Prom, and Caddy told about when she went a-roaming to Ukraine and how she used a cruise as a feint to throw the elves off her trail.

"I should be grateful the cruise ship kept to its schedule!"

"Why?"

"Because you can say that if it weren't for a cruise leaving exactly on time, you might not have made it across the Channel undetected, and I wouldn't be with you today. "

She hugged his arm.

"I would have found you eventually. I'm pretty determined when I put my mind to something."

He smiled down at her. "Determined" was an understatement.

Kyrylo

The next morning, they started the return journey to Ukraine, and travelling between their homes always involved a lot of fuss and bother. Since the UK and Ukraine were separated by the Channel, it meant that an unbroken porting chain directly from one place to the other wasn't possible because the stretch of water was too wide for elves to cross. When elves first came to ancient Britain, there had been a land bridge called Doggerland. Now the space between modern France and Great Britain was water, and no elves lived within porting distance.

They could take the train, which was two to three hours from London to Brussels, and from there they could port home and be at their door in Ukraine in fifteen minutes – if all the ports worked as they should. Or they could fly to a secure elf-owned landing strip in France and again be in Ukraine in fifteen minutes. The hour-and-a-half by helicopter from Lowestoft to France was a pain, although Caddy frequently reminded herself and anyone who would listen that it was a marker of how spoiled they were that they would complain about a two-hour commute door-to-door when her first trip to The Wall in Ukraine took four days.

As they waited for the helicopter, Kyrylo took Norma aside and asked how she had worked out the cruise trip. The elf rolled her eyes.

"Oh, I had it all planned. It was going to be lovely. Ms Caddy seemed excited about it, although what she really wanted was one of the big ships where she could get lost in the crowd. But for me, it was perfect. I could put lots of security on there, and they wouldn't be intrusive, and it was pretty secure." Then the elf glowered. "But it was only secure if she was on the freaking thing in the first place. She scarpered, and our security guys were trapped on the ship, and it was all a fucking disaster."

"Are there any cruise ships that go to New York?" Kyrylo laughed. "And you have to stop rolling your eyes at me. They'll get stuck."

"Look, I'll send you some links."

"At this point, this is just between us, Norma."

Norma nodded and did the key thing with fingers and lips. She could keep a secret.

Kyrylo

Kyrylo liked England, but he loved Ukraine and going back home meant he could speak Ukrainian, eat real food, and watch some football on his sofa in the sitting room. It was home. Of course, Caddy felt the same way about Lowestoft, so she had worked hard to establish a chain of elf ports across Europe so they could go quickly from western France to eastern Ukraine, and that allowed them to live in both places. Many people had worse commutes.

Now that he was back home, Kyrylo could go visit the training compounds that had been set up to train both elves and pro-elf humans how to deal with orcs and the humans who worked with them.

Lester lived on the other side of The Wall, and Kyrylo knew he was always pushing and probing for weak spots. Incursions happened regularly, and while the Ukrainian border guards took care of most of the raids, they weren't private bodyguards for lords and elves, and that's why Kyrylo took their own security personally in hand. When Caddy was kidnapped, that laid bare how vulnerable they could be. It was only Lester's stupidity that kept her alive long enough for Kyrylo to plan her rescue. Next time, he would kill her the first minute he could.

Caddy went out once a week, usually on Thursday, to wake up elves and establish a new node. Where she went was determined in a meeting every Monday. Was the location a part of their strategic plan? Was it secure? Was the weather favourable? Did the elf-parazzi and elf-stalkers on social media have it staked out? And, most of all, did Caddy sense that there were elves there, waiting to come out of hibernation? Not every place had elves, and there was no use going to the fuss and bother of scheduling an elf re-birthing if there were no elves underground to call up.

Today's meeting discussed the issues with Belarus. Belarus was still under the influence of Russia, so that meant Lester pulled the strings in that government. If Lester convinced the Russians to reboot their failed invasion, Belarus was a risk. Most of the Russian populace were kind, decent people, but that didn't matter if the government was not. Russia wasn't a democracy; the people were firmly under control, although most didn't realise their controllers were orcs and a rogue lord. The ones who didn't care. Lester kept them rich and pampered.

Poland and Lithuania were eager for Caddy to work her way up the Belarusian border, while Ukraine wanted to concentrate on covering the entire Ukrainian interior, not just the borders. The Ukrainians wanted complete coverage, just like she had established in England. Once she had opened up a node, the "pioneer" elves who lived in that area would go and wake up their friends and relatives, so it wasn't like she had to wake up millions of elves across Ukraine herself.

Ukraine, however, was a very large country and would need many more than the eight nodes that Caddy had started in the UK. Many, many more.

Caddy and Kyrylo

The meeting room was large, but then it had to be. There were a lot of people in there. This Monday meeting included small delegations from Ukraine, NATO, the EU, Poland, and Lithuania, along with representatives from the elf security team, the Ukrainian border guards, and observers from Korea, the United States, and the UK. The delegations were small, but if you have enough small delegations, you still end up with a very crowded room.

Kyrylo and Caddy arrived early to walk around the room, shake hands, and welcome their visitors. Elves bustled around with coffee, trays of snacks, and helped their guests set up their wifi. Their visitors always came in a good mood. Each of them had had an elf visit their work, embassy, or hotel in Warsaw or Kyiv and personally port them to the meeting, which was a very impressive perk to show off to your colleagues. A limo? That was nothing. Having an elf in uniform show up in your waiting room and port you out – that impressed whoever was watching. For some reason, all the generals and diplomats liked porting in public, even though it was just as easy to port out from the privacy of their offices.

Bram announced that everyone should please take their seats, and Lord Kyrylo would open the meeting and do a quick overview of the issues they were here to discuss.

And so the meeting started, and it took all morning. Pros and cons of different locations were debated, and everyone had a few minutes to sell their point of view and subtly disparage everyone else's.

The elves served a massive lunch for their guests, and Caddy went around to every table and talked to all the delegates. Kyrylo could tell that some, especially anyone new to meeting a lord, didn't quite know what to think of her. He thought she was gorgeous, but then he looked at her through the lens of love.

Anyone else, though, would think she was cute, but it was her lord and elf characteristics that made her striking. She was at full health now, which meant she looked neither young nor old. The little wrinkled face that Kyrylo first saw on that snowy day in Ukraine was now firm and mostly smooth with just a few lines around the eyes that only showed when she laughed. The only thing that betrayed her great age was her snow white hair. And from a distance, if you couldn't see her otherworldly green eyes, the only thing that showed she was a lord was her ears. They were getting a bit pointy as her body shed its human genes, but she had done a complete morph to escape her kidnap prison, and when she had come out of the shape-change, she had full-on elf ears. Because he had never morphed, Kyrylo's ears were changing much more slowly, but now they were distinctly elfen. And both lords' ears twitched.

Caddy laughed and talked with the delegates, doing her best to charm them. It was her mission to build human support for her elves, and this backroom work was how she did it. These were all men and women with important jobs, and most of them had egos to match. A few bold ones were a bit, as Caddy would say, handsy.

An affair with the Queen of the Fairies! Now wouldn't that be something to write in your memoirs!

Kyrylo was deep in discussion with the EU delegation and hinting at a possible visit to Brussels when he looked up and saw him. An American colonel assigned to NATO reached over and touched Caddy's ear. She was turned away from him, talking with someone else, and he stroked her ear.

The EU men saw the lord freeze. They looked at what the lord was looking at, and one later told his wife that he had never seen anyone so angry in his life. They knew the lords were magical. Lord Cadence's famous line, "I don't *do* magic, I *am* magic," was known everywhere and printed on t-shirts. But they had never seen a lord's eyes glow with fury. They certainly had never seen one lift his hand, flick it, and send a man flying across the room for touching his wife.

The colonel went flying, hit the wall with a splat, and then did a slow-motion slump to the floor. A soldier elf ran up to him, and both immediately disappeared, leaving nothing but a streak of blood and a big dent on the wall.

The room froze.

Caddy looked around, and her eyes glowed bright green, but the corner of her mouth twitched. She stood up.

"Gentlemen. This meeting is over. We're so happy you came and hope to see you again very soon. Our decision on the location of the next node will be made and will be relayed to your offices. Any personnel [and she looked to the spot where the colonel met the unfortunate wall] left behind will be returned as soon as they are ambulatory. Goodbye!"

The tension broke, the delegates babbled nervously, and everyone wrote notes for long reports of the meeting when they got back home. What Lord Kyrylo did took a chapter all by itself.

Caddy and Kyrylo ported out.

Kyrylo and Caddy

"Fucking bastard is lucky I didn't kill him!" Kyrylo was still furious. Not with Caddy; she hadn't even known the man was going to touch her, but with that idiot.

"That wouldn't have been proportional and would have meant a lot of cleaning up." She wasn't mad at K for teaching the colonel a lesson; he was just defending her. But killing him? That would have been unfortunate.

He was calming down and started thinking about the ramifications.

"I lost my temper."

"Oh, yes."

"Are you mad at me?"

"No, he was wrong and certainly cheeky. You just caught him before I did."

She looked at him and then smiled. Caveman Kyrylo was a bit intriguing. He was normally so disciplined and controlled.

She leaned over and kissed him on the cheek.

"You can touch my ears any time you want."

"I will, but later when I can do them justice. I think I should go visit with my victim and send him on his way."

"Should I come with you?"

"No, he might do a Trump pussy grab. The man has no manners at all."

Kyrylo

Kyrylo walked into the infirmary where the colonel was sitting on a gurney, rubbing his neck. Healer elves had him patched up and had fixed a broken shoulder blade and a slipped disc he already had.

The man looked up as the lord walked in and had the common sense to be terrified.

Kyrylo had to pause and adjust his thinking. He had just been speaking elvish with the healers, and he spoke Ukrainian in Ukraine, but this guy was American, so English now. His English was very good, but he still had a Ukrainian accent. That would never go away.

"What is your name?"

"Whitman, sir. Lord Kyrylo."

"You touched Lord Cadence's ear."

"I – yes – I deeply apologise. I don't know what came over me. I'm really sorry to have offended her. And you."

Kyrylo frowned at Whitman, his one good eye snapping with sparks of blue.

"Are you married?"

Whitman looked confused.

"Yes, Lord Kyrylo, I am. Eighteen years. Four kids."

"And what part of your wife's body do you allow strangers to touch?"

The colonel turned bright red.

"None, sir. I don't know how to apologise more. If it helps, I'll have to explain this whole incident to my wife and my superior officers. I'll probably lose my career over this. It won't do my marriage any good either."

He looked glum.

"If I'm lucky, they'll let me work to retirement scheduling the Vermont National Guard's spring training."

Kyrylo nodded.

"I was in the Soviet Army and then for many years, the Ukrainian Army. I'm sure you know that. I know how the military works when an officer disgraces himself."

Whitman winced. Disgrace. Conduct unbecoming. He could get court-martialed for common assault if this thing snowballed. He really fucked up.

"I will tell your people that you have apologised, and I have accepted your apology. Lord Cadence will back this up. She is much softer than I am and will feel sympathy for your wife and children. What your superiors decide to do to you is up to them. I will not try to influence them one way or the other."

He paused.

"The elves have fixed any broken bones as well as an old back problem. You are fit now, and they will take you back to your office."

Kyrylo turned and left without another word.

Whitman put his head in his hands, but he didn't have to wait long. Two elves, probably their version of military police, popped in and took him back to work.

Kyrylo

That afternoon, Kyrylo's office sent a letter to the relevant NATO and American Army officers saying that Whitman had apologised to both lords' satisfaction, and the colonel's apology was accepted. As far as they were concerned, the incident was over.

Caddy was unperturbed by the entire brouhaha. It would get around the diplomatic gossip chain quickly, and that might prevent other handsy guys with ideas from copping a feel. It was also a hint at what they could do when provoked. She was sure there were a lot of analysts thinking about the military implications of Kyrylos's body slam. A little fear and uncertainty when negotiating with the guy on the other side of the table was not always a bad thing.

The next morning, they received hand-delivered letters of apology to their embassy in Kyiv.

Kyrylo

He opened the letter and read it again. There it was. "We sincerely and deeply apologise for any upset this unfortunate incident has given you and your wife…"

Wife.

He was going to have to do something. He felt like he was wearing an unearned medal. He felt like a fraud. Everyone thought she was his wife and treated *him* like he was the husband of the Queen of the Fairies, and he hadn't even asked her to marry him.

Caddy had married twice. Her first husband had only lasted six months and was a bigamist. He used her, and it broke her heart. Her second husband loved her, and they were married for fifty-five years. Then he died, and it broke her heart.

Kyrylo didn't know if those two marriages would turn her off the idea or not. His own bad luck with Katya hadn't spoiled his opinion of marriage, but then, he wasn't Caddy.

He was totally lost. If he asked her and she said no –

If this were a military campaign, he would know exactly what to do.

So that's what he did. Caddy had once sat down and mapped out how she was going to integrate the elves into the modern world, so now Kyrylo decided to map out a campaign to marry Caddy. Only his campaign wasn't to gradually integrate; it was to conquer.

Alizah

The Breakfast Room of the stately home was sunny and cheerful and simply oozed comfort. Caddy was quite pleased with the old house when she first saw it. It was huge and wonderfully eccentric as it mished-mashed architecture from the fifteenth century to modern times. She especially liked the turrets. She always liked a good turret.

The estate was purchased to house Alizah through her rehab and training. Caddy wanted a place that was a calm retreat and utterly private, with huge grounds that would allow whoever lived there to practise their abilities in peace. She also wanted it to be well within range of the Lowestoft elves. So the Lowestoft clans found a place in rural Suffolk that could be purchased with a minimum of fuss and met all of Caddy's requirements. It was then totally modernised and now boasted stables, a heliport, a pool, and all the mod cons. Then they proceeded to erase the entire estate from all records, road signs, and maps, and went so far as to raid all the old bookstores to capture every physical book or magazine that mentioned it in any way. When they were done, it essentially ceased to exist. Like House and The Rum Lot's front door, you only found the entrance if you were meant to.

Alizah was the only lord who lived there, but the staff was pretty big, so Caddy was sure she wasn't lonely. There was a massive security presence, not to keep her in, but to keep others out. There were as many humans who worked there as there were elves to include a full-time psychologist, and Caddy hoped that Alizah wouldn't feel like she was the weird one in a sea of elves.

The estate, now known as Aelfeham House, was to be the place where newly found lords could rehabilitate, be trained, and be evaluated. Caddy knew not everyone would be as wonderful as Kyrylo, so new members to their club would have to be handled carefully.

Alizah was fifty-five, looked like she was seventy-five, and was a drug addict. She had lived on the streets of London, turning tricks and getting high since she was fourteen and was probably one of the most damaged individuals Caddy had ever come across. With no education, no hope, and absolutely sure she was crazy, she had turned to drugs, and her body showed every homemade tattoo, self-mutilation, broken tooth, needle track, abscess, frostbite damage, and scar she had earned from her years on the street. Caddy looked old as a supercentenarian, but when Alizah first walked in, she looked older at half the age. The elf healers didn't think she would have had more than a few months to live if she had gone on the way she was. Her body couldn't take another overdose.

But four months after that fateful day when she had somehow gotten through the gates at the London embassy and run to Caddy, she was a changed woman. She could pass for sixty now, but more importantly, she was drug, scar, and (mostly) tattoo free. She still carried hidden psychological damage and probably would for years, but she was, as she said, in a good place now.

Today, Alizah was to meet Kyrylo and Jack for the first time. Caddy visited with her every time she came to Lowestoft and talked to her daily by videoconference. She was very involved with the psychologists and the elf healers who worked with Alizah.

The psychologist's name was Zoya, and she was a little fireball of a woman with experience in dealing with war veterans and torture victims, and if anyone had been through a lifetime of wars, it was Alizah. It was Zoya who escorted Alizah into the room to meet the other lords and make the introductions. Caddy knew that they had been practising this for weeks, so Alizah would know exactly what to expect.

She bowed and shook Kyrylo's hand and called him Lord Kyrylo. She bowed to Jack and called him Lord Jack, and then bowed to Caddy, but Caddy earned a huge smile as well as a bow. Alizah was painfully, pitifully grateful she had been rescued by the lords, and Caddy was her lodestone.

They sat down for tea, something else Alizah had been practising. While it seemed that this was all a bit Eliza Doolittle, the goal was that she would feel comfortable in social situations, as it was discomfort, embarrassment, and insecurity that would make her fall into old thought patterns – and the comfort of drugs.

They chatted and laughed, and as she relaxed, Alizah felt more and more at home with her lord peers. She learned that Jack would be flying in every day to talk to her about being a lord and to talk about their history. Maybe a raven wasn't the best example of being a lord, but Caddy and Kyrylo couldn't spend the time with her that she needed, Neptune was off the grid, so that left House and Lester. House was occupied being a house, and Lester was occupied being an asshole, so Jack volunteered to pick up the reins.

Kyrylo (under previous instructions) spontaneously asked if Alizah could show them around the grounds, which she readily agreed to do.

It was a bit overcast and breezy, but what's a little wind? They walked out to the paddocks and Alizah showed them the horses, then out past the herb gardens and the parterre, and that's when Alizah blew away.

A stiff gust danced by, and the woman simply tumbled head over heels down the wide lawns like an out-of-control party balloon. Caddy and Kyrylo looked at each other, mouths agape, and then both started running after the bouncing lord.

Jack flew as hard as he could and caught up with her after a very high bounce and grabbed a piece of her dress, but he didn't have the weight, and he wasn't able to hang on. Kyrylo tried to grab her with the tractor beam version of his ability, but she was bouncing around too erratically for him to get a good fix on, and he was afraid of hurting her if he messed up.

Eventually, she was snagged by a tree branch, and that allowed Kyrylo to catch up to her, grab her by the ankle, and pull her down. By the time Zoya and Caddy ran up, Aliza was in tears. She was so embarrassed she didn't know what to do.

"I'm so sorry, Ms Caddy! I didn't mean –" And she started sobbing again.

Caddy went up and hugged her fiercely and laughed. "I think, dear Alizah, that we have figured out your talent! You can fly on the wind!" Alizah gulped and looked at the lord dancing around. "How wonderful!"

"I thought I just fell down a lot. I'm always falling down. I'm really clumsy."

Jack tilted his head and made a raven chuckle. "Alizah, I think you've been falling *up*. Since humans can't fall up, they told you that you were falling down, and, of course, you believed them."

Kyrylo and Caddy nodded in agreement, and while Zoya looked a bit stunned, she was professional enough to make this a positive moment.

"A very good day indeed! Alizah, I'm so proud of you!" And that made Alizah cry again.

After some thought, Jack suggested that Alizah wasn't flying on the wind, and he wondered if she was controlling her own gravity. Caddy asked him to be the lead in helping train her because the woman would need to learn how to deal with flying, wind, weather, and such. She also needed to learn how to come down without hurting herself. Jack was enthusiastic, and Caddy felt Alizah was in good hands. Or claws. Or whatever.

Zoya tendered her resignation that afternoon, which was disappointing, but it wasn't like they could keep her there if she didn't feel comfortable working with lords. It turned out that while she was fine dealing with elves, and she was fine dealing with Caddy on Zoom, when she actually saw a glowing-eyed lord doing lordy things, she was not fine; she was terrified. The talking raven was really the last straw, and if Jack was going to be there every day, Zoya said she had to go.

She was reminded about her non-disclosure agreements and given a nice going-away bonus and sent packing.

HR started advertising for replacements the next day, but it turned out Alizah didn't need them. She had Jack.

Caddy and Kyrylo

Brenda showed off her new earrings to Caddy during breakfast. Normally, Kyrylo would pay absolutely no attention to her primping and preening, but today he was interested. Without looking up from his tablet, he typed the name of the elf who made them.

Caddy thought they were very pretty and told the elf so, and she bent down to look at them more closely. Kyrylo looked up and peered at the elf's ears.

"Do you want a pair, Caddy?"

Caddy laughed. "K! Have you ever seen me in earrings?"

"Why not? You have very pretty ears. That Whitman man couldn't keep his hands off them."

"I'm not a jewellery girl, I guess. No one has ever bought me jewellery, and I'm too cheap to buy it for myself. I think you have to get used to the idea of wearing it."

"You used to wear that necklace. That gold coin."

She looked at Kyrylo with something like pity. "That was a credit card carrier."

"Oh, yeah. Well, you had engagement rings, didn't you?"

"Nope. I had two wedding rings. One of them was sold, and the other is in the bedroom in Lowestoft, in a box next to Conary's ashes. That is the full extent of the Aeldor Family Jewels."

Kyrylo was appalled. Who didn't buy their woman jewellery? She was married for fifty-five years! Ricky loved her! Katya demanded jewellery for every holiday. Shit, she would probably have demanded a bangle for National Pancake Day if she had known the holiday existed. Then he remembered he had never bought Caddy anything remotely like jewellery.

How could he have neglected that?

Kyrylo

"BRAM!"

Kyrylo was in his office at work. Caddy was at home practising her violin, so he had some time to himself.

"Yes, Boss?"

"Have you heard of this guy?" And he shoved the tablet at the elf. Bram stroked his beard and then looked up, puzzled.

"Jared of the Zakarpattia clan? Yeah, I've heard of him. He's the best in the business, but he makes jewellery, not weapons. He'll make you a pretty knife hilt, but you'll have to get the blade from a knifesmith."

"Take me to him."

"Sure, Boss. When?"

"Now."

Jared

Jared was sitting at his bench working on a particularly tricky bit of enamelling when the lord popped in unannounced. He looked up. It must be Lord Kyrylo because who else would it be? There weren't many lords around. Then he went back to his work.

The lord stood there patiently, waiting for the craftsman to finish his task. The workshop was a dark clutter of strange machines, presses, forges, and racks and racks of neatly arranged tools. The place was immaculate. The workbench looked like you could do surgery on it.

The elf stood up and bowed to the lord. In the back of the room, Kyrylo saw a door inch open and a woman with a baby peeked out. When she saw him look at he,r she squeaked and ducked back in.

"Lord Kyrylo, how can I help you?"

"I've heard you make pretty things, and I have a job for you."

Kyrylo

That night, Kyrylo went to his tablet, pulled up the Caddy plan, and ticked off the ring task. Done.

Then he spent the evening looking at the links Norma had sent him. Transatlantic cruises to New York City out of Southampton. It seemed there were a lot of them.

Neptune

The merman hauled his bulk onto the sand on the South Beach and waited. A few minutes later, an elf appeared, and he gave him the message. The elf delivered the message to Norma and then returned to the beach with a six-pack of lager to give to the merman.

Norma opened the message, scanned it, and sent it to Kyrylo's private box.

It was from Neptune, and it was simple. "Don't forget to bring Caddy to me."

Kyrylo could not have been more upset if Neptune had poked out his remaining eye.

Kyrylo and Caddy

Kyrylo walked to the sitting room like a man walking to the gallows. Caddy was sitting on the couch playing the guitar he had bought her in Odessa during that wonderful weekend they had become a couple.

She looked up and gave him one of her beautiful smiles, and then the smile faded. Something was wrong.

"Caddy." And he cleared his throat. "I have received a message from Neptune."

"Oh! Really? What does he want?" And she held out her hand for the tablet and read it. She raised an eyebrow, shrugged, and handed the tablet back.

"Oh, no worries. I'm fine with that. You and the team can arrange it, and I'll go and make him a happy chappy."

Fully expecting Kyrylo to be relieved and pleased, no one was more surprised than Caddy when he went pale, then red, and then threw his tablet to the ground and stormed outside, slamming the door so hard her teeth rattled.

Shocked, Caddy followed him out to the porch. There were no elves around, and usually there were, but as soon as they saw the lord and his thundercloud face, they had disappeared.

"K, what's wrong, I don't –"

He swung around and glared, then he threw up his hands and turned to lean on the porch railing.

"Caddy, I'm a simple man in many ways. I know I wear this lord thing now, but I was brought up human. I know that elves and some people have much more liberal or just different ideas about fidelity and sex and all that." He turned to her, and he was so upset that his eye glowed and his voice shook. "In my world, a man doesn't give his wife away to someone else to fuck. I did. And now I have to arrange it. "

"Kyrylo…"

"AND YOU ARE OKAY WITH IT!" And he turned and looked out over the garden.

"KYRYLO!"

Caddy didn't know whether to be furious or hysterical with laughter. She opted for fury, and when Kyrylo turned back to her, he met with Fury Caddy. She stood with one hand on her hip, and she poked him hard in the chest with her finger. He remembered the last time she did that.

"Now you *listen* to me!"

"For one thing, I am NOT going to sleep with Neptune. I don't want to. Besides, he wasn't asking for that. He was asking –" and she poked him again. " – for me to perform *music, not* sex acts! He wants me to sing for him and his people."

"Caddy –" Kyrylo wasn't buying it, but he listened.

"If he wanted to bonk me, he wouldn't ask you for permission. From his point of view, what do you have to do with that? You don't own me. He'd just ask me directly. He's not shy."

She poked him again.

"And another thing, have you ever seen a dolphin penis? Well, that man is half fish, and the fish bits are below the waist. The ONLY people he can screw with are other merfolk. Men, women – he's not too picky. The ONLY way for him to have relations with human types is to morph and go on land so his bottom half matches his top. He didn't say anything about meeting me on land to visit, did he? He reminded you to bring me to him, *which would be to the sea.* He didn't say anything about screwing, did he?

And she poked again.

"That was all in your head. You assumed. And you assumed you had the right to say yes or no. And you don't. The ONLY person who decides who I fuck is me. Not elves, not Neptune, and not you. *Me.*"

And she spun around and stomped off, closing the door firmly behind her.

Kyrylo watched the door close, stunned. Then he took a big, shuddering gulp of air and sighed. Oh, shit. Out of the corner of his eye, he saw Bram port in.

"Boss?"

"Bram, I think I might have screwed up."

"Yes, Boss, I think you have."

He sighed again.

"Now, I think I should go fix this."

"Yes, Boss. The longer you wait, the worse it will get. You know women; they brood over things for a long time, holding it all in. Making assumptions."

"Bram, if I knew women, I wouldn't be in this mess.""You said it, Boss, not me."

He glared at his PA and then, with another sigh, went inside to face the music. And Caddy was the master of music, not him.

Caddy lay on the bed, staring at the ceiling, still not knowing if she should laugh or cry. The silly man must have been moping over this for months now! She knew something was bothering him, but she had no idea he was agonising over Neptune's casual invitation. There was no doubt in her mind that Neptune just wanted a concert. The merfolk would probably have a party and dance and get roaring drunk, and then it would end with the inevitable spawning ball, but she wouldn't take part in any of that. She wasn't much of a drinker, and group sex wasn't her thing.

He was jealous and insecure, and he didn't say anything because he was afraid of what she would say.

That made her angry, and the more she thought about it, the angrier she got. It wasn't only that he had given himself permission to pass her on like a breeding mare, even if it was tearing him up inside; it was also that he didn't have faith in her, that he didn't believe she was as committed to him as he was to her. He thought his mare would bolt.

THEN he had the audacity to call her his wife. Well, that was going to come to a head today. They were *not* married. He had never asked her, and she had never asked him, and the last time she looked into it, there was more to the marriage thing than just assuming.

Someone knocked on the door.

She knew it would be Kyrylo; elves don't knock. They just port in. It had taken a long time to train them not to do that, and she had given them windows of time when they absolutely could not come in unannounced. Having an elf peer over the side of a bed when one was in *flagrante delicto* was unnerving. She even kicked the dogs out of the bedroom when she and Ricky were doing it.

She waited.

He knocked again. "Caddy?"

He looked in. She was lying on the bed, staring at the ceiling. She didn't say anything, but she wasn't crying, and that told Kyrylo she was still very, very angry.

He went to his side of the bed, and like her, lay down fully clothed and stared at the ceiling. He didn't even try to touch her.

"I'm sorry, Caddy." His voice was rough. "You are absolutely right. I assumed, and I assumed totally wrong. I can't tell you how badly I feel for hurting you. "

She didn't look at him. If she did, she'd have to kiss him, and that would be letting him off too easily.

"You didn't have faith in me. I'm not mad about you saying, 'I was okay with it.' What really hurts is that you've been carrying this around because you didn't have the faith in me to say no to Neptune *if* he asked me (and he didn't)." She turned her head to look at him. "If you had said something when this first started to bother you, I would've told you what he meant and just laughed it off. But you were jealous, and you didn't trust me."

Kyrylo didn't look at her. He just closed his eye and said, "Yeah, I was jealous. I'm still jealous. You slept with him in the past, so you must have loved him, and he's a fully intact, very powerful Lord of the Sea." His voice broke. "It's a miracle you are here with me. God knows I love you. But there he is – Lord of the Sea. He's hot. I don't even bend that way, and I can see he's hot. I was afraid you'd leave me and go back to him, given half a chance. I'm still afraid you'll leave me for someone better. I can't help it."

Caddy sniffled and took his hand, all promises to herself that he needed to be taught a lesson swept away.

"Of course, I love Neptune. I loved him then, and I love him now, just not in the same way and certainly not the way I love you. He taught me a lot about myself, and I had a lot of good times with him. He was exactly the right man for me for *that short time of my life*, and then it was over. K, you are exactly the right man for me for now and for *all* of my life.

"He took a month or so of my past. You are all of my future, and from what I've been told, I have a very long future to look forward to. I love you madly, sweetheart, but I can't change my past, and I really don't want to. Before I met you, Neptune and I split up. I could've gone back to him at any time, and I know he would've gladly taken me back – on his terms – but I didn't want him then, and I don't want him now."

He squeezed her hand so hard it hurt.

"K, no matter what men come and go around me, whether they are lords or kings or film stars, you must promise me you'll always have faith in me just as I have faith in you. I won't let you down, I promise."

He turned to her, his eye bright. "I'll never let you down, Caddy, I promise. I told Neptune I'd die for you, and I meant it. I love you, Caddy."

"I know you do, love. I know. I heard you tell Neptune, 'My life for hers.' I was an octopus then and not in the best of shape, but I could still hear fine. And he laughed and said you were being dramatic. So you see, I heard the whole thing and didn't think anything of it. I had no idea you were brooding over it until fifteen minutes ago."

Kyrylo sighed. What could he say to that? That he was an idiot, and he was sorry?

"I'm an idiot. I am so sorry, Caddy."

She kissed him on the cheek and jumped up before he could take advantage of the opening.

"You're not an idiot. Apologies accepted and I'm not mad any more. There's a new cake in the kitchen; let's go down and have a slice. I think it's chocolate!"

So they went down and had cake, which fixes everything.

Kyrylo

Kyrylo sprang up bolt upright in bed and just had to go to his tablet. The idea was just too good to wait, and possibly forget, until morning. Caddy snuffled and gave a little snore, but she didn't wake up.

Norma was narrowing down their trans-Atlantic sailing prospects, and they almost had it nailed down. Could she persuade – and pay – the shipping company to have a four or five-hour stop in the middle of the trip? Somewhere over the rift valley that follows the Mid-Atlantic ridge, right in the centre of the Atlantic. If they stopped, Caddy could go out there on a tender or lifeboat and play for Neptune.

Kyrylo could fulfil his promise to bring Caddy to Neptune, and it wouldn't be on some seductive tropical island. She wouldn't go off on her own; Kyrylo could be there the whole time. The location could be in deep water, which would make the merfolk happy, and if Caddy woke up a few merfolk sleeping in the trench with her music, then Neptune would be happy.

After the concert, they would continue their voyage, all debts paid in full.

He hoped Norma could make it work.

The next day, Norma video-called him and they had a long talk. Everything with the ship, including the stop, was a go. The only thing that would prevent them from stopping was weather, and Cunard's was adamant that the EN understood that it *was* the Atlantic and that the ship's captain had the final call on whether to pause or not. Otherwise, it was just a matter of money to pay for the time and trouble, and the elves had that.

Norma and Ellen were still working on the diplomatic itinerary for when they landed and where they were going to stay. Once that was set, the return trip would be booked. It was all coming together.

It was time to tell Caddy.

Kyrylo and Caddy

After dinner, Kyrylo asked Caddy if he could talk to her in the sitting room. He was nervous, and it showed. What if she objected to his Neptune plans or sighed and went along with it? What if she said a flat no? He knew she wouldn't, but his life was filled with improbable impossibilities, so he never took anything as given. There were no sure things in Kyrylo's world.

Caddy sat on the edge of the couch and looked at him expectantly. She knew something was up. There was a football match tonight on the telly, and if this took a long time, K was going to miss the start. Shakhtar Donetsk was playing Dynamo Kyiv. This must be important.

He cleared his throat, and Caddy smiled encouragingly. *Get on with it, man.*

Then he dove right in, flipping through his tablet's PowerPoint as he talked. He told her what he and Norma planned, all about the ship, the stop mid-Atlantic to play for Neptune, and a rough idea of the itinerary in New York. As he was going on about the meeting at the UN, the most important bit, she put her hand on his arm to stop him. He looked up at her, and her face was all scrunched up.

Oh, shit.

"You're taking me on a cruise? We're not flying?"

"No, I thought a cruise would be more fun for you. And we can get that blasted Neptune out of the way. A jet wouldn't be –"

And she threw her arms around him and screamed. "A CRUISE!! You're taking me on a holiday!"

"Well, yes, that's what I planned. You deserve a real holiday, and you've said you've never been on a cruise."

Caddy started to sniffle, "That's the sweetest thing anyone's ever done for me."

"A real holiday," she marvelled, "No visiting relatives or working during the day or hauling kids to uni and calling it a holiday. No one's ever taken me on a real, proper vacation with silly drinks with umbrellas and pools and eating out every night and music."

Kyrylo pulled her into his lap and let her give him a teary hug. He was so relieved he could have cried, too, but he didn't. It was all the reaction he could have hoped for.

Caddy was thrilled all out of proportion to the event. If Kyrylo had known how much a cruise meant to her, he would have done it ages ago.

She pestered him with questions all through the game. He missed seeing a goal while he looked up the suite Norma had booked on the internet, so she could look it over.

When he asked if there was anything Caddy wanted to change, she was startled. Of course, not; it was all perfect.

"Even the bit in the middle with Neptune? This cruise is supposed to be a holiday, and I've scheduled work in the middle of it. And New York is going to be work, I know."

Impatiently, Caddy waved concerns about Neptune away. She wasn't worried about him at all. She could put a concert together with her eyes closed that would make the old grouper happy, and she would play whatever she wanted, so that would be fun for her, too.

As they went to bed, Caddy turned to him and gave him a hug.

"Y'know, K, this is the nicest thing anyone's ever done for me. Really. I know this took a lot of planning and messing with, and I know it's not something you'd do if you had your choice of holidays. I've spent my whole life taking care of other people, and now you're taking care of me. I really appreciate that."

There were more tears in her eyes, and all Kyrylo could do was hug her and kiss the top of her head.

From then on, it was Cruise Prep 24/7 in the Aeldor-Melnyk household. Outfits were planned for two weeks at sea (seven days there and five days back on two different ships) and four days of hardcore diplomatic elbow-rubbing in the US. They were invited to Washington, but Caddy vetoed that idea. It was too early for that high-level stuff. They needed to concentrate on winning over the public, so she told Ellen to schedule an interview with someone major and some sort of charity gig. They were to emphasise Caddy's time in Texas. Maybe take in a ball game. This was going to be a charm offensive; diplomacy would be much easier later when they had the American public on their side.

None of the upper staff had ever been to the US. They didn't even know many Americans, so Caddy warned them not to underestimate the cultural differences. She had lived and worked in Texas for forty-seven years, and they were weird. Americans dominated popular culture worldwide, but that didn't mean people from outside really knew what Yanks were like in the privacy of their own homes. People in the US thought differently from Europeans and made no apologies for it.

With no elves on the North American continent and no way for European elves to reach them, security for the lords was a big issue. There weren't any plans to wake up elves because once they hit land, there would be no privacy at all, and Caddy wouldn't work her magic out in the open when the re-birthed elves would be at their most vulnerable.

It would be entirely old-school travelling and guarding, and New York was sure to be filled with orcs. It was decided that Rahim would not go as the security chief but would be the man in charge in Europe while Kyrylo was gone. Instead, a newer guy, Jameson, would be the lead during the trip. He was American and ex-Secret Service, so that would be a plus.

Kyrylo planned and obsessed over the security. There was Lester to worry about, of course, but there were also radical Christian extremists making threats, something that surprised everyone but Caddy. The lords' and elves' very existence was an affront to their literal interpretation of the Bible, and "do not suffer a witch to live" had a long, long history. The Salem witchcraft trials were not as much an aberration as they were an indication.

But the biggest worries were with crowds. There were no elves in America and no lords that anyone knew of. The American public had read and watched the emergence of the two tribes in Europe with rapt and sometimes hysterical fascination. Now the two lords were coming over, and, if they were lucky, they could be seen in person. The crowds were expected to be huge.

Cruise day approached, and Caddy and Kyrylo moved to Lowestoft for the final preparations.

Captain Wilson and LeeAnne

Captain Wilson rubbed his temples, and LeeAnne knew her dad was pissed. Really pissed. Her mother had that cheerful frozen look where her mouth smiled, but her eyes didn't. It meant she was really pissed.

They were both really pissed at her. They were being *so-o* unreasonable.

"Lee, sweetie, it would mean a lot to me –"

"DADDY! It's not fair. I've been planning on this convention for months! All of my friends will be there!" She wailed with all the fine, high drama a sixteen-year-old girl could wail. "I have all my clothes!"

Her mother soothed. "Darling, we know cancelling is a disappointment, but –"

Wilson looked at his distraught daughter. He was at sea, on a video call, so there was that psychological distance that talking through a screen always brought. He could call her every day, but that wouldn't make up for not being there, and he knew that. All her life, he was Zoom Daddy, and only rarely was he Home Daddy. That's what she used to call him. Zoom Daddy and Home Daddy. She loved Home Daddy more and said so.

But you don't make captain on a trans-Atlantic ocean liner by neglecting your career. Choices were made, and he provided a very comfortable living for his wife and daughter. They could sail with him whenever they wanted, and when LeeAnne was little, that's what they did. But as his baby girl grew up and her friends at school became more important, those family trips became fewer and fewer.

There wouldn't be many after this one, he knew, when boyfriends and uni and jobs would get in the way.

Captain Wilson looked at LeeAnne, and his eyes were so sad. There she was, his little girl, still sitting in her bedroom at home. You couldn't get any pinker, frillier, lacier, or more flowery than that bedroom, and on the walls were poster after poster of AI paintings of elves and drawings of the Fairy King and Queen. Like a lot of girls in the last year, she was elf mad. The convention she was so desperate to go to was about elves and fairies and all that nonsense. They had a singer as a headliner who dressed like Lord Cadence and sang K-pop and E-pop. Those tickets were hard to get, and all of her friends were going.

Poppy looked at her daughter and sighed. Daddy looked so disappointed. LeeAnne wailed a heart-wrenching "ARRGHH…" then sobbed out an *okay*, and she cut off the call. She had no choice but to go. But she didn't have to be happy about it. This was going to scar her forever. This was going to ruin her life.

She cried all night and then cried the next day when she had to tell her friends she wasn't going with them. She cried when she sold her concert ticket to her best friend's new boyfriend so he could go, too.

She would go with her parents on this stupid trip on his stupid boat with all the stupid old people, and he would get his stupid award to go on his stupid wall with all the others, and she would stand there with her proud mum and pretend to be a proud daughter, and they would all be in the stupid photo.

But she absolutely refused to have a good time. That was *not* going to happen. This was going to be a life-altering event. She'd never get over it.

Lester

The wide veranda at Putin's Sochi palace was bathed in bright sunlight. Underneath the gently swaying white curtains of the marquee, Putin and Lord Lester shared an al fresco lunch. Off to the side, a contortionist in an incredible and vaguely obscene pose was playing a balalaika with her feet. She wasn't very good at it, but the music was hardly the point.

Lord Lester looked at the old man with undisguised calculation. He had a conundrum that he had never encountered before in the three thousand five hundred years he had been the Earth's supreme lord. It's *only* lord for all practical purposes.

Should he stay anonymous, a shadowy figure in the background of the Russian government, or should he take his proper and rightful place in the forefront as a leader of the country?

Specifically, how was he going to handle this Putin matter if Lester was the leader of Russia? The old dear was as senile as a slug and was well past his sell-by date, which was unusual for a garden-variety dictator. Usually, they flamed out, and Lester simply found another to take their place, but Putin had been useful for a long time and had clung on despite the odds and the animosity of the West.

Normally, Lester's habit was to find a powerful but weak leader and simply take him over and so rule from behind the throne with the patsy taking all of the blame if things went sour.

The lord had no illusions that if humans and orcs got fed up with him, they could kill him just like they did with all of the other weak lords they found. His powers were in fomenting doubt, anxiety, and depression in the susceptible and then making them feel that he, Lester, was the solution to all of that unhappiness. Past that, he was pretty small cheese in the lord business. He couldn't even lift things, and he certainly couldn't shape-change. If a band of furious humans came after him with a pitchfork, there wouldn't be much he could do against a tidal wave of emotion other than try to talk himself out of the danger. He could manage two or three people at a time. He couldn't manage a mob.

But he could manage a small group of psychopaths, sociopaths, and neurotics that rose to the top of the heap because they were almost always humans and didn't have the nose of the orcs. To keep the orcs in line, all he had to do was take frequent baths to keep down his own scent and surround himself with a layer of humans between himself and the orcs.

Hitler was a good example. He had been a true find. He had talents in oratory and a devious mind, but gods, was he insecure. Lester played him and his jolly band of sociopaths like puppets until they imploded. Then he simply changed uniforms and stepped into Stalin's court.

Russia was a good gig for him. It had the natural resources and a large human population mixed in with plenty of stupid orcs to send out if a baby lord showed up and needed to be eliminated. For centuries, Lester hadn't had any other lords to worry about. He didn't know about the hidden ones like Neptune, but if any remained hidden, he was fine with that. They were as good as dead.

If a lord soul found its way out of the Void and managed to find a fertile human or orc female and get born, the odds against them even making it out of childhood were astronomical. Usually, the humans and orcs eliminated them without Lester having to bother, and that was how huge parts of the world stayed in line. The weak and the weird and the ones who smelled bad to the orcs were labelled as witches and demons, and the humans played along and killed them. Who wanted a baby whose eyes glowed?

Lester, Neptune, and any hidden lords didn't have human parents, so they weren't infected with human cells to age into senescence. As long as they ate well and didn't get in the way of an arrow or bullet to the brain, they would live forever.

Human-born lords had to live long enough to use their abilities, and only then would they gradually erase their human side and become full lords. With no elves around to encourage them to use their powers and gradually wipe out their human genes, the human-bred lords who did manage to live to adulthood eventually succumbed to their human old age and died. It was a Catch-22. Use your powers and start to smell like a lord to an orc, and they kill you. Don't use your powers and keep your human side dominant, and eventually you die of some human disease or old age.

But now things were changing. Somehow, that idiot Kyrylo had stirred some elves up. He was obviously an Elemental. That woman of his had smelled bad to his orcs, but Lester had assumed it was just because Kyrylo was banging her, and his smell rubbed off. Lester was sure the odds of two lords meeting were astronomical, but he was wrong. Now he had to assume she was a lord, too.

But two lords *did* meet, they did bring back elves, and now they set themselves up as king and queen of the elves and came out to the public, which meant they weren't afraid of orcs or Lester. They knew Lester existed and both took his attempt to kill Kyrylo personally, so the pair of them turned into a direct threat to Lester. For the first time, he had to deal with a real opponent. An Elemental opponent.

A mature Elemental opponent with elves and another lord to back him up. Kyrylo scared Lester shitless.

The question ran in tight circles in his brain like a mouse caught in a bottle. Should he remain hidden or come out like they did and publicly gather his own power base?

Putin tried to spread some butter on a piece of bread and was having a hard time of it. One of the contortionists released her pose, trotted over in her bare feet, and spread the butter for him, and then returned to another impossible position.

The gentle wind and hot sun of Sochi competed for dominance on the wide terrace. Lester sat on the fading and fraying garden furniture that couldn't be replaced because of the West's ridiculous sanctions and watched the old man eat his lunch while he pondered his future.

Lester made his decision. He would come out. He would leave the shadows and emerge as the new leader of Russia. After all, the people who mattered in Russia already called him the Tsar in a half-joking way. It wouldn't take much to make it official.

He wasn't going to mess around with elections either. That nonsense was not for him. It was demeaning to run around and beg for votes from toothless old women in cheap puffer jackets. He wouldn't do it.

Instead, he simply convinced the Patriarch and the right oligarchs that it was time to openly reestablish the Court of the Tsar. He would be the new Tsar and unite all of Russia under one double-headed black eagle. They had wanted to bring back the Tsar and a true monarchy ever since the Russian War, so it wasn't a hard sell. He just had to convince them he was the anointed one. Easy.

He even had a beautiful Tsarina in mind so he could pose as a stud (which he was, of course) and a family man, which appealed to the average Russian. He could always buy a kid if need be.

Lena was still around after that disastrous attempt to capture Kyrylo using that Cadence woman as bait, and she lived in an apartment near the Kremlin. Maybe by marrying her, Kyrylo would be less inclined to bomb the crap out of Lester's home, especially if he thought his daughter was sleeping next to the Tsar. You don't assassinate your son-in-law, can you? Well, actually, history was rife with murdering royal relatives, but Lester needed all the insurance he could buy.

Yes, she was Ukrainian but spoke Russian, too, and she was highly decorative and completely controllable. When he didn't need her any more, he would divorce her, and, in any case, she would age out of the job in a few years.

So, Lester I, Tsar of all the Russias, was secretly crowned in St. Basil's along with the love of his life, Tsarina Lena. Putin made a statesmanlike, heavily enhanced, and edited video giving Lester his blessing and returned to Sochi to forget what he had just done and cavort with the Russian national gymnastics team.

Now, Lester just had to find a flashy way to announce his God-endorsed ascension to the world..

Caddy and Kyrylo

Outfits were packed, and a ridiculous amount of luggage mysteriously appeared in the Grand Duplex Suites, as well as the dozens of less grand cabins booked for the RumLot Security team, a lady's maid, and a valet. There was a lot of security, but the shipboard agents were just part of the overall operation. An advance team was flying to New York City.

No one on the *Queen Catherine* ever saw an elf, but they were all over the ship checking security and making note of any orcs on board with the passengers and crew. There were only three – two below-deck kitchen help and one in the purser's office – and all three suddenly became violently ill and had to go onshore to the hospital, where they miraculously recovered as soon as the ship left Southampton.

At the appointed time, Caddy and Kyrylo ported to a private waiting room on the dock where everyone showed their passports, and then, as a group, they boarded the ship.

Caddy would have skipped with excitement, but she was wearing high heels.

Thank goodness they didn't have to walk far.

The Wilsons

Poppy and LeeAnne stood at the end of the gangplank where the guests boarded the ship. It wasn't really a "gangplank" but more of a bridgeway like you see in an airport, but that's what they still called it. Jeremy had insisted they come, and he insisted they dress "presentable," so Poppy spent the morning fighting with LeeAnne as to whose definition of presentable was going to prevail.

Poppy was confused because Jeremy usually didn't ask her to be at the Welcome Event for VIPs, but today he insisted, and she suspected that a very, very VIP was coming on board. When she asked directly, he wouldn't say. He almost seemed afraid to. That only deepened her suspicions, and while she didn't say anything to LeeAnne, Poppy was on her toes, alert for whoever was coming on board. A movie star? The Prime Minister? She couldn't imagine who. Tip-top bigwigs didn't take cruise ships for obvious privacy and security reasons; they had their own yachts, and those who didn't rented them. Wilson's ship was a Cunard luxury ocean liner, but their passengers were drawn from the upper middle classes, sensible old money, new richies, and rock stars who didn't like flying, and it wasn't often they lured in the really big beasts.

Jeremy had a wire in his ear. Poppy could see it. This meant something. He turned to her, grinned and winked, and Poppy gripped LeeAnne's arm and gave it a shake.

"Mummy! You're hurting me!" LeeAnne grumbled and returned to sulking. She was on a roll.

"Look!"

And they walked out of the gate. The King and Queen of the Fairies. Surrounded by about a dozen uniformed human Rumlot Security guards, all dressed in their dark green elf-made livery. Gawd, they were all gorgeous.

The guards, male and female, were hard, sleek, and dangerous-looking. Their livery was an Eisenhower jacket of finely embroidered green wool picked out in dark red or dark blue, matching trousers, and soft black knee boots hiding holsters with elaborate hilts peeking out of them. The bodyguards openly wore pistols in finely-tooled belts, and one wore a sword. They all had jaunty elf-caps on with a long feather stuck in. They were as sexy as hell.

Lord Cadence wore a smart green and brown pencil-skirted suit, a jacket with a peplum, and a hat that tilted at a dangerous angle. She was dressed exactly like a 1940s film star. Lord Kyrylo was in a dark brown jacket, tan wool trousers, a crisp white shirt, and a tie. He wore a fedora and brown-and-white derby shoes. With his eyepatch, trim beard, and waxed moustache, he lived up to the Danger Santa meme and more. LeeAnne could have cried.

Lord Cadence walked up, beaming, and anyone could see she was absolutely delighted to be there. LeeAnne seriously thought she was going to faint. Her knees got weak, but her mum kept her steady. Daddy was already leaning forward to shake the lord's hand.

"Lord Cadence, welcome aboard the *Queen Catherine*! May I introduce my wife, Poppy and my daughter LeeAnne?"

After a panicked moment of indecision about curtsying or not, LeeAnne shook the lord's hand. She actually got to touch her. AND Lord Kyrylo! Oh, god, she touched him, and she looked right into that dead sexy blue eye, and he said "Pleased to meet you, LeeAnne," in his rumbly Ukrainian-accented voice.

The welcome aboard was over in a minute, and the lords continued to their suite, their stunned cabin steward and butler leading the way. No one was told lords were boarding. Only Captain Wilson knew.

As they walked away, LeeAnne heard Lord Cadence say something to Lord Kyrylo in Elvish, and he smiled back at LeeAnne and winked. OMG!!!

Captain Wilson turned to Poppy and Leanne.

"*That* was my award. I have been honoured to be chosen to take the lords across to New York. If you want to leave the ship, LeeAnne, you can still make it to your convention. The ship leaves in an hour. Or you can stay for the entire trip. The *real* elf lords are going to New York, and you can sail with them."

"*Ohh, Daddy!*" And LeeAnne burst into tears. Zoom Daddy was the best daddy ever.

She wouldn't leave for the world.

Caddy and Kyrylo

They walked from the boarding area to the Grand Lobby, which was already crowded with passengers. It was hard to avoid seeing the phalanx of security guards in their dark uniforms contrasting with the lords they guarded as they marched through the crowds of casually dressed passengers.

They made quite a stir, which is what Caddy had hoped for. The ostentatious security scrum had a purpose. She wanted the passengers to know they were on board and to know there were guards. The way she explained it to K was that anyone who saw them would recognise the lords because of all the press, and while there weren't any photos, there were plenty of drawings and paintings, and some were very good and very detailed. There was no hiding their ears, so they might as well make a virtue of it and make the passengers think they were just wonderful, but not too approachable. She wanted them to leave the ship, saying, "Oh, yes, I met them, lovely people. Lots of security, but to be expected. I don't see why anyone would want to hurt them, but you know, nutters."

They all walked at Caddy's pace, and she was wearing high heels, so it wasn't exactly a fast clip. She walked by a sea of cell phones, all pointed at them, and she waved a couple of times and smiled. Kyrylo nodded and smiled, and when a woman in a zimmer frame passed in front, he stopped the whole group as he waved the old woman on. She had no clue who he was, but wasn't he a polite man? Lovely manners.

By the time they crossed the lobby, everyone who was anyone knew the King and Queen of the Fairies were on board their ship, and life on board was going to get a bit more interesting.

As soon as they walked into the suite, the butler brought a tray of ridiculous drinks with paper umbrellas in them. That's exactly what Kyrylo had ordered. "Please bring Lord Cadence a ridiculous drink with an umbrella in it." And that's what she got. Caddy was very happy, and they went to their balcony to watch the sail-away.

When they returned to dress for dinner, Kyrylo had a surprise for Caddy. Cunard was a bit more formal than other cruise lines, and while other people might be wearing "nice casual" on the first night, Caddy said they needed to be a bit more dressy because on the first night they would be on show. So Kyrylo wore one of his dark military style suits with all the frogging and epaulettes, and Caddy was in a classic full-skirted cocktail dress in brilliant emerald green silk. She figured that when people got used to them, they could be more casual.

She came out, gave a little twirl, and the dress floated around her like a cloud. "Isn't this beautiful? The tailors outdid themselves with my clothes on this trip!"

"You're always beautiful!"

"You can't lie to a lord, K – just so you know!"

"You must learn to take a compliment, *Zaychik*! But look, I have something for you." And he picked up a little box from the coffee table. "A present!"

Caddy gave him a little air kiss so she wouldn't mess up her makeup and opened it up. Inside were the most intricate and striking set of elf ear cuffs. They were green enamel and emeralds and had a pattern woven in like a Celtic knot. The workmanship took Caddy's breath away.

"I'm going to cry and smear my makeup!" She looked up at Kyrylo, and her lip trembled. "If I kiss you like you deserve, I'm going to get red lipstick all over your beard."

He grinned. "Then we'll do that later when I can take proper advantage of your gratitude. Let's put them on and see what you think."

She put them on and, of course, she loved them and wore them to dinner.

One down, six more to go, and the campaign, Kyrylo thought, was progressing brilliantly.

Every night, Kyrylo was going to give her a new piece of jewellery. They had seven nights at sea, so he had the ear cuffs, bangles, a tiara for formal night, a necklace, an arm cuff, a broach, and finally, an engagement ring. That was the plan. If everything worked out as well as the ear cuffs, he might move the ring up a few days. Flexibility was important in any battle plan.

Dinner went very well. Two security guards sat nearby and pretended to be passengers, and a couple were posted in the hall, so they weren't overbearing. The other diners, after a bit of initial shock, were very polite and tried not to stare. Caddy and Kyrylo ate until they couldn't stuff down another bite, and if it weren't for a sudden sharp pang of indigestion, she would have had dessert.

As they left, Caddy spotted the captain's family, Poppy and LeeAnne, and she and Kyrylo stopped at their table to say hello and to tell Poppy to let her husband know how happy they were with the suite.

"It's just lovely!" And she turned to LeeAnne. "And it was very kind of you to welcome us at the gangplank! We were told not to expect anyone, so it was a nice surprise."

LeeAnne blushed and blurted out, "I didn't know what to do! I didn't know if I was supposed to curtsy to the Queen of the Fairies!"

Caddy chuckled. "No curtsies. First, I'm not your liege lord, so a little head bow is enough of a greeting. Or if we are in a formal line, a namaste." And she demonstrated. "But secondly, I'm not the Queen of the Fairies. That's something the press has latched on to."

Her voice went low as if she were telling a secret. "Actually, the elves hate being called fairies. It's quite insulting."

Shocked, LeeAnned asked why.

"Because, darling, fairies don't exist. Anatomically impossible to have both wings and arms unless you're a bug, and elves aren't bugs. I am a lord, which is both a title and what I am."

She turned to Kyrylo, who was standing there with an amused expression on his face, watching them both. Caddy picked a crumb off his jacket and smiled at him.

"Lord Kyrylo is a lord by title, but it's also what he is. Lords are lords, elves are elves, and humans are humans. No fairies around."

"So he calls you Lord Cadence, and you call him Lord Kyrylo?"

Kyrylo laughed out loud at that. "Good gods no. That would be a mouthful when you're being called to breakfast!" He grinned at LeeAnne. "She calls me many names and titles, not all of them flattering, but the only title that I want to hear is 'husband.'"

Caddy turned to him, stunned.

"Are you asking me to marry you?"

He turned white, then bright red. This was not how his carefully planned proposal was supposed to happen, not at all. Not in public. Not in the middle of a restaurant with security people, waiters, diners, and sixteen-year-olds all in earshot. Kyrylo couldn't say no to her direct question. He would never say no to Caddy and break her heart.

"Yes."

Caddy swayed a bit and then gave him one of her wonderful smiles. She could have kissed him, but they were in public and standards must be upheld. Instead, she took a big, shuddering breath. "Okay."

Caddy steadied herself and turned back to the Wilsons, "LeeAnne, Mrs Wilson, do have a lovely meal, and we'll see you around. Good night!"

They turned to leave, and Caddy took Kyrylo's hand and said in Elvish, "I'm not going to let you back out, you know."

"I'll never back out. I love you. I've been planning on asking you for months, but that damn girl –"

"Don't blame her! Planning for months?" Caddy turned to Kyrylo and frowned. "I bet you have a ring!" And she bolted down the corridor, but he was faster and made it to the elevator first and laughed when the door closed on her, leaving her fuming in the hall, the security guards trotting behind. "That's not fair. I'm in heels!"

When she ran into the suite, he was standing there waiting, a small box in his hand.

Caddy and Kyrylo

Day two was spent exploring the huge ship, eating sweets and snacks at every little kiosk, and sitting by the pool listening to the bands and sipping on ridiculous cocktails with umbrellas in them. If they stood in a queue, which they insisted on doing just like the other passengers, they chatted with guests and generally made themselves agreeable. If someone asked an impertinent question, they smiled and moved on.

The Wilsons

Captain Wilson and LeeAnne were sitting down to breakfast in his quarters when there was a knock at the door. Poppy was in the shower, so LeeAnne answered it, and two of the lord's security employees stood there. One was the guy with the sword she had seen on the first day, and standing a bit behind him was a slightly taller man in a different uniform. He was certainly the cutest guy she had seen in a long time. It helped that he wasn't one of the geezers. The man with the sword politely introduced himself as Jameson, Head of the RumLot Security unit and asked if he could have a word with Captain Wilson. It would only take a minute, and it wasn't an emergency.

Of course, her daddy said yes, and she brought the two to the dining room where they were offered a seat but declined. They would be quick, Mr Jameson said.

"Captain Wilson, I'm sure you understand the logistics of the pause tomorrow night."

Wilson nodded. It was weird, but HQ said that if weather permitted, they were going to pause for four hours between ten at night and two in the morning at a certain coordinate, and the mooring platform was to be deployed. The Rum Lot people were adamant that no boats would be coming or going, just that the lords would be sitting on it for some time. Wilson wondered if they were going to scatter some ashes or if they were doing some religious thing. People had asked to do that in the past. In any case, they were paying a huge amount for the privilege, and as long as whatever they were doing was legal and safe, he had no problem with it.

Jameson paused.

"Captain Wilson, have you ever seen a mermaid?"

Wilson's head snapped back. "A mermaid? Only at SeaWorld."
Jameson smiled. "No, sir, a real one. Humanoid top, dolphinish bottom. The elves of the sea."

LeeAnne's mouth was a little o, and her eyes grew as wide as dinner plates. The man with Jameson looked at his hands and had a little smile. Gawd, he was cute.

Wilson slowly shook his head. "No, I can't say I have."

"Lord Cadence owes Neptune, the Lord of the Sea, a favour. He did a great service for her, and I won't go into that now, but all he asked is that she sing for him, so that's what she's going to do. She's going to give him a little concert, and that's why she needs the ship to stop and the mooring platform deployed. She's going to sing to him from there."

"Shit."

"Yes, sir. Tomorrow night, there will be a bunch of merfolk swimming up here to have a little sing-along. I expect your passengers will enjoy it. As you can understand, this was top secret because we don't want a bunch of private boats and yachts, not to mention press helicopters and god knows what, to be out there. One of the reasons we chose this spot was because by the time word got back to shore, they wouldn't have time to come out here." Jameson nodded and continued. "Someone always shoots off their mouth, Captain. Always."

Captain Wilson took a deep breath. "Mermaids."

"Merfolk, sir. Lord Neptune himself, the same guy in all the Greek myths, and male and female merfolk, are being sung to by Lord Cadence. It will be quite a spectacle. They'll be dancing in the sea. There will be a lot of sea creatures with them, too – whales and such. They'll sing back to her."

"Oh, Daddy –"

Jameson continued. "So I've come here to tell you that, but I also came to tender an invitation to your daughter, LeeAnne, to be on the platform when this is going on. Lord Cadence said LeaAnne did her a favour, too, and she would like to pay it back. As her father, I want to tell you what to expect if LeeAnne joins us. This isn't going to be a Disney film, sir."

"Jameson, I'm still wrapping my head around mermaids and Neptune. But go ahead. What's the downside, because I assume that's what you mean."

"Yes, sir. They don't wear cute seashell bras. They don't wear anything. The men can get, well, excited. It'll be full-frontal Full Monty, sir. If they decide to have intercourse nearby, they will. They won't go up on the platform and probably not very close to the ship at all, but Lord Cadence won't stop the concert or say anything. It's their ocean, sir; they have their own ideas on privacy and sex."

Jameson paused to let Captain Wilson absorb that image and then continued. "They won't touch LeeAnne; they don't like humans. She'll be perfectly safe, and I've assigned this Ranger to watch out for her the entire time, but Lord Cadence just wants you to know that if you go on safari and watch the elephants, sometimes elephants do what elephants do."

LeeAnne jumped up. "Oh, I accept! I would LOVE to go! No problems at all!"

"LeeAnne –"

"Daddy, you just can't say no. You can't!"

"Lee, sweetie, I –"

LeeAnne crossed her arms and glared at her dad. "Daddy, don't be a prude. I have no problems handling a man's penis."

And with that, she spun and went running to the bedroom, yelling for Poppy. "Mummy, guess what!!"

The three men looked at each other, and then Wilson rubbed his temples. "I hope I live through the next few years. God save me from sixteen-year-old girls."

The Ranger looked like he was choking, and Jameson looked at the ground, his shoulders shaking.

"Well, sir, I guess that's settled then. Her escort is Ranger Bunn here, and he'll be here at exactly nine-thirty. I suggest she dress for the weather. Have a good day, sir, and if you have any questions, just contact me."

They left, and the door closed behind them with a quiet click, but Wilson could hear them out in the hall just howling. He put his head in his hands.

Wendell

Wendell knocked on the Captain's stateroom door at exactly nine-thirty. Captain Wilson wasn't there; he was on the bridge, which was to be expected, and so the person who opened the door was Poppy Wilson. She was an attractive little bird of a woman with jet black hair and a rather brittle air about her, but she was friendly to the Ranger and led him to the living room where he waited while she fetched LeeAnne.

Wendell didn't mind this LeeAnne duty. He wasn't part of the security team but was on the staff as basically a go-fer and emergency fill-in. It was a training and observation mission for him so that he could get used to seeing how the security team worked and what went on behind the scenes at an embassy, crowd control, and so forth. While he was observing and learning, he might as well be useful, so he did whatever odd jobs Jameson assigned him, and that could be everything from handling luggage, cleaning gear, or babysitting spoiled sixteen-year-olds.

Besides, she was very pretty and not that much younger than he was. She was almost seventeen, and he had just turned twenty-one, so the age difference wasn't vast. They could at least speak the same language, which didn't often happen between Wendell and the more mature security people, some of whom were old enough to be his parents. Most treated him like the go-fer he was and pretty much ignored the Ranger. Between themselves, the security agents had no idea what a Ranger was, anyway, and when they asked Wendell, he just shrugged and grinned. He was told not to talk about it, and he didn't.

But Jameson wasn't stupid and knew human nature, which was why he was everyone's boss. He came down hard on the Ranger when he handed him this assignment and made sure Wendell understood he was *on duty*. No flirting, no trading of phone numbers, no touching, and, God knows, no screwing. None. If he did anything unprofessional, he would be fired. For Wendell, no girl, no matter how pretty, was worth his job as a Ranger, so LeeAnne was strictly off limits, probably forever. That's just the way it was going to be.

Part of Wendell's training was etiquette. He didn't understand why a Ranger needed to know how to dance or eat with the right fork when he was first sent to classes, but Caddy wanted the Rangers to blend in seamlessly in any environment, and that meant knowing how to act and be confident in formal situations. When LeeAnne walked into the living room, he knew how to greet her without acting like a geek, help her on with her coat without strangling her, and generally act like a gentleman without making a big deal of it. Back home, it didn't take long for the hated etiquette lessons to become valued because they certainly helped him pick up girls.

When he opened the door for her as they left and didn't charge down the hall ahead of her like a friggin' golden retriever puppy like her previous boyfriends all had, LeeAnne was smitten.

"Wendell, what's a Ranger? Are you, like, in the army?"

"No, not an Army Ranger, more of a fantasy game Ranger. Do you role-play, LeeAnne?" She said no, but she went to cosplay conventions, did that count? Wendell nodded and smiled.

"Well, I'm in Ranger training and probably will be all of my life. In gaming and a lot of fantasy novels, Rangers are skilled woodsmen and known for their stealth and wilderness survival skills. They are usually lone wolves. I'm getting some of that woodsman training, but much of my training is about working in cities. I'm being trained to work alone and do assignments for the elves that they can't do."

"What kind of assignments?"

He grinned. "Oh, it can be anything! Right now I'm taking a pretty girl to see the merfolk!"

LeeAnne blushed. OMG.

There was no formal announcement of what was going on, but people seemed to know something was brewing. The lords hadn't been seen all day; they were holed up in their quarters, yet the security people were out in full uniform, and it was getting late. Then the ship gradually came to a stop, and the engines went idle. You didn't notice the hum of the engines until they died, then the quiet became very loud.

When passengers asked the crew why they were anchoring in the middle of the sea, the crew simply said that the lords had asked for a four-hour stopover, but it would probably be less than that. When they were asked why, all the staff could do was shrug. They didn't know either.

But secrets can't be kept, and somehow it got out that the mooring dock was being deployed, and the Fairy Queen was going to sing on it. Passengers started to gather on the portside, and every cabin with a balcony had people leaning out, watching, but they didn't know what they were looking for.

LeeAnne was given a life vest and told that if she didn't put it on, she couldn't go out, so with no fuss, she put it on. Wendell wore his, but didn't bother to tie it up. The dock had a couple of the ship's crew members on it who looked frightened and excited at the same time. They knew. The crewman next to her, a Filipino guy LeeAnne knew worked on board for years, was breathing heavily. His hands were shaking.

Lord Kyrylo, two security guys, and Lord Cadence were all there. The humans all had vests on, but the two lords did not.

"Why aren't they wearing vests?" whispered LeeAnne. Wendell leaned over and whispered back. "Can't drown them because the merfolk would just bring them back up. You and me – maybe, maybe not."

They stood next to the ship, back and in the shadows, leaving the large floating dock empty as a stage. There was no light on Lord Cadence, but she didn't need one. Subtly, she started to glow.

Lord Cadence walked to the edge of the dock, holding her violin and bow. She bowed to the sea. Then she turned, and LeeAnne gasped. The lord's eyes were bright points of green light. She bowed to the ship and the passengers. They became as silent as ghosts.

Watching.

Waiting.

Wondering.

The lord turned to the sea and began to play. The sea was glass, and the sound of the violin was unnaturally piercing and clear. It wasn't volume, the music was *in* the audience and reached the farthest corner of the ship as clearly as if it were a foot away.

She played a short song, a lilting song that reminded LeeAnne of Celtic music. It was happy and sad at the same time, and in her heart, she could hear the words. *Come to me. I'm here, don't let me sing alone.*

Then the unnaturally calm Atlantic began to boil. At first, there were a few bubbles, then some ripples and then the merfolk.

Oh, the merfolk!

They burst from the sea like rockets, all at once, reaching fantastic heights in a chaos of spinning, flipping, twirling joy. There were tens of thousands of them – as far as the eye could see, they sparkled and danced and leapt.

Lord Cadence played. She played the violin, but what LeeAnne and everyone heard was a full, impossibly beautiful orchestra. She heard sounds she had never heard before, sounds that vibrated in her bones, rhythms that took her breath away.

The mermaids sparkled in their jewels, and their colourful fins caught the light because it was no longer dark. Lord Cadence was a glowing, pulsing orb of light, and LeeAnne could see her magical radiance swirl and ripple like the Northern Lights, and the light caught the merfolk and the sea creatures who swam with them.

Lord Cadence played for about an hour, maybe more. To LeeAnne, time had stopped long ago. As the last note played, LeeAnne let out a great shuddering sigh. Without realising it, she had been gripping Wendell's hand the entire time, and it was the pain of letting go, of coming back down to earth and flexing her fingers that brought her back to the real world.

At the same time, the crowds on the balcony let out a collective sigh and murmur and then clapped and cheered. At any other time, their noise would have been described as a roar, but against what they had just witnessed, that would be comparing a breeze to a hurricane.

Later, books were written and films were made about Lord Cadence's performance and the dance of the merfolk, but – but – but – human imagination paled against magical reality.

Wendell

LeeAnne didn't notice when Lord Neptune swam up to the platform and had a word with Kyrylo, then nodded and swam away. Wendell's earpiece was buzzing. Something was happening on the other side of the ship. Not good.

The earpiece buzzed during Lord Cadence's final crescendo, and instead of magic, Wendell heard Jameson's flat American twang say that there was an incursion, and as soon as the lords were secured in their suite for everyone was to go to stations. LeeAnne, still enthralled with the music, didn't hear the curt, "Bunn here. I'll take my package to the bridge unless told otherwise." Jameson acknowledged, and the connection went dead. The emergency plan had always been for Wendell to take LeeAnne to her mum and dad to the bridge, which was probably the safest place on the ship, and then for Wendell to go back to Jameson and do whatever he was told.

The last note was playing when Wendell pulled LeeAnne to the side and told her they had to leave. Now. She almost had a LeeAnne meltdown because no, she did *not* want to go now, but the man's eyes told her not to argue, and she closed her mouth with a snap.

He threw off the life vest, grabbed her hand, and pulled her along like a rag doll, elbowing through the crowded gangway and onto the ship and towards the banks of elevators. They were about as far from the bridge as they could be and so would have to climb a dozen floors and cross the length of the huge ship to get there, and Wendell was in a hurry.

"What's wrong! Stop pulling!" LeeAnne hissed, and Wendell looked at her with something very close to annoyance. She didn't like that, not at all.

"I don't know, but I'm on duty, something's going down, and I have to get you to the bridge. I need you to cooperate."

The elevator banks were mobbed. The stairs were packed solid. People on the upper floors wanted to come down to their cabins, people in the cabins wanted to go have drinks and get something to eat, crew couldn't get through to go to their stations, and of course, every last one of them had to stop and talk about the miracle they had just seen. It was gridlock.

Wendell spotted a couple of Rumlot Security standing on the other side of the room, scanning the mob. They weren't looking for him. They were looking for something else.

"Wendell!" LeeAnne pointed and yelled over the ear-splitting chaos in the elevator atrium. "That door. Crew access. We can take the stairs."

There was a plain, unmarked door, and it was blocked by a very grumpy man in a mobility scooter. They shoved their way to him, but the man refused to move, and Wendell lifted the entire rig and shifted it over a few feet. LeeAnne almost laughed at the expression on the old geezer's face, but she remembered why they needed the door and squeezed past him, slapped her hand in the centre, the door read her palm, and opened. Wendell went in first, did a quick scan and pulled her in, and they ran towards a stairwell. LeeAnne let the door automatically close behind her.

Only it didn't. Not immediately.

Not so quickly, a shadow couldn't slip through and close the door softly behind him.

Joab

Joab was hiding in the crush of the elevator mob, trying to blend in. They were packed in so tightly that the cruise passengers never noticed that he was dressed rather oddly for a cruise on the luxury liner *Queen Catherine*. Black cargo trousers and heavy webbed belts were not *de rigueur* for the cruising set.

But he saw the man, not much more than a boy, dressed up in one of those stupid elf uniforms they liked to prance around in, and while Joab was avoiding him, he heard the girl yell. When he saw she could get past the security doors, he took his chance.

He wasn't trying to follow them, but they were going in the same direction he was. The bitch was chattering. Would not shut up, which was fine for Joab. Her noise hid his footsteps. Then, as clear as a bell, echoing down a long, empty corridor, "Daddy doesn't need me on the bridge –" Perfect! She was related to someone on the bridge. Joab wanted to get on the bridge! Jesus be praised, she was going to be his entry key to the bridge.

The boy did all the right things. When they came to a corner, he would look around first, and he would go first. He didn't go charging down narrow corridors like an idiot, so he had some training. Joab wasn't worried and soon got the rhythm of the kid, and then, when she was a bit too slow behind the boy, he pounced. He grabbed the stupid bitch by her ponytail and yanked back, instantly gripping her in a headlock. Oh, Jesus, she screamed! She struggled, but it was too late. Joab had done this before. He knew how to keep a woman quiet, even if the RumLot kid didn't. He squeezed, and she went limp.

Wendell

Wendell spun around and to his horror, he saw LeeAnne being choked by – an orc.

He had no doubt, the purple, glittering eyes gave the monster away. The orc was enjoying himself.

Suddenly, the corridor lights went red, and the automatic hatches flew shut, trapping them in a thirty-foot section of the corridor.

The ship's security AI heard LeeAnn's scream, noted their direction of travel, and the algorithms interpreted the images on the cameras that someone was being held at knifepoint. In its computerised wisdom, it locked down the entire ship.

Wilson

On the bridge, Captain Wilson saw the AI lockdown the ship, and immediately, his years of experience and training kicked in. The computer system showed him why it had locked down the ship. One cell experienced an incident. The camera was slow to focus and blinked on and off, a maintenance issue he automatically noted to himself. The rest of the ship was deemed safe by the AI, so he immediately unlocked the rest of the ship, and the lockdown and release happened so fast that his passengers only saw a flicker in the lights and a hesitation in the lifts. Wilson sent his security people to the lockdown area, but they were scattered all over the ship and struggled to get through the masses of people blocking the lifts and corridors. Unknown to him, Jameson was tapped into their comms, and he saw immediately what was going on and directed four of his people to the cell. The rest of his people were cleaning up other issues.

Back in the UK and Ukraine, the security comms room knew something was going on the minute the ship's AI alarms went off.

Then the camera snapped into focus, and all four places – the bridge, Jameson, UK, and Ukraine – all saw the same desperate video at the same time.

Captain Wilson frantically tried to override the locks on the doors to allow Wendell and LeeAnne to run away, but something was wrong with the electric switches. In both Ukraine and Lowestoft, technicians used every bit of their skill to look for alternative routes to bypass the break, but in the end, AI can only do so much. Mechanics are mechanics, and a jammed piece of metal can't be fixed with a software patch.

In the very narrow, red-lit corridor, Wendell faced off with a man in military gear who had LeeAnne in a headlock, pressing a huge, black knife into her throat. They were trapped in a stretch of windowless, doorless utility corridor with locked emergency hatches trapping them in a space about four feet wide and about thirty feet long.

"Let her go!" Wendell hissed. He was in a semi-crouch, poised to jump and holding his only weapon, the elf-knife kept tucked in his boot. The elvish blade looked pitifully small in his hand. He was armed with a jackknife and was up against a machete.

The orc laughed. "Shit, no, pansy. She's my ticket to the bridge. Now you get out of the way if you want to keep your balls."

Months ago, Timothy sat around the pub after his morning routine of beating Wendell to a pulp and waxing philosophical about orcs. He had fought a lot of them, and he turned to Wendell (whom he liked and Wendell appreciated that as not all elves liked humans) and leaned forward, tapping a gnarled finger on the table to emphasise his words. "Lad, if you're ever trapped by one, keep'm talking. They're stupid, and talking confuses them. They make mistakes when they're talking and listening."

So Wendell talked.

"You're not going to kill her. They won't let you in with a dead body."

"No, pansy, but I can sure cut her up. I can make her not so pretty." And he grinned. "Daddy can have her in pieces." Then he kissed the side of her head, and Wendell saw her eyes fly open. "Maybe I'll even have time to have some fun with her after I kill you, pansy."

Pansy. The orc said it twice.

Wendell went to a rough school. He was a quiet kid who didn't play sports and loved his role-playing and computer games. He read everything he could get his hands on. He hung around with the other eggheads, misfits, and nerds, and if he heard it once, he heard it a thousand times during lunch and PE and on the sports field – pansy, pouff, fag – he heard them all, the complete dictionary of homophobic slurs favoured by bullies worldwide.

"You don't want her, you fuckin' fag. You want me, don't you? That's the way you swing – you like the little boys. Do you think I can't tell?" and Wendell puckered his lips and blew a kiss.

If Wendell hit Joab with a poleax, he couldn't have gotten a more satisfying reaction. Joab threw LeeAnne behind him and, with a roar of rage, dived at the Ranger. Wendell leapt up, and his training –

and all those beatings from the warrior elves – kicked in, and he fought on instinct.

But Joab was trained, too, and he was meaner, more experienced, and bigger. A former US Navy SEAL until they kicked him out for that stupid hazing issue with the newbie in the barracks. Six months in the brig and then dishonourable discharge. Some people just couldn't take a joke.

Legs and arms flew everywhere, both connected and both drew blood. They rolled around on the ground, and the orc got on top. Just as Wendell got the leverage to throw him off, LeeAnne jumped on the back of her attacker, the orc screamed, jerked up, threw her off, and she went flying into the wall.

Wendell wriggled away and jumped to his feet. The orc swung around and took a swipe with his combat knife at Wendell, giving him a long, shallow cut across his stomach. But the wild swing also left him open, and the Ranger leapt forward, and his many hours of practice of avoiding body armour and aiming for soft, weak spots paid off. He slit the orc's throat.

At that very moment, the camera went dead.

There was frantic pounding on both ends of the corridor on the closed hatches. On one side were *Queen Catherine*'s security personnel, and on the other side were the Rumlot's.

The electrical fault that made the camera blink on and off affected the heavy water-tight steel doors, and it took the ship's engineers a good twenty minutes to drill through the locks. When they finally pried open the door, the corridor was empty, and LeeAnne was already on the bridge, telling her hysterical mother she was just fine. The other door had a melted man-sized hole in it as if a plasma welder had burnt through it._____

Victor

In Lowestoft, Victor, the Senior Warrior Elf trainer and Wendell's Ranger instructor watched the entire fight on the big screen in the conference room, and when he saw Jameson burst through the melted door, he grinned at Tony.

"I *knew* the lad could do it! Popped his cherry, he did." He looked profoundly pleased with himself. "Bagged his first orc on his first assignment. Not too bad. Not too bad at all."

Caddy

Expressionless, Caddy watched a replay of the footage. There was no gloating from her. She stayed out of the way until Wendell was examined by their own medic, and then she visited him the first minute she could without getting in the way.

The slash across his stomach that came within millimetres of disembowelling him was very shallow, and the medic patched him up with a bit of superglue, tape, and some impressive Frankenstein stitches.

Kyrylo

Kyrylo went to see Captain Wilson, Poppy, and LeeAnne.

The captain didn't know whether to be furious that the lords were on board and the target of some sort of assassination attempt that meant hijacking his ship or profoundly glad that they had security to take care of it.

LeeAnne was bruised, but pretty cheerful. She had an adventure! Poppy was still upset, but she didn't see the video feed and never learnt the full story of what had happened. The more LeeAnne and her dad talked it down, the more the incident became just an ugly encounter with a drunk passenger, and that nice Wendell man stood up for her daughter.

But privately, Captain Wilson was worried and said so to Kyrylo.

"I don't know how I'm going to explain this. It's going to be a hell of a report. And I have a dead body to deal with."

Kyrylo raised an eyebrow. "What dead body?"

Wilson looked at the lord, and you could see the wheels in his brain turning. "The dead body on the video?"

"What video?"

"The video half my bridge saw?" Wilson was incredulous. Was the Lord being thick?

"Oh, the video of a drunk passenger fighting in the corridor? The one that the electronic glitch erased? That video?"

"The video that's sent on a live feed to Southampton. Automatic alarms have been triggered in our central offices. They've already seen it!"

Kyrylo smiled and simply said, "Before you write anything to your superiors, make sure you review the video again. You don't want to make any unfortunate mistakes. And if your crew on the bridge or anyone says differently, you have evidence that they weren't thinking straight. There was a lot to absorb tonight. There were mermaids in the water! People get confused."

Captain Wilson looked at the lord. The lord looked at the captain. Both nodded and bid each other goodnight.

Kyrylo

Kyrylo sat on the balcony, his feet up on the railing and smoked a forbidden cigar. Passengers weren't allowed to smoke on the balconies, but who was going to stop him, especially tonight?

Smoking a victory cigar was a bad habit he picked up from the Americans he trained with during the Russian War. Back a thousand years ago, when he was a young officer in the Soviet Army, everyone smoked cigarettes, but he gave those up when he was in the hospital. The doctor said every cigarette he smoked would delay his healing by a day, and he had a lot of healing to do.

But when the Americans won a firefight or had any victory, they broke out a Cuban and had a little group smoke. It was bonding, it was a reward, it calmed nerves, and, frankly, it tasted good. He enjoyed a cigar when he really felt in control of his abilities and shot that first ball of plasma through the target tank. He had a cigar the night he first bedded Caddy; even though the day began disastrously, the way it ended could only be described as a great victory. He used to have a cigar every time they had sex, but that soon became excessive. And he had a cigar when he gave her the engagement ring.

Caddy walked up behind him, and he felt her hands on his shoulders, kneading the tight muscles. She knew what the cigar meant.

"Okay, tell me what happened."

"There was a submarine. We think it was Chinese, but we aren't sure. The intel people will figure it out. We didn't know it was there because of all the whales, mermaids, and general crap going on. The merfolk knew it was there, but thought it was ours and ignored it."

He took a puff.

"It surfaced in the middle of your concert and released three RIBs of infiltrators. We assume now that the plan was to take over the bridge and hold the ship for ransom, probably in return for us. Don't know, because they're all dead. Anyway, two of the RIBs got to the ship, threw up abseiling hooks, and climbed aboard. A good-sized force, about twenty of them. Our guys were right there and took care of all of them, encouraging them back into the sea. No passengers were around; they were all on the other side of the ship watching you. I told Neptune, and he sent his people to finish them off. Then he made sure the sub had a hole or two inserted in it, and the entire lot went down to the bottom of the sea, which is very, very deep here. There won't be any survivors."

"The third RIB snuck in by boarding further down and a bit later. By the time our guys caught up with them, they were all on board. There was a bit of a fuss, and seven were tossed overboard. That left three. We found two inside, hiding in an empty cabin, and that left one. Wendell took care of him. We are very sure that all have gone to meet their reward in Hell. The merfolk will make sure the orcs in the group can't recover."

Caddy rubbed his shoulders. She was exhausted and would go to bed in a few minutes, but she had to know what had happened so she could get to sleep.

"So, any idea who funded that? A submarine! That's real money. Government money."

"Someone who doesn't want to use nukes. Maybe to capture us alive. Don't know. Someone who wants deniability, I think. Someone who didn't think we could sink a sub."

"This could make the second sub the Chinese have lost in the last eighteen months or so."

"It's very careless of them." And he stubbed out the remaining half of the cigar and carefully put it into a cigar case for later. Time for bed. He was tired, too.

Wendell

It was day four of the seven-day transatlantic crossing, and the lords slept through most of the day. Several passengers asked the security team about them, concerned that they were ill, but they were reassured that Lord Cadence was simply exhausted and sleeping. She *did* put on an amazing show! Lord Kyrylo was just staying with her. Not a single passenger of the five thousand on board had any idea of the other raid, and certainly no idea that he was up all night dealing with the ramifications of that.

Wendell was recovering from his slashed stomach, so he rested, too, along with a couple of the team who also had some bumps and bruises. Everyone was tired.

Jameson did wake Wendell up long enough for him to take an elf-filtered video call from the Warrior elves in Lowestoft. There they were, gathered in the pub after their normal morning training, with someone panning a shaky phone across the group, and after some hoots and claps, they all stood up and saluted him with their pints. He had killed his first orc. He was one of them.

Wendell could have cried, but of course, he didn't.

Wendell and LeeAnne

It was Gala Dinner night, and while Caddy wouldn't have minded sleeping through it, the lords had a long-standing invitation to sit at the Captain's table on Gala night. Everyone was to dress in their best gowns and tuxedos and enjoy the dance band.

Caddy had a very low-cut, very tight, black velvet bodice paired with a full, calf-length skirt of stiff, bronze satin brocade. She was grateful the matching shoes were made for dancing, and the heels weren't stupidly high. The elf fashion designers had decided to allow her to walk tonight. Kyrylo gave her his Day Four jewellery present, and it was a tiara. It was, like the other jewellery he gave her, elegant and perfect in every way, and after getting several pieces, she could see how everything worked together and was obviously part of a set.

She was, she thought, starting to look like a Christmas tree and opted not to wear the ear cuffs. It was all getting to be a bit much. She wore her ring, of course, and the tiara and that was plenty.

They set out for the main dining room with the security team, who were all dressed in their best civilian clothes; the men were all handsome and James-Bond deadly in black tuxedos. Three of the women wore dresses that would allow them to work if they needed to, and a couple wore tuxedos like the guys. Even Wendell was there, albeit walking a bit stiffly. He dressed in a tuxedo, too, and looked very debonair. Kyrylo was, in Caddy's unbiased opinion, the most handsome of the lot, but that went without saying.

The security team met in their conference room, and Jameson made a quick inspection before they set out to pick up the lords. Right before the team left, he pulled Wendell aside.

"Son, I need to have a word with you."

This is not good, Wendell said to himself. He called me son.

"Wendell [even worse, thought Wendell, now he's using my first name], I know you're going to see the captain's daughter at dinner tonight. That LeeAnne girl." He coughed.

"And I want you to – well – be careful. Let her down gently. She's only sixteen."

Wendell raised an eyebrow. He wasn't stupid. *Let her down gently* really meant *Stay the fuck away*.

"Sir, as far as I'm concerned, I'm still on duty. Is that what you mean?"

Jameson looked relieved. "Yeah, that's what I mean. Look, I've been around war zones for years. After a high-risk incident – well, to put it bluntly, being almost killed can make people horny. Especially women. It would be the most normal thing in the world for a kid like her to think you're a knight in shining armour and get frisky. Just keep your cool and be kind to her without getting her hopes up. That's all I'm asking."

Jameson looked at Wendell. "I have daughters at home. It's what I would want for them. And you have a career. Keep business and pleasure separate, and you can't go wrong. Right now, she's business."

"Yes, sir, I understand."

"Good man. Let's go and get this job done, then."

Wendell

Dinner was winding down, and the dance floor was filling up. Wendell sat at a table with eight of the guards, and they all rotated between having a good time and doing half-hour stints of work. Of course, none of them talked at all about the incidents the other night because they didn't want anyone to overhear their conversations, so they talked about football, exercise regimes and whether Chinese food was better than Mexican. Passengers stopped by and tried to strike up conversations and buy them drinks. Not a few of them hit on the guards. Like Jameson had said, there was nothing like the frisson of danger to pique one's interest and get the blood running, and just knowing these people were the lord's security guards was enough for some people.

The eight started keeping a running score with the winner being the one who had the most propositions by the time they left for the evening. Joan, who was wearing a stunning red sequined cocktail dress that didn't leave much for speculation, was winning at ten o'clock with six propositions, all by guys old enough to be her father. Being gay and in a committed relationship back home, she thought it was hysterical.

The lords danced, and anyone who looked could see they were having a good time. Kyrylo was quite a good ballroom dancer, and Caddy only stepped on his toes twice.

LeeAnne sat with her parents and looked bored.

Wendell was threading his way back to his table after a stint on guard when LeeAnne caught up with him. She was waiting for him.

"Wendell –" She was nervous, and it showed. "Would you dance with me?"

He gave her a lovely, genuine smile. "Of course, I will! But don't expect any *Strictly Come Dancing* moves. I'm still really sore."

She immediately relaxed and beamed at him. "Oh, I'll be gentle."

There were bruises on her neck that make-up couldn't hide, but she didn't mention them.

He led her to the floor and into a staid waltz, forever grateful Norma had arranged the etiquette and dance lessons, although he had moaned at the time.

"So where did you learn to dance, LeeAnne?"

"In PT class. Dance is more interesting than running laps." She paused and then dove right into the deep water. "Wendell, can we set up a chat group? Just the two of us?"

He looked down at her and smiled, but she could see that his eyes were sad.

"No, I'm sorry, LeeAnne. I can't do that."

"Can't? Why not? I want to!" She looked up. "Wendell, I know all the arguments. Mummy made sure today I knew every little negative. She wouldn't shut up. But you're not coming on to me. And I'm not jailbait. Next month I'll be seventeen. All I'm asking is for a simple WhatsApp."

"Nothing with you is simple, LeeAnne. I can't. I have my job and I don't mix business with pleasure, no matter how beautiful the pleasure is. And I'm not going to be around, anyway." He gave her a little twirl and winced. The stitches pulled. "I'm a Ranger, LeeAnne, and Rangers range."

Wendell gave her that sad smile again. "Let's just enjoy this dance, and then I have to go."

She nodded, blinked back any tears, and changed the subject. A few minutes later, the dance was finished and Wendell escorted her back to her table, shook hands with the Captain and Mrs Wilson, said goodbye to LeeAnne and left. He didn't look back.

Poppy looked at her daughter. Wendell said "goodbye", not "see you later". He didn't ask for any contact details or mention seeing any of them after the cruise.

Her daughter was oddly calm when Poppy expected a pout at best, tears at worst. But no, she was quite reasonable. Maybe she was growing up, after all.

For her part, LeeAnne expected Wendell to brush her off. Mummy was quite clear about that earlier today when she made sure LeeAnne understood that the Ranger was not going to jeopardise his job by dating a sixteen-year-old going on seventeen, whom he was tasked with protecting. Mummy pointed out he wouldn't be around like a normal boyfriend, and God knows what risks he took when he was doing whatever it was he did. It would be like dating a soldier deployed in a war. And he was four years older than her! He surely had a girlfriend somewhere back home, wherever home was. Maybe a wife and kids!

LeeAnne listened to everything Mummy said and, oddly, it all made Wendell more attractive, if that was possible. He had called her beautiful, and that must mean he liked her.

She wasn't worried about any brush off; Plan A didn't work out. LeeAnne already had a Plan B.

Caddy and Kyrylo

The cruise was almost over. The lords caught up with their sleeping and eating, and the sixth day was dedicated to working on the last-minute details of their whirlwind diplomatic trip. They would have three days in New York and then simply take a different cruise line back to the UK. There would be no pauses on the trip back.

They would also be escorted back by a Norwegian sub, which just happened to be rerouted to the area.

Thirty Rumlot security officers had flown into New York a week earlier to work with the NYPD and the American Secret Service, and they were ready and waiting. Everyone was staying at the Lotte, an elite hotel near the UN that catered to visiting diplomats, sheikhs, presidents and premiers, and this time, the leaders of the Elf Nation and their retinue.

The visit to the United Nations General Assembly was not going to finish with a petition from the Elf Nation for membership in the organisation, and that was made clear from the beginning. Caddy wasn't too sure if membership would end up being beneficial for elves if it made them obligated to follow UN rules and guidelines. Membership in the UN didn't prevent Russia from invading Ukraine in 2022, a member of the UN that sits on the Security Council.

What could the UN do to help them in return for being subservient to their rules? From Caddy's point of view, it seemed that membership would be a one-way relationship. She would have to be convinced otherwise.

What mutual obligations they would agree to would all come out in time, but from her point of view, it wasn't wise to be too eager to join. The lords would visit, get to know people, talk to a bigwig or two, and observe.

Disembarkation day dawned bright and clear, which was a pity because it encouraged huge crowds to gather on the routes the lords' motorcade expected to take. The security team was not happy with the number of police on the streets, which they felt was far too few for the masses of onlookers. It seemed that the NYPD didn't think a visiting head of the Elf Nation would be that interesting to blasé New Yorkers. They were wrong. Whether they loved the magical people or hated them, it seemed like half the East Coast wanted to be able to tell their children that they saw the Queen of the Fairies on her first official visit to the US.

They didn't see much. The motorcade was fast, and the windows were heavily tinted and the most they saw were the usual shiny limousines, only these were painted in dark red livery.

The cars drove into an underground garage, and the lords went up to the main atrium the normal, human way, by elevator. They didn't port in, which was a disappointment to the office workers and families who were waiting on the interior balconies of the huge atrium. People had no idea about *terroir*, and that was something that was considered to be off limits when talking to humans who weren't employed by the elves. They kept that to themselves as much as possible.

But Lord Cadence and Lord Kyrylo were in full flower on this initial visit. The late Queen Elizabeth was known for saying, "I must be seen to be believed," and Caddy took that lesson from the master.

They *looked* elvish, with Caddy in a bright green suit, so there was no missing her from the furthest gallery. She had a pill-box hat on and wore her hair pulled back so that her pointed ears were out there for all to see. They wanted ears; they got ears. Ears with K's ear cuffs giving them sparkle. Kyrylo wore an all black, high-necked military jacket with loads of loops and frogs and buttons. His hair was pulled back, too, so his ears showed. They weren't as pointy as Caddy's, but they weren't human, either. Ellen wanted him to wear a sword and a tricorn hat, which he resisted as too ridiculous, but in the end, he wore the sword because there was no denying it was a beautiful piece of elf craftsmanship. He drew the line at the damn hat.

They shook hands until their hands were numb. They waved to the gallery and were rewarded with a cheer. They were only out in the atrium for a few minutes because other ambassadors and staff were coming in, and then they were escorted to their observer seats to watch the proceedings for an hour and a half.

Kyrylo walked over and held Caddy's chair, and as she sat down, he scanned the room and froze. He only had one eye, but it was a very good one. When he sat down, he whispered to Caddy, and she stiffened, but that was the only indication that anything was different. Kyrylo started tapping on his phone. She looked, and Kyrylo was right. How he spotted her, Caddy would never know.

Down at the Russian desk sat Lena.

Lena.

Kyrylo's daughter Lena. The same Lena who betrayed her father and her father's true love to Lord Lester, so that he could murder them.

That meant Lester was somewhere in the building.

Kyrylo patted Caddy on the knee and looked at her, raising an eyebrow.. She met his eyes and nodded; she was all right. Sometimes a couple doesn't need to say a word.

She turned to him and whispered, "We'll honour this place. It's not the time nor the place for revenge," and he leaned back, patting her knee again. Good girl. If anyone was going to get revenge on Lester, it would be him, but as Caddy said, not here and not at this time.

They listened to the speeches. They weren't there to honour or acknowledge the lords, so most of the ambassadors didn't mention them at all. A couple said nice things about "bringing all races and tribes together in peace" and that sort of thing, which earned a smile from the lords. Then it was the Russian delegation's turn. The itinerary said that the UN Ambassador from Russia would speak, but he walked to the podium and announced he was giving his turn up to the Tsar, so he could offer a few words to the world.

The crowd stirred. There was no Tsar. Russia's head of state was President-for-Life Putin; what happened to him?

Lester walked to the podium. The ambassador gave him a low bow and left the stage. He was wearing Tsar Nicholas' old state uniform or a close reproduction of it, complete with cape, and his chest was covered in medals down to his crotch, like a North Korean general. Even the old Tsar didn't have that many medals.

"And I thought I was overdressed," murmured Kyrylo. "I wonder if any of those are a Good Conduct Medal."

Caddy kicked his shoe, but the corner of her mouth turned up. Lester did look ridiculous.

"That hat he's wearing. It's hiding his ears," she whispered.

Kyrylo frowned and nodded. So Lester didn't want anyone to know he was a lord. Then he checked his phone. Was this being broadcast live? It was. Lester was a grey blob on the screen; like all elves and lords, he wasn't photographable. Kyrylo showed his phone to Caddy, who nodded. She wondered if Lester knew that. He might hide his ears, but he couldn't hide who he was. It was a careless oversight.

The speech started with the usual boilerplate. Lester thanked the body for allowing him to speak in this august chamber. He wished all nations well and said that Russia was ready to lead the world to a new peace and prosperity for all. Then he announced *he*, Lester, the Tsar of all of the Russias and anointed by God, would be leading Russia to a new enlightenment and that the revered ex-president Putin was retiring to a well-deserved rest in Sochi as befitting an elder statesman.

Then he asked for forgiveness for Russia's past sins and said he would be working the rest of his life to bring the Russian people into the community of man, especially as a member of international trade organisations. It was pretty obvious he was asking for the sanctions to be lifted.

Finally, he thanked the world for allowing him to speak, and he appealed for unity, and just as he could marry a former Ukrainian and make her his Tsarina, he appealed to Ukraine, Poland, the Baltic States, and Georgia to set aside their past animosity and move forward in friendship and unity with Mother Russia.

He never mentioned elves, orcs, or lords. Everyone but the lords clapped politely, and he left.

The poor guy who followed Lester never had a chance. No one paid any attention to him at all. Lester stole the show.

"Well," said Caddy.

"Well," said Kyrylo.
And since it was their time to go, they left. There was a banquet at the American Embassy to prepare for.

Caddy and Kyrylo

Caddy settled in the limo and turned to Kyrylo.

"So, K, what do you think of your new son-in-law?"

"Shit, that's right. Lester *is* my son-in-law if he married Lena and isn't lying about it." Kyrylo looked out of the window, and then he shrugged. "It doesn't change what he's done. Doesn't change that she tried to get us both killed."

Then he looked at Caddy and grinned. "When we're married, he'll be your son-in-law, too!"

"And if they have kids, you'll be Danger Grandpa!"

"You'd be Danger Grandma, then."

"I guess this means Christmas holidays in Moscow."

"No, I don't see that happening. I didn't even spend Christmas with Lena when she was growing up, and we were still talking."

Caddy turned serious.

"Yes, this is an attempt to bring Russia back into the modern world and get sanctions lifted, but it's also an attempt to set up an alternative power base and marginalise us. He didn't have to choose today to give his little speech. He knew we were there, watching."

Kyrylo nodded. "He's giving the world a choice, I think, of magic folk versus his religious folk. And he is going to set himself up as the one who is integrating with the world. We mustn't forget that only a few people know about his kidnapping of you or that he keeps sending raiding parties over the wall into Ukraine and the Baltic. He's going to make sure the nasty parts stay hidden and try to charm the world with lies. Lies worked for Putin for a long time. Lester will think he's better at it than the old man. Most of the world doesn't care about Ukraine now that the war is over, so this is his time."

Caddy held his hand. "We'll just have to do our best."

And then they pulled into the parking garage, and it was time to move on to their next appointment.

Caddy and Kyrylo

The American UN delegation invited the lords to a banquet in their honour at the American Consulate. This wasn't a state banquet, but President Meecham and the First Lady would be there, as well as a slew of celebrities, especially from the music industry. Lord Cadence was known to love music, so that was going to be the theme of the evening.

Caddy dressed in a frothy silver and gold confection with a low neck and loads of tulle. As she told Kyrylo, she was going "full fairy" tonight. She wore the tiara and thought for a moment about the matching necklace, but changed her mind. The tiara and her engagement ring were enough.

A sweet woman from the Lotte's spa was brought in to do her hair and makeup, and for a while, Caddy wondered if she would have to do it herself, the woman's hands were shaking so much. In the end, she did a lovely job, and Caddy let her take a selfie with the Fairy Queen. Caddy didn't show up at all, but that was fine to the beautician because it meant the pic was real.

It took her over an hour to get ready. Kyrylo wore his standard tuxedo,o and it took him fifteen minutes to get dressed and out the door, which Caddy thought was not very fair.

"Next time, you can wear the tuxedo and I will wear the dress, and we'll see who gets ready faster." Kyrylo led her out the door, and the security guard took them to the limo. "I think you will still take an hour to dress, and I will still take fifteen minutes."
"You'd look ridiculous in a dress like this."

"How do you know? Have you ever seen me in a dress? I think I could look fetching, although I think I would not have so much of this netting stuff." He batted down the tulle so he could get in the back seat. "It's taking over the car."

They walked into the embassy and through to the reception line, where Caddy had her first shock of the night. There was the President Meecham smiling and waiting to greet them, and next to him was his wife, a striking if very hard-edge woman.

The first lady was an orc. She didn't know she was an orc because her visceral reaction to the two lords was as unexpected to her as her orc-iness was to them. Caddy walked into the foyer, and immediately her eyes started to water and she sneezed. Kyrylo had a sharp intake of breath over the stench, but at least he didn't have an allergic reaction like Caddy did. The First Lady saw them walk up, and she had her best formal smile on, but the minute she took a whiff of the two lords, the smile turned into a skull's grin, and she swayed a bit.

The woman turned as green as Caddy's tiara. Caddy walked up, a bit unsteady on the high heels as it was, but when she leaned forward to shake the First Lady's hand, Kyrylo had to hold her elbow to keep her from tipping over. When Kyrylo shook the President's wife's hand, she retched.

Caddy had moved over to shake the President's hand with Kyrylo following as fast as he dared. Behind him, the First Lady turned and barfed all over the carpet.

The two lords almost ran up the reception line and into the next room, where celebrities, diplomats, and dignitaries gathered for cocktails. Behind them, there was a lot of fuss and banging as staff cleaned up the carpet, and the First Lady was escorted to an upstairs bedroom to recover. She didn't come back down.

After some judicious application of hand sanitiser, the lords were given a glass of champagne, and they began the serious work of mingling. At least the air conditioning system took care of the odours of orc and vomit and orc vomit.

The President didn't make any effort to talk to them, and at first Kyrylo didn't notice; they were busy. But the room felt odd to him, and he couldn't quite put his finger on it. It was normal for men at these occasions to want to talk and joke with their exotic partner. There were always women around who wanted to flirt with Kyrylo, and yet the two lords seemed to be encased in a sort of invisible bubble to be avoided by about a quarter of the room. There was no overt hostility; no one was rude. They just found a reason to walk to the opposite side of the room when the lords moved.

Dinner was announced, and they sat down to dine; it was there that Caddy realised there was a group of politicians, all Representatives, who appeared to be avoiding them. A couple moved place cards and changed seats to be a bit further away from the lords. It was subtle; no one made a big fuss, but it happened, and Caddy noticed. They weren't orcs who would be offended by the lords' scent, so that wasn't the reason they moved.

Now that the FLOTUS was indisposed with her violent bout of stomach flu, her seat was taken over by a female senator who came across as friendly enough and was on her third glass of wine. So Caddy asked her why that table wanted to sit together. Were they part of a club?

"In a way, Lord Cadence. They're a group of Representatives who are afraid of people like you. They're afraid of everyone. They want to ban all immigration to the US, and elves are just another group they don't want to let in."

"Really? What about elves who had already lived here for millennia, before the Vikings or Columbus? What do they expect to do with them?"

Senator Billings laughed. "You don't expect them to have thought this through, do you? There is no logic to bigotry."

"I'm surprised they came tonight. I must make them uncomfortable."

The senator gave the lord a sideways glance and took a sip of her wine.

"The president invited them. They are his friends."

Cadence nodded. That explained the coolness.

"What is new is always scary. We understand that."

Nodding, Sen. Billings raised her glass and took another drink, "You have to be aware that they've been briefed on you and Lord Kyrylo by our intelligence agencies. Your personal powers are scary. They don't know what you can and cannot do to them directly."

"You're not too scared to talk to me!"

"Oh, I'm scared, but you don't deal with the unknown by putting your head in the sand, do you?"

Caddy smiled at the woman, a genuine, undiplomatic smile from the heart. "You are a very wise woman, Senator Billings. Thank you for giving me a chance. I am –" she paused, "– a fierce defender of my people, as you are, but I wouldn't be here if I didn't want us to live in peace with the world. It would be very easy for me to stay home. I think that by getting out and being a part of the world, we'll be less scary, and everyone will benefit."

Billings smiled back, "I understand you lived in Texas for a long time. They seemed to have survived you quite well." And the conversation turned to Texas, then Tex-Mex food and on to the extreme weather there, which is always a safe topic.

The cheese course was brought out, the president stood up and offered some toasts and a very short after-dinner speech and the banquet ended because the gods are kind and they get bored, too.

As they were leaving, Caddy saw the table she had pointed out to Senator Billings huddled in a tight group, and she walked up to them. They froze and turned to her, some with tight smiles and a couple with open scowls. An image of schoolroom cliques and the bullies she faced when she was a teenager flashed through her mind. Some things never change.

"Ladies. Gentlemen. I'm very sorry I couldn't talk with any of you tonight. Maybe one day soon we can have a more relaxed chat. I would love to meet all of you in person– "

"Demon, begone!" a woman hissed. A man grabbed her elbow. "Janet! Remember where you are! Don't provoke her!"

Caddy stiffened and drew up to her full height and simply looked at the woman gravely.

Janet spun to the man, her face bright red. She was obviously in her cups. "I don't care. She's the spawn of the devil, and we've been sitting here all night as if this was *normal*. I won't have her casting her spells on me!"

The room went dead silent.

The men and women in the little clique mumbled. Someone said, "Oh, Jesus help us." Some were embarrassed, and some were afraid, but some had a hint of satisfaction in their eyes.

Kyrylo walked up and stood behind Caddy and said it was time to go; the car was waiting. Those who sat through the classified intelligence briefings on Lord Kyrylo started to sweat.

Lord Cadence made an almost invisible nod to the lord and then gave the group a low curtsy. "I'm sorry if I upset anyone; that was not my intention. Anyone here who wishes to have a civilised, adult, *sober* conversation with me can contact my office. For now, a very good evening to all of you. It's the witching hour and my broomstick awaits."

And she turned, put her hand on his elbow and left with Kyrylo, who chuckled the whole way out.

The next morning at breakfast, Caddy received a handwritten apology from the President for the discourtesy shown to Lord Cadence. Kyrylo looked at it and gave it to their PA. "You can file this with the others. We're getting a collection now. I can see a book coming out in a few years – *Apologies to the Fairy Queen, Volume One.*"

Caddy scowled at him. "K, she was as drunk as a skunk. Horrible woman. But she spoke for others; this bigotry is just what we're going to have to deal with and work around."

Kyrylo shrugged and nodded. That was why they were here.

Later that day, twelve men and women in the US House of Representatives held a press conference on the Capitol steps announcing a bill they were introducing to the committee. It would –

- Limit all rights and protections in US law to humans
- Make all activity that permits the importation or immigration of elves or other non-humans illegal
- void any previous US passports granted to non-humans
- allow for the immediate detainment and deportation of all non-humans
- require all non-humans to identify themselves with a permanent and visible marking

It was called, with no sense of irony whatsoever, the "Americans for Humanity Bill".

Caddy watched C-Span from the living room of their suite and gave a great, shuddering sigh. They were getting ready for lunch at the French embassy, and the room was packed with their PR people and security. They all went quiet.

Kyrylo spoke first, slowly. He was thinking about the ramifications as he was talking.

"This is just a proposed bill and hasn't gone through any of their processes. I don't know what they need to do to make this abomination a law, but this is just a few Congressmen, not everyone in their government. If this passes, it would be legal in the US to kill an elf or lord on sight, as they wouldn't have any legal rights or protections under US law. So some people will take just announcing this as permission for an open hunting season against us."

He looked at the security people, "and people working for us will be fair game. There will be a small, very small group who will think they are doing humanity a favour by getting rid of humans who help elves and lords. A tiny group, but it will only take one idiot to cause a lot of damage."

Everyone nodded. They understood. Security would be ramped up, if that were possible. It was already very tight. They just had a couple more days to go, and then they'd be on their way back home.

"Freedom of Speech means freedom to make an asshole out of yourself," Caddy spoke in clipped tones. "They haven't thought this through. They don't know that orcs are non-human, too. The President is married to an orc and doesn't know it. The First Lady doesn't know what she is."

Caddy stood up. It was time to go.

"At the moment, I have tried very hard not to stir up the orcs and to keep the ones who think they're human in their state of blissful ignorance. I don't want orcs here to organise any more than they are in Russia, so for now, I want the policy of not talking about them to continue. It won't be possible to ignore them forever, but every day we delay their awakening is a day we can use to build defences against them. Does everyone understand that, too?"

"Yes, ma'am"

"Then the French are waiting for us. Let's go to work."

The French were lovely.

Of course, they heard all about the incident the previous night with the Americans, so they made an extra effort to be gracious to their guests. Showing up the Americans was a national sport, and the Americans' own goal with the lords was gleefully exploited by the French Ambassador.

There were already enclaves of elf clans in France, but only on a small part of the coast and in areas where they created a porting chain across Europe. The French government was eager for the lords to visit other areas and do whatever it was they did to wake up elves and establish more nodes. They had been talking privately with the Ukrainians and the Poles, and of course, the Brits, and the other countries' experiences with elf clans. Paris couldn't see any negatives at all. Having an elf clan pop up in a rural area was an immediate economic boost to the local human population, and crime went down. Elves minded their own business, didn't put any strain on schools or hospitals, and, *comme un aubaine pour la communauté*, paid taxes. They spoke French perfectly. They were the perfect immigrants.

Paris certainly wasn't going to let the Americans' fetish with isolationism and their tolerance (and intolerance) of certain religious sects influence French policies.

So excellent wine was drunk, excellent food was eaten, and aside from a few snide comments about American manners on the French side, everyone was on their best behaviour, and it was a very pleasant two hours. The Ambassador's wife insisted that Caddy come to France and be shown around the best couture houses, and maybe an opera? And the Ambassador was very pleased at the reception he received from the lords regarding his suggestion that more elf nodes be established along the remaining coastline. The lords hadn't visited Paris yet, but they had an open invitation.

The crowd waiting outside the French embassy was huge, but then every single event the lords went to in New York drew huge crowds.

Demonstrators were screaming for and against every possible variation on every possible subject. Each group hoped their placard or sign would earn a few seconds of air time from the masses of TV cameras that panned over the crowds as pundits filled in air time as they waited for Lord Kyrylo and Lord Cadence to leave the embassy. While a large majority were simply people who wanted a glimpse of a real, live fairy king and queen, there were others with more sinister agendas.

"Death to Demons!" "Thou shalt not suffer a witch to live!" "Jesus is the ONLY Lord!" and "Save us from Satan" were just the more moderate anti-elf, anti-lord sentiments. Not everyone thought the returning elves were cute, and lords were charming.

The scruffy young man squatted next to a wall, sipping an overpriced **Coke** he had bought from a street vendor. He looked like any college kid milling around on the fringes of the crowd, people-watching and occasionally snapping a selfie with his phone. He wore a cheap tourist t-shirt that said "I (heart) Elves," non-too-clean jeans, and broken-down trainers. His shabby black backpack had a collection of keyrings and charms dangling from it and a bottle of sunscreen in the side pocket. Underneath his t-shirt, tucked in the white bandage that circled his stomach, was an elf-knife.

There were orcs everywhere, and for the first time, Wendell realised that the knife knew it. It was warm, and he could feel it vibrate next to his skin like a phone, making sure he didn't miss an urgent call.

Most of the orcs milled around a very noisy religious cult that was demonstrating next to the barriers. They had a front row seat, and there were a lot of them; they waved banners, held up signs, and had a huge American flag with a cross on it that they held up like a canopy so they could say they were literally under God and country.

Wendell saw the NY police watching them closely from both sides of the metal crowd barrier. There were a couple of orcs in police uniforms, but they weren't nearby.

Then a man pushing a wheelchair with an old woman hunched in it walked in front of him and stopped, which was really annoying because it meant Wendell had to stand up to see around him.

The crowd roared. The door to the embassy opened, and out walked Lord Kyrylo, Lord Cadence, and the French Ambassador, along with a scrum of security guards, officials, and anyone with a reason, or no reason at all, to be there.

The lords waved to the crowd, raising another roar and then turned and shook hands with the French Ambassador's party. They then walked to the waiting RumLot limousine.

And that's when it all happened.

With perfect choreography, the cult members parted, and in the middle of their mob was a kneeling man with a sniper rifle.

Wendell shouted, "Shooter!" His mic picked it up and relayed it to the team, and the security guards sprang into action. At the same time, the man pushing the wheelchair levitated a rock into his hand, and, with unnatural speed and accuracy, threw it at the shooter, hitting him hard in the ear. The path of the rock had to bend around some of the cultists to get there.

The millisecond before the rock hit, the sniper rifle shot three automatic rounds. One clipped Lord Kyrylo's arm, barely grazing it before hitting a security guard full in the stomach (Was that Luke?). The second hit the open door of the limousine and shattered, but didn't penetrate the bulletproof glass. The third skimmed between the car and the glass, ricocheted off the bonnet, killing a woman spectator.

Lord Cadence spun around, there was a brilliant flash of green, and the shooter, who was now holding his head and halfway to standing up, simply boiled away in a thunderclap of green light, along with parts of the orcs standing near him.

One of the security team (Joan?) shoved Lord Cadence in the car, the door slammed, and in the chaos, they sped off.

It took a second for Wendell to process everything he had seen. Should he run to his team and help them? The remaining team and half of the NYPD ran to the hit guard and the dead woman. The other half of the police had their guns trained on the demonstrators. Then he looked at the man pushing the wheelchair. He was running away.

He had levitated a rock.

He was a lord.

Wendell ran after him.

Wendell

When Wendell wrote in his report later that "he ran after the man with the wheelchair", it wasn't as simple in real life as it sounded in his dry report.

The road in front of the embassy was a boiling mass of panicked people running away from the gunshots and police with guns drawn, taking down some of the cultists and running after others. A pack of orc/cultists tried to escape by ploughing a van through the crowd, causing more deaths and more chaos with the living. Everyone screamed. Someone shot off tear gas.

The man ran, pushing the wheelchair as fast as he could, the old woman wailing as she was jostled and tossed like a cork in the heaving tsunami of the mob. He was a stocky, short man, the wheelchair was heavy, and he was slowing down.

Wendell caught up with him at the top of a long flight of steps leading down into a subway. He looked around – surely there was a lift for the disabled – but he saw orcs running behind them. The man took a careful step forward to roll the woman down the steep stairs, one step at a time.

Pushing ahead, Wendell grabbed the foot of the wheelchair and yelled, "Let's go!" The man didn't say a word; he just lifted his end, and they scrambled down the stairs, the old woman loudly crying the entire way.

At the bottom, the man tried to thank Wendell, but Wendell shoved him ahead; there were orcs behind them. He put his backpack on the woman's lap and yelled over the crush of the crowds, "Take the next car, wherever it goes. I'll come behind. We've got orcs."

In the crush, the handicapped turnstile was forced open, and they sped through it. No one worried about paying their fare.

Wendell didn't know whether or not the orcs he spotted were following them or just running in the same direction. All he knew was that orcs could smell lords and elves, and they didn't like either. If this was indeed a lord, then he was in danger, and they needed to get away.

Confused, the man hesitated, but did as he was told. He pushed to the platform and somehow rolled onto the next car, with Wendell barely able to squeeze in the crush of humans inside.

As the door slid shut, Wendell saw through the window the enraged faces and purple eyes of three orcs; so they *were* chasing him. He heard them pound on the side of the subway car as it pulled away. He didn't see three of them get in the last car of the train.

The Ranger scanned the car for orcs, but he was in a tightly packed car of humans, many of them crying and jabbering on their phones. They were okay for now.

He turned to the man and held out his hand. "Wendell Bunn. And your name, sir?"

The man looked dazed and his steely blue eyes glowed weakly, "Sam Steinsmiour. And thank you." He shook Wendell's hand and then turned to comfort the old woman who was still crying and whimpering in the chair.

Wendell leaned in to get close to Sam's ear, hoping that the clatter of the train would cover his voice.

"Lord Sam, we were chased by orcs. Do you know them?"

Sam went pale. "Orcs? What are orcs?"

Wendell looked back, speculating. "Orcs are orcs. Can't you smell them, Lord Sam?"

Who was this man? Who was this person who appeared out of nowhere to help him and Vera get away from the Stinkers? Why did he talk so funny? Sam started to wonder if he jumped from the frying pan into the fire.

"The Stinkers?"

Wendell grinned and held on to the strap as the carriage swayed, "That's as good a name for them as any, Lord Sam! I like it."

The car slowed.

"Where's your stop? Are you going the right way home?"

"I need to transfer at the next stop after this."

"I'm going to escort you home and make sure you and your mother are safe."

"This isn't my mother. This is Vera, my wife." Wendell bowed to her as much as he could in the jam-packed carriage.

Sam stroked Vera's head, but she didn't respond. "Vera is a bit muddled nowadays. She has old-timers. Maybe I shouldn't have taken her to see the fairies, but I thought it would be a good day out. Get some fresh air. But you don't have to take me home. We'll be fine now."

Wendell looked at Lord Sam and shook his head.

"No, sir, I sure *do* have to take you home. I would get fired if I didn't."

"Who? Who is going to fire you?"

Wendell just smiled and scanned the carriage again as the doors opened and closed and people got on and left. No orcs so far.

At Sam's transfer stop, they left the carriage, and Sam pushed Vera to the next platform. Now the subway was almost empty, and Wendell could look down the long platform at the small clusters of commuters who arranged themselves to be in front of the next train's doors. He didn't see any orcs, but the platform was long and curving.

"Do you smell any Stinkers, Lord Sam?"

Sam looked up at the tall man. Why was he calling him "lord"? Couldn't he smell the Stinkers himself?

"No, not fresh ones."

"Yeah, I imagine in a closed place like this, their scent would linger. You make sure you tell me right away if you smell anything."

Wendell wondered if his phone and the tracker in his backpack would work down here. His earpiece had long ago stopped receiving.

He opened his phone; there were only two bars on the signal, but he sent a quick, secure text anyway. If they couldn't get it now, they'd get it as soon as he was above ground.

"Found a lord. Possible orcs. Track me." That would do it, he hoped. Wendell knew they would be taking care of their lords first, but when the team was able to, they would find him.

Their train came, and they boarded. This time, they were the only ones in the carriage, which was a blessed relief.

Vera stopped crying and was asleep, mumbling in her dreams. She smelled like pee.

"Okay, Lord Sam, as long as this car is empty, you can ask me questions. I'm sure you have a few."

Sam looked at the young man with the serious eyes. A big guy, to be sure, and there was something of the athlete about him. He worked out. But he was so young!

Just as Sam opened his mouth to ask his first question, the carriage doors between the cars opened, and a stinker walked in. He was wearing the cult's t-shirt. Sam had never seen anyone move so fast as Wendell did. He flew into the stinker and, with one swift movement, slit his throat. Behind him were two more, but with their buddy ahead blocking the door, they had to crawl over him, and Wendell took care of each of them in turn.

All Sam could do was stare, open-mouthed. It was like watching an action film, only this was real life. That man killed three people without a word of warning and with no hesitation whatsoever. Yeah, they were stinkers, but this was some serious shit, and here he was sitting next to a killer with Vera snoozing next to him.

The carriage slowed down and came to a stop. The door opened to the platform, and on the platform were six Rumlot security guards, waiting for them.

Sam didn't know what to do. Now he had Men in Black to deal with.

Jameson walked into the carriage and sighed.

"Mr Bunn, I can't take you anywhere nice, now, can I?"

"No, sir. Sorry about the mess."

Jameson hit the button that delayed the train long enough for wheelchairs to exit, and the guards hauled out the three bodies onto the platform through the other door and propped them up, more or less, on the subway wall and then the train went on its way. A headphoned girl singing to herself and tapping on a phone walked by and, without skipping a beat, stepped over the bodies and continued up the stairs.

Wendell turned to Lord Sam and bowed.

"Lord Sam, Ms Vera, I have to go, but Mr Jameson here will take good care of you and make sure you are safe. I'm sure I'll see you soon. Goodbye for now!"

As Wendell walked up the stairs, Sam heard him say to one of the guards, "I think I busted a stitch"

Caddy and Kyrylo

Luke's bullet to the stomach was serious, but he had on elf-made body armour, and the bullet didn't pierce it. The bullet gave him a nasty bruise, and he was checked out in the hospital to make sure there were no internal injuries.

Joan burnt her hand badly when she pushed Caddy into the limo, and that was going to require skin grafts. Once it was determined they could travel, both Luke and Joan were bundled up and medevaced back to Heathrow. It took five hours of flight time, but once there, they were immediately under the care of elves. Both agreed it was worth the trip back home.

The unfortunate woman who died on the scene was not forgotten, and a day later, Caddy and Kyrylo had a long private talk with the family. That was rough, but had to be done. She was a huge fan of elves and the lords and was looking forward to catching a glimpse of the lords. She had three children and five grandchildren, and while her family mourned her loss deeply, they didn't blame the lords. There were crazies out there, they said. Handwritten letters of condolences from the lords were delivered, the funeral was paid for, and when the grandkids went to uni, they never had a bill. It could never be enough.

Kyrylo had a flesh wound. It might leave a scar since they didn't have elf healers around, but he was unconcerned. It would just add to his already existing inventory and would blend in with the other battle trophies.

The biggest after-effect from the assassination attempt for Kyrylo was Caddy's complete and total meltdown afterwards. Incandescent with rage, she was going to go to Moscow and personally tear off Lester's balls and stuff them in his ears.

All she had to do was get in the same room with him, and he would be dead. All she had to do was see him, and he would never hurt any of her people again. He didn't have to be alive for balance to be achieved.

She was going to war.

It took Kyrylo a good half hour to talk her down.

Out in the hall, the security guards could hear everything; Lord Cadence was not discreet. They had never seen her like this, and all they could do was hope to hell she never got that mad at them.

Everyone thought that Kyrylo was the big power lord, although he never claimed anything of the sort. Oh, they knew Lord Cadence was powerful; they had seen with their own eyes how she could sing up the elves, and they felt with their own feet the tremors that her songs sent down to the centre of the earth. They saw the lights dancing in the sky when she played for the merfolk. But those were pretty things. Really, it was all rather girly. Not real raw power that could kill; not like shooting out bolts of lightning like Kyrylo could do. But there she was, furious that her man had been hurt, as well as her security guards, who put their lives on the line for her. *"All she had to do was get in the same room with him, and he would be dead. All she had to do was see him..."* And that's just what she did to that sniper. She just looked at him and he vapourised in a cloud of steam and ash.

It was an eye-opener for the team. Thank goodness, one said later, she was on their side.

She was not angry at her security team. Their people were not allowed to fly drones or post themselves on the rooftops, and the Americans had said they would handle that bit. The flag was used as a canopy by the cultists to prevent them from being seen from above, so that was a lesson learnt.

She was furious at Lester, whom she was convinced was behind this, but Kyrylo was not so sure. That would take some investigation. Religious cults certainly existed everywhere and popped up and died like nasty little brushfires, but that didn't mean Lester was involved. He was not their only enemy.

So Kyrylo counselled that going to war half cocked would do them no good in the end. It would just tip Lester off and give credence to the anti-elf factions amongst the humans. It wouldn't help the elves in any way.

So far, their actions have been defensive, but if Caddy went on the offensive, that would change the dynamics of their integration campaign. It was too early to even consider that. It would prove that the lords were indeed serious offensive threats, and neither the lords nor the elves were strong enough to battle against three billion humans.

Caddy's plan was a good one, and they needed to stick to it. This incident was a wake-up call that they would have more dangers ahead than one stupid lord and that they needed to stay vigilant.

Secretly, Kyrylo's biggest fear was that Caddy would lose her temper and go off in a rage like she did when the raiding orcs attacked the female guards in Ukraine. That time, she shape-changed into a monster and sliced the orcs into pieces. Getting her back to normal was traumatic for everyone, although they dealt with it. The problem that kept Kyrylo awake at night was that she would go a-roaming by herself. If she ran off on some self-directed mission, she was vulnerable to whatever was out there. If she put her mind to it, he wouldn't be able to find her or stop her.

However, that move she did today when the shooter was boiled to nothing but vapour was pretty impressive. He had never seen her do that before. When she was calmed down, he'd ask her about it.

When the tears came, he knew she was climbing down from her fury. It was the cold rage that scared him.

"They could have killed you! It was only a few inches off!" she sobbed.

"*Zaychik*, if I'm hurt that bad, just keep me breathing and dump me in a cauldron. I'm pretty tough. They can't kill me that easily." He hugged her. "If you can be re-birthed, so can I."

He wiped her eyes and made her blow her nose, then he had an inspired coda. "The only way they can kill us is with a nuclear bomb. If you are always with me, then at least we'll go out together with a big bang. I like banging."

"Don't be silly." But she smiled, and the storm was over. He hoped.

He was so glad he put trackers in all of her jewellery, including her engagement ring. Those were anti-theft precautions, but if he ever had to activate them, they were there.

Sam

Jameson sat in Lord Sam's cluttered, dark living room. The man was very close to having a nervous breakdown, and he didn't want to push him too hard.

Sam's eyes darted around the room as if looking for escape. Actually, he was; everything that happened today was overwhelming.

The military man in the hand-tailored suit sitting in front of him looked as hard as granite, but there was some sympathy in his eyes. What he was telling Sam was insane. Fantastic. Crazy.

True.

He knew it was true because he could do magic.

Sam was a stonesmith. A mason. He carved architectural pieces to order, usually for buildings under restoration. He worked on the Cathedral of St. John the Divine and St. Patrick's Cathedral when they needed some restoration done, and he took on a lot of private work. If you needed a gargoyle, Sam was the man to go to. The average person would be surprised, but a lot of people in New York needed hand-carved gargoyles, finials, cornices, and special artwork for headstones. Sam made a good living.

About twenty years ago, a large block of stone toppled over on him and should've crushed him, only it didn't. He told it not to fall. He was always talking to his stone when he carved, telling it what he wanted it to do, but he never expected it to listen. Then he found he could "feel" stone. He could make rocks move. He could do magic.

At first, he practised his parlour tricks in secret, but eventually, if only to make sure he wasn't going crazy, he showed Vera what he could do.

She was amazed. As a good Catholic, you'd think she'd say her husband of thirty years was possessed by the devil, but she never once thought that. She said he had a gift from God and encouraged him to practise. One day, she said, God will use you, and you have to be ready.

Vera kept him sane, but when she was about seventy-five, she started to forget things, and one of the things she forgot was herself. She started walking at night. And then she became afraid of the TV because it was talking to her, except for old videos of The Addams Family. Sam put Morticia and Gomez on a loop, and every day she spent hours watching them.

And then one day, she forgot how to stand up.

She aged and got sicker and sicker. And Sam? He didn't, at least not as fast. He was still able to get around and take care of her, even though he was only a couple of years younger, and that was a blessing. His reasonably good health was able to keep her out of one of those hellhole nursing homes. He could afford to put her in a good one, but he absolutely refused to do so. Even the best ones were horrible, in his opinion. None were good enough for his Vera.

He had a couple of women come in to help him during the day, but he provided most of Vera's care. It was tiring at best, frustrating at worst, especially when she stopped being Vera and became mean and hit him. But good care was what the old Vera deserved, and every now and then she rewarded him with a smile or a sensible word.

She didn't have long, he knew it in his heart, and now his goal was simply to allow her to die at home. That's all he wanted, for Vera to die at home, with him holding her hand when she passed over. He would give up his magic for that.

So when this hard man with the sympathetic eyes told him that his magic was not a fluke, that it was part of who he was, and that there were others like him, he didn't object to the magic bit. He was overwhelmed that he wasn't alone.

Being alone, that was tough. Vera's mind wandered away years ago, and while her body was still there, it didn't matter. Sam was alone. His life revolved around his work and taking care of Vera and leaving no time for a visit to a cafe or taking a walk to clear his head. He didn't talk to anyone. The LPNs who came in to help with Vera were pleasant, but they didn't want to hang around and talk. They had their own lives. The architects and designers he worked with had a purely professional relationship with the odd genius who lived in the old garage in an unfashionable part of Queens. Sam was fossilised, buried deep in the centre of one of the largest cities in the world and was utterly alone.

"I would very much like you to come and meet Lord Cadence and Lord Kyrylo. They are wonderful people and started alone, just like you. Would you come back to their hotel with me?"

"No, I can't do that. Can't happen. I have to take care of Vera."

"I'll leave two guards with Vera. She'll be as safe as houses. And I'll get a professional nurse to come in and sit with her. We have them on call. You'll only be gone a few hours, I think."

Jameson didn't tell Lord Sam that he would be under round-the-clock guard forever now. That detail would be revealed soon enough.

Sam thought about it and slowly shook his head. No, he just couldn't.

"What would Vera tell you to do, Sam, if she could?"

Tears welled up, and Sam had to look away. Men don't cry, do they?

"Vera would tell me to go."

Ellen

Ellen called. First, she just wanted to hear Caddy's and Kyrlo's voices and make sure they were all right. After a few tearful minutes, personal feelings were set aside for professionalism, which was why Ellen was now the VP in charge of Public and Governmental Relations.

She wanted the lords to hold a press conference. Caddy had vapourized a person so thoroughly that some people were already saying that he never existed and the whole thing was staged. Whatever the conspiracy theorists said, there were hundreds of witnesses, and they were being interviewed right this minute. They needed to get their side of the story out and fill the information vacuum, and it was important that Lords Cadence and Kyrylo were seen as the victims.

So a hasty presser was called, a conference room at the Lotte was booked, and Ellen hoped that they could get one or two of the major stations and papers to send stringers.

Three orcs in the press were turned away, and while they made a huge fuss, they were told they didn't pass security protocols, and their organisations could send subs. Three and a half hours after the assassination attempt and during the evening news, a press conference was convened, and some stations carried it live.

Kyrylo spoke first and made a statement about the incident. He wore a very impressive white sling that showed up nicely in person, even if it didn't in video. He said that everyone on their team who suffered wounds was being taken care of, and no one had life-changing injuries. He spoke of the innocent bystander who died and how deeply they felt about such a tragic waste of life.

Caddy then stood up and spoke again about the woman who died. Then she continued, "Everyone who died this afternoon, and that includes the terrorist shooter, is a tragedy that should never have happened. We came to New York in peace to forge relationships with the American people, and that mission won't be ended by terrorists. We know that the vast majority of Americans are wonderful, hard-working, peaceful people who want to get along with their neighbours and keep their families happy and healthy. We stand with those Americans.

However, like Americans, I will defend my family and my life when the first shot is fired with the intent to kill.

I want to make it crystal clear to everyone that every single one of those terrorists will be brought to justice. Evidence will be gathered, terrorists located, and my legal team will give them to the American justice system to be tried. There will be no hiding, no forgetting, no forgiveness.

Now, Lord Kyrylo and I will take questions."

The press conference took about half an hour, and Kyrylo and Caddy patiently answered questions, whether sensible or silly.

She was asked why she didn't just disappear the terrorist to another location, and she said that she would not answer any questions about what she could or could not do.

Kyrylo was asked if his wound would affect his magical abilities, and after a very puzzled look at the questioner, he answered no.

When Kyrylo was asked why he didn't use his magic on the shooter, he just answered, "Lord Cadence got there first. I was otherwise engaged."

One reporter asked why Lord Cadence didn't simply wait for the police to handle the shooter, which earned an audible groan from the rest of the press.

"Sir, how many bullets am I and Lord Kyrylo supposed to endure before we fight back? The terrorist shot first. When I fought back, three bullets were shot at us with the intent to kill. That's not enough?"

At that point, the press secretary took the podium and closed the session.

As they were leaving, a reporter yelled out, "Lord Kyrylo, what now?"

Kyrylo turned and answered, "Dinner. I'm thinking pizza. Then we'll turn in early because it's been a big day, and we're tired."

But Caddy and Kyrylo weren't done yet.

Sam

Sam waited in the living room with Jameson and spent his time taking in the architecture and pricing the granite in that fireplace. He had been in many ritzy Manhattan houses during installations and often worked with top interior designers and architects, so Sam was not overawed by his surroundings, but he could tell that these elf people weren't worried about cash.

The lady fairy came in. She looked really tired, but she smiled and held out her hand, and Sam shook it. She was a little bit taller than Sam and had a nice look to her. She was more stacked than the fashionable animated skeletons that Sam worked for, and she was pretty average-looking, really, until you saw those pointed ears. And the eyes. He had never seen eyes like that. Bright, bright green with black rims like something you'd see on a cat or owl. She had silky snow white hair, and it was hard to estimate her age. Maybe in her mid to late 40s, he guessed. Neither old nor young.

The fairy king was taller, 6'1' or 6'2 with broad shoulders and an athlete's build. He also had bright white hair, but his eye, because there was only one and the other was covered by an eyepatch, was an intense blue. He had curly hair and a short beard, and a curled moustache, like out of an old photograph. The side of his face with the eyepatch showed major scars, scars that travelled down his neck, where they continued under his collar. He also shook Sam's hand and gestured to the sofa, so they could all sit down again.

His arm was in a sling, but as soon as he sat down, he took it off.

Caddy was the first to talk. "Lord Sam, may I call you Sam?"

Sam nodded.

"Sure, ma'am, I don't go by *lord* anyways."

Caddy smiled. "Well, you do now, whether you want it or not; it will take some getting used to. We have different names for different roles. To the world, I'm Lord Cadence, to my employees and some others, I'm Ms Caddy, and to other lords and friends, I'm Caddy."

"I call her *Zaychik*, but you can't call her that. Do you want a beer?"

Sam turned to Kyrylo, and for the first time all day, he smiled. "A beer would be great."

"We have pizza coming and something from room service. We'll see what they dig up."

That was how Sam became the next lord, sitting with Caddy and Kyrylo over pizza and beer and learning what it was like not to be alone.

Sam

Sam said he'd think about it.

They wanted him to go to a place in England where he could have some training in this lord stuff. Vera could come with him and would have round-the-clock specialist nursing care. He and Vera could leave at any time, and they'd pay all expenses. He was not at all under any obligation; they just wanted to make sure the orcs didn't get him before he could defend himself.

They knew all about the stinkers. Sam lived in a rough area, and he had his fill of stinkers. It seemed like they were getting much worse, too. He had some break-ins, and that was one reason he didn't like leaving Vera, even for a minute. If they broke in when he was out running around, she would be stuck in her chair, totally helpless. They would dump her or do worse, just for the fun of it.

Kyrylo guessed that the orcs were getting worse because Sam was getting stronger, and they could smell it on him. The smell of lords and elves made them aggressive. That made sense to Sam, and that was just one example of the things he would be learning if he went to England.

If he and Vera moved to their elf school, Vera would be cared for and safe.

He trusted Caddy and Kyrylo. He would know if they were lying; he was good at that.

Jameson rode with him back to the house, and as they walked to his door, he turned to the guard [what was he exactly?] and said, "Tell Caddy and Kyrylo I'll do it."

"Can you be ready in the morning? All you have to do is pack what is special for you that you want to keep with you. You don't need any clothes, and neither does Vera. You can leave everything here, we'll have people take care of the house. You can tell them what to do and they'll do it. The rest of us are leaving by boat tomorrow evening, but you'll be flying to Heathrow on a medical evacuation plane. I don't know the exact time it will be leaving yet. I need to make sure we have nurses and everything set up for Vera."

Sam shrugged. Sure, why not? There was no point in struggling against the avalanche, and he really didn't want to.

He woke this morning and took Vera out for a stroll. Twenty-four hours from now, he'd take Vera on a flight to England. But this time he wouldn't be alone.

Caddy and Kyrylo

At nine in the morning, detectives appeared at the hotel to interview Lord Cadence, and they were escorted to a conference room to wait for them. Despite all the witnesses and the obvious assassination attempt, protocols still had to be adhered to. There was a death in their jurisdiction, and they needed to take her statement, along with that of any witnesses on her staff.

Det Lopez was in charge, and he brought along three of his best so that they could take multiple statements at the same time, if needed. He'd worked high-profile cases before, and he knew they wouldn't get many chances to see the celebrities and their staff face to face. Once they went to ground, it would all be conference calls and delays. These lords were leaving the country tonight, and once they were gone, getting anything out of them was going to be hard. Of course, this was all just a formality; anyone could see her actions were self-defence.

Under the law, an individual can use the amount of force needed to defend themselves or others who are in imminent danger. The only question was whether the force Lord Cadence used was proportional or not.

A Mr Jameson came in to tell them that Lord Cadence and Lord Kyrylo would be down as soon as their American lawyer arrived. They would not be talking to anyone without counsel. There wasn't much the police could do about that, so they sat down to wait.

And they waited. And waited.

The lords were busy. Their lawyers weren't here yet. This was their last day in the US, and they had meetings and such, and would the detectives like a cup of coffee?

And they waited. The longer they waited, the more nervous the detectives became, and they weren't the nervous types. That woman just *looked* at the shooter, and he evaporated into dust. What if she could read minds?

At eleven, the door abruptly opened and in walked Lord Cadence, Lord Kyrylo (sporting his sling), and two heavyweight criminal defence lawyers, along with five of their uniformed security guards.

The minute they walked in, one of the detectives fainted dead away. This caused a bit of a delay.

Lopez turned to the lords, who were sitting on the couch across from him, looking with mild curiosity at the detective who was now awake and rolling on the floor, retching. They had to wait for the Lotte staff to drag him away and get medical help. Lopez wouldn't let the Rumlot security people touch him.

"Are you doing something to him? Stop it now."

Offended, Kyrylo answered, "No, of course not. What a suggestion!"

"Sometimes," Caddy offered, "People find us overwhelming. Maybe he's a fan?"

Lopez looked at the lord. From a distance, she seemed so ordinary. But up close, it was different. She had those ears. And something in her green eyes glinted.

"I don't think he'll be asking for a selfie with you."

Then Lopez got down to business and started his questions, beginning with Lord Cadence. The lawyers jumped in. There was the usual sparring as dominance was tested and established, and the first formal questions were asked. They immediately hit snags. Lopez already knew their official names, but when Lord Cadence told him her birth date was Feb. 2, 1925, his tablet wouldn't allow the year for a living person, only as a corpse.

There was more messing around with their official home address, which they said was simply *House, Ukraine*. ("...but you can't send post there because it's not accessible to humans...") So they ended up using the The Rum Lot shop in some podunk berg called Lowestoft in the UK.

Lopez sighed.

Then came the statement. Lord Cadence, as expected, was quite firm that this was a case of self-defence and that she was defending Lord Kyrylo and her staff and that she was sure her life was in danger. She pointed out, much to her lawyer's satisfaction, that the shooter shot off three bullets before she acted. She didn't know that man, nor did she have any prior contact with him. He was a total stranger, so there was no premeditation history to sort through.

Lopez then got to the question he wanted to ask all morning.

"Mrs Cadence –"

"Lord Cadence. Please use her correct title," Kyrylo interrupted firmly.

"Lord Cadence, what was the weapon you used to kill the shooter? If a gun was involved, we need to confiscate it and enter it as evidence. You can't keep it. You weren't close enough to use your body as a weapon…" and there he trailed off.

Caddy looked at her lawyer, who nodded. They had talked about this earlier when the detectives were cooling their heels waiting in the conference room.

"Detective Lopez, I did use my body as my only weapon. I sent a targeted high-frequency sound wave out that hit 270 decibels and boiled all the water in the man's body. Anyone standing next to him was affected by the very intense heat emitted by the terrorist. The parts that couldn't boil burned in the heat."

Her eyes glowed.

"Would you like a demonstration?"

"No, thank you, ma'am. I'll take your word for it." And he snapped his tablet shut and got the hell out of there as fast as he could.

After the detectives left, the lawyers told the lords not to worry, they would take care of everything. They could do the rest of the witness statements by remote.

Kyrylo looked at his fiancée, who constantly amazed him. "I didn't know you could do that! When did you learn to boil things with sound?"

She shrugged. "Oh, I don't know. I think I've been doing it for years without realising it. I'm British. I drink a lot of tea. It's a handy skill, heating up a teacup of water by humming."

As they walked out, Jameson heard her say, "But I didn't know I could use it as a weapon until yesterday, I wish I'd known earlier."

Caddy and Kyrylo

The party was getting ready to leave the Lotte for the ship when their PA walked in.

"Lord Kyrylo, the Canadian ambassador to the UN and another person – I don't know who she is – just walked into the lobby and have asked for a meeting. They said it would only be ten minutes, and it's important that it's face-to-face. But they won't say why. Jameson is running checks on them now. What should I tell them?"

"If Jameson is okay with it, then send them up." Kyrylo turned to Caddy.

"*Zaychik*, we have guests! Why don't you put the kettle on? Oh, that's right – you don't need a kettle."

"Shut up."

Ambassador Blanchet and Martha

Ambassador Blanchet walked into the living room and was met by Lordy Kyrylo, who had put his sling back on after losing it behind the couch. He and Lord Cadence were both dressed to leave, and around them there was a bustle of security personnel, personal assistants, and PR people moving luggage and piled by the door was an impressive number of aluminium cases holding goodness knows what.

She even had her hat on, which Canadian intelligence had told the Ambassador was "the sign" that she was going to step out the door. Without hesitating, he reached forward to shake her hand.

"Thank you so much for seeing us, Lord Cadence, Lord Kyrylo. I know this is not a good time, but there is something that the government of Canada would like to communicate to you in person."

"I'm sure it's important, Ambassador Blanchet, otherwise you wouldn't be here. So please, let's get on with it."

"Yes, um, well, I want to introduce Martha, a representative from the Stoney Nakoda people. I've known Martha since I was a child, and please take my assurance that she is a serious and well-respected person. She came to see me to tell me a story because she didn't think she had a chance to meet you without some official pull. I thought her story was interesting enough that I cancelled my afternoon appointments in the hope we could meet you today."

Everyone looked at Martha, a plump elderly woman with a very tired face. The lords didn't know she had been travelling for four days from her rural home in Banff Mountains to New York, which terrified her, and that she had camped outside the Canadian Consulate waiting to snag Ambassador Blanchet, whom she knew as the son of the owner of the local Ford dealership.

"Lord Cadence –" And there she stopped, overwhelmed and mute, and she stared at her feet. These were not human people with their strange ears and sparkling eyes. But they weren't Little People, either.

Then Caddy told her in Elvish not to be nervous, which Martha heard as her native Stoney, and she looked up, awed. The lord spoke Stoney! So she spoke Stoney back.

Both Caddy and Kyrylo heard her speak in Elvish and listened intently.

"My story is this. My father was a mountain climber. He loved the mountains and climbed up all the tallest peaks in the Banff. He left my mother for a mountain woman. He told us she was not a human woman and lived deep inside a mountain, and that she was thousands of years old. He said he fell off a ledge and hurt his leg, and she rescued him and took him to her home. Now he was her man. We all thought he was crazy and that maybe that fall had knocked the sense out of him.

"He came back every now and then to visit us kids and make sure we were all right. Whenever we needed money, like to go to school or set up a business, he would bring us gems and gold nuggets. And we bought him stuff to take back to her because he never had cash. Then one day he said to me, 'Do you want to come back with me for a week and see where I live?' I think he was drunk or maybe just – I don't know – but he asked, and I said, 'Sure, why not?' I was twelve; I wanted to be with my dad.

And so we hiked back, and it was a long, long hike. I don't know where we ended up, but I later figured out it was the mountain at least. The woman was there. She was very short and old, but not old if you know what I mean."

Martha looked at Caddy and Kyrylo.

"She had white hair, like you do. And her eyes were dark green, like malachite. Sometimes her eyes glowed, like there was a fire in there. Her name is Ratna, which she said means 'Jewel'. She said she was the last of her kind and lived in the mountains. I stayed there for a week, and she thought I was very funny. She said I made her laugh, but when I went back to the world, I wasn't ever to talk about her again. To prove she was real, so I wouldn't think I was crazy when I grew up, she gave me a gift."

And Martha pulled out a little bundle.

"My father died an old man and was happy with his life, I think. I never went back to see Ratna. But when I saw you on the news, I had to come and tell you my story. Because she was kind to my dad and was kind to me, I came looking for you. She was lonely in her mountain, and if she is not the last of her kind, that would be good for her to find out, wouldn't it?"

She handed the bundle to Caddy, who carefully unfolded it. In it was an elf knife.

Kyrylo took a sharp intake of breath. Caddy handed it to him, and he looked at it – there was no doubt. He handed it back, and she wrapped it up again and gave it back to Martha.

This time she bowed to Martha and said in English, "You have done the right thing. We'll find her. Not today, but in good time." Caddy looked at Martha sadly. "She must be very lonely. When you think you're the last one or the only one, it's very hard. Thank you so much for telling us your story. I'm sure coming here was not an easy decision to make."

Caddy turned to Lily, her PA on this trip, and told her to make sure they got all of Martha's details and that she got escorted back home properly. Then she turned to Ambassador Blanchet and thanked him profusely for bringing Martha to them.

He grinned, delighted that his instincts were right.

"The Elf Nation will have a hearty welcome in Canada. We would love to have you set up an embassy or consulate there. And maybe establish some elf colonies; I think we're a very welcoming people."

Caddy smiled, but didn't make any commitments. However, Blanchet reported back to Ottawa that he thought everything went very well, indeed, and that maybe, just maybe, they had their own lord living somewhere in the west.

In the meantime, the lords and their staff had a boat to catch, and they were already late.

Martha

Martha was escorted all the way to her front door by a very nice woman security guard. They flew her back first class! And she didn't have to lift a finger, not even to carry her own bags through customs at Calgary.

The PA got all of her contact details, and on the plane, Martha spoke with a friendly woman in England named Norma, who asked her a lot of questions about the mountain. She understood that it was over fifty years ago, and Martha was just a kid, but she said, in her funny accent, that they had a lot of clever people over there in Lowestoft, and they would work with what Martha said.

She was asked not to tell anyone else.

"There's a reason that Ratna stayed hidden, Martha. There are people who want to kill lords and elves. Look at what happened to Lords Cadence and Kyrylo in New York! So we need to keep her hidden and safe in her mountain for a while longer."

Martha understood.

Caddy and Kyrylo

The trip to the Manhattan dock to pick up the cruise leg back home was uneventful, unless you count that someone somewhere adjusted every single traffic light to be green from the hotel to the dockside.

They were the last passengers on the boat, and if Caddy hadn't been wearing heels, she would have run. But, given that she could barely move in the things she thought she was doing pretty good with a wobbly walk. Kyrylo threatened to throw her over his shoulder and haul her in that way if she didn't hustle, but she just made a face and went at her own speed.

This was a pleasure cruise ship on a repositioning voyage, not an ocean liner like the *Queen Catherine*, and the vibe on board was completely different. It was three times the size of the Cunard liner and had all of the modern bits of theme park theatre that new cruise ships were known for, like water slides, cinemas, and big shows. They even had an ice rink! This meant that there were many more young families and a much more casual and hectic atmosphere.

Caddy and Kyrylo had five very silly days at sea surfing on the wave rider, hurtling down the water slides, and drinking lots of ridiculous concoctions with umbrellas in them. There was nothing to worry about, no stop in the middle for work, and only a few orcs, who all came down with a mysterious gastric problem whenever they walked by either of the lords.

Southampton arrived too soon, and they were back in Lowestoft within minutes. By the time they went to bed, New York was almost a rather unpleasant dream.

LeeAnne

LeeAnne's plan to snag the elusive Ranger Wendell Bunn was simple. He wasn't allowed by his stuffy and unreasonable bosses to set up a simple WhatsApp with her? Okay, she could deal with that. He didn't give her a phone number or address? She could deal with that, too.

She knew where he worked.

If they couldn't hold a conversation like ordinary modern humans, then she would go back to olden times, just like what people did in World War II. LeeAnne paid attention to her history classes, and last year her favourite teacher taught a unit on letter writing during the war, and what the letters could teach historians about social history. He talked about epistolary romances. She would have one of her own.

It wasn't like there were boys at school who liked her. LeeAnne was clever; too clever by half, some people said. Wendell might think she was gorgeous, and her parents spoiled her rotten, but out in the real world, life wasn't so rosy. In the vicious scrum that was sixth form, she wasn't fashionably cute and since her sharp tongue didn't suffer fools gladly, her circle of friends was very tight. There was no boyfriend to take her mind off the Ranger, and frankly, she wasn't going to look for one.

The first step was to handwrite a thank-you note and send it to his work to be forwarded. It would, of course, have her return address on the envelope. If he wrote back to say not to contact him, she would honour that; she wasn't going to be a pain. But if he didn't outright tell her to get lost, that was another matter.

She would wait a month or so, and after her seventeenth birthday, she would pop a card in the post and see what happened.

Roman Kasianov

Professor Emeritus Roman Kasianov was old. Not as old as the languages he studied as a **professor of historical linguistics at Mechnykov National University**, but some days it felt like it. He taught an occasional class when enough foolish students signed up for it, but on the whole, he was long retired. As a courtesy, he still had an office at the university, which gave him a reason to get out of the house every day, and from that office he researched whatever took his fancy and the University was happy to have their name associated with any scholarly papers he published, at no real expense to the institution.

When he overheard the married couple speaking their beautiful language at McDonald's, he was just finishing up a paper called "The Evolution of Sanskrit: From Proto-Indo-European to Medieval Era Sanskrit." Roman was a collector of languages, but Sanskrit was one of his favourites, probably because it was fascinating to get into the minds of an ancient people. There was no better way to study the soul of a people than to study their language.

The couple, for whatever reason, didn't want to tell him what they were speaking about and gave him a very lame explanation. He wasn't fooled for a second that it was two lovers' baby talk. Their evasiveness just made him more curious. Why on earth would anyone not want to share their language? In all of his eighty-seven years, that had never once happened. People always wanted to share their language.

But he had his Rosetta Stone on his phone – the same phrase spoken in both languages – and with a bit of tracking down and AI, he could at least figure out what language it was, even if he couldn't translate what they were talking about.

He was wrong. What they were speaking was not in any database, no matter how obscure or ancient the language. Roman couldn't believe it, and as a professional researcher, he didn't believe it. They spoke to each other with the rapid-fire fluency of a couple who used the language daily, without thinking about it at all.

His AI program filtered out the background noise of the busy McDonald's, and it matched up a few sounds that he recorded with a very obscure database in Finland. It said the language in the recording had some matches with ancient Sanskrit, which was right up his street.

Roman started a dictionary, really only about two typewritten pages and there it sat for some months. Then one night he was watching television, and the news was wall-to-wall about an assassination attempt in New York on the King of the Fairies. And there he was, the man Roman had seen in McDonald's. The television didn't show a photo, but a drawing, and there was no mistaking the tall, bearded, white-haired man with the scars and the eyepatch. The woman in the drawings also matched the other person he saw in McDonald's.

Like many academics with very obscure specialities, Roman lived in his own little world, and he had no idea about the emergence of lords and elves. He didn't have any students now, so no young people came to sit and chat. Besides, he didn't keep up with popular culture, and the few people he talked to only talked about linguistics. Elves? Lords? What were they? So he put away the ancient Sanskrit he loved and spent the next two days getting caught up with modern life.

The more he read, the more he was sure he was listening to their language, the language of lords and elves. There was no dictionary, no translations, no nothing about their language in any format anywhere.

If he could create a dictionary of their language, it would put his name in the history books; it would be the cap of a respectable career.

No one would remember him if he died today, but if he created this dictionary, at least in academia, he would never be forgotten.

He desperately wanted to speak with Lord Kyrylo again; just one interview would do it. When Roman read on the internet that Lord Kyrylo once served in the Ukrainian Army, it seemed quite logical to write to the military and ask if they knew his current address. So he wrote an email and explained what he was doing and sent it off to the head of the Ukrainian Army Military Intelligence (where Kyrylo once worked), prepared to wait for a few weeks. They wouldn't answer on the first inquiry, but he'd just try again, and persistence usually paid off.

Instead, he had a UA Major knocking on his office door the next day. They were very interested in what he had to say.

Jack

Jack was falling for Alizah. He was falling hard, and he didn't like it.

For 3,500 years, he was content to fly around as a raven and have a little raven hen to care for. Oh, they only lasted about twenty years or so, if he was lucky, but each one was a little different, and they kept him interested in life. He helped rear thousands of raven chicks. He watched humans evolve and change, but his hens never did. They were a comforting continuity.

In his time as a lord stuck in his shape-change, he never once thought, "I would like to have a piece of that" when he saw a pretty human girl. He was so thoroughly a raven that the only being he was attracted to was another raven, and that certainly made life much simpler.

In the two millennia he lived, he never met another lord, at least, not one a living one. He saw a couple get burnt as witches, and he saw one die in the Battle of Hastings, but never a live one he could talk to. And only one of the witches was female.

But Alizah! Oh Alizah. Alizah was so badly damaged, yet she survived. She wasn't as clever as the other lords, but she was kind, and when she was relaxed, she had a sharp sense of humour. She was very unhealthy, but was getting better every day. She smelled really good.

Really, really good.

The joy she took in learning to control her abilities made Jack's heart sing, too. To go from fearing her powers and doing her best to hide them to embracing who she was – the transformation made her a different woman from the zombie who jumped the embassy gates and ran in desperation to Caddy.

Jack showed her how to catch the wind and use it. He taught her how to soar and sit on the updrafts. They flew very, very high, higher than he was comfortable with, and they raced to the earth. She learned to use the air to break her fall, and she learned the dangers of friction if she fell to Earth too fast. Most of her hair was burnt off during one such fast descent.

Alizah wasn't worried. It would grow back.

And all this was fun. He was having fun with her. They laughed and joked, and she would ruffle his feathers and scratch the back of his neck. And then one day, totally out of the blue, he thought, what if I turned back into a man?
He never told her that as man-lord he could fly, too.

He never told her why he became a raven. He never told anyone, mostly because for 3,500 years, there wasn't anyone to tell his story to who would understand. The raven hens certainly wouldn't.

It was the very end of the Before Times. The elf genocide was coming to its sorry finish, and the few remaining elves were escaping into hibernation. Orcs and humans were trapping and systematically killing off the lords as if they were vermin. All of the strongest lords died with Gaia, so there was no protection for weaker ones like Jack, and nothing they did could counter the aggression of the humans and orcs. Jack didn't know about lords like Neptune who went to ground; the only thing he knew was that he was alone and that all the elves were gone.

In the end, Jack was a survivor, but he was also prey. He could fly. Not as well or as high as Alizah, but he could fly. He could also move things, something Alizah couldn't do- yet.

He was surviving, but only if he totally hid his abilities and kept his eyes down when he was around humans. He still had to eat and didn't know how to hunt or grow his own food because that's what elves did, and they were gone. He had no money, because lords didn't need money, they had elves to deal with that. He constantly looked for more of his own kind, and they would be living with humans, or so he thought. Then the last of the elves disappeared. After they left, he lived on the fringes of society, adapting to human life by covering his eyes, pretending to be blind and begging for coins. He kept to himself, and for a couple of years, that worked.

Back then, humans and orcs were keen to catch lords; it was a sport, so they were always looking. One day, he was buying bread in a market, and as he handed the coin to the girl in the stall, something fell behind her. He looked up, startled, and she saw his blue eyes glow, and she screamed "LORD!" and that's all it took. An ugly, jeering crowd gathered around him, and most were orcs. The only way to escape was straight up, and that's what he did. He bolted straight up, and he almost got away, too. But someone unleashed an arrow, it grazed his skull, and his eye popped out. He shot up as high as he could go, screaming in unbearable pain and half blind.

Then he passed out and fell like a rock, out of control.

As he fell spinning and screaming from the sky, some deep survival instinct kicked in, and he shape-changed into a raven and glided to a tree. There he hid, shaking and cawing in agony. On the ground, the orcs didn't look for a raven; they searched for a man, and he escaped.

He never turned back into a man. Now he didn't know if he ever could.

Sam

Aelfeham House was just weird. There was no other way to put it. From what Sam could see architecturally, some of it was very, very old, and other parts were relatively new, and none of the parts matched. It was not laid out in any logical fashion, and that made orienting yourself inside hard, so it took him a good week to realise that the inside didn't match the outside.

A guy would walk down a hall in a wing and see five rooms on one side and five on the other, and each one would have two windows overlooking the garden. However, when you walked outside, you'd only see three sets of windows. Or you'd walk up a flight of stairs to the second floor and then up another flight to the third, and outside there would only be two stories. Sam was absolutely sure the Breakfast Room expanded and contracted based on how many people were in it at any one time.

He ate breakfast, lunch, and dinner there, even though it was called the Breakfast Room. When he asked an elf why they called it that, the man just looked puzzled. "Because that's its name. It's where you break your fast, and you lords are always hungry, aren't you?" Which, of course, made sense when you thought about it.

There was only one other lord who lived there full time – a rough-looking woman named Alizah who reminded Sam of a starving chicken. Painfully thin and nervous, every time he spoke to her, she flinched, and then she'd smile shyly and chatter back. She worked with a bird lord named Jack, learning to fly and all the lord stuff Sam was learning, too. Sometimes they sat in the same lectures with Jack, but mostly they learned as they went on.

Sam didn't have time for many lectures. Vera was dying, and that took up all of his spare headspace.

Alizah

The wind was wild and bitterly cold at this altitude, and while the air was very thin, Alizah didn't plan on being up here very long. She was dressed for it. The trick was to control her descent so that she flew precisely at the speed where friction warmed her up a bit, but not so fast that it burned her up. She was still regrowing her hair from the last time she lost control, and if she came back with singed hair, Jack would fuss and cackle at her. He didn't like her going this high.

But how was she to learn if she didn't practise?

It was hard to believe that she was terrified of using her ability and treated her talent as a rogue bit of insanity caged firmly in a box in her mind, under lock and key and with chains around it.

Oh, The Curse escaped every now and then, usually when she was relaxed and sober, and always with fekkin' disastrous results. Stuff would break, people would scream at her for being so clumsy, and her mother would beat her. So Alizah stayed as high as she could as often as possible and kept on constant alert for any hint that her weird Curse would spring out of its cramped little box.

But she was sober and happy the day Ms Caddy came to visit with Lord Kyrylo and Lord Jack, and, as it always did in such unusual circumstances, the box sprang open. She lost all connection with the ground and went bouncing across the fields and lawns of Aelfeham House like a wayward carnival balloon.

Only they were happy! Thrilled at her talent, to be precise. The lords laughed and cried and gave her hugs and made her feel that there was nothing to be ashamed of and that Alizah was a rare and special person. Every time she thought of that day, she got choked up. Every single time.

Lord Jack was assigned to help her learn how to control her ability and to teach her about being a lord, and he took it all very seriously. He visited her every day.

He yelled at her, but he was kind, too. He only yelled if he thought she was going to hurt herself. He wanted her to go much slower. She smiled and nodded, but Alizah had spent her entire life throttling back. Now she wanted to soar.

Her goal today was to fly very high – about 30 miles up to the edge of the stratosphere – and then return at an angle and end up hundreds of miles away. Over 2,300 miles to be precise. If she could do it, she could go from Suffolk to Caddy and Kyrylo's house in Ukraine in about forty-five minutes. Faster than they could do it with porting and helicopters!

They'd be *so* surprised when she showed up for lunch without using any porting at all!

Going up wasn't the problem. It was controlling her descent that made her tired, but she could do it. She just had to get the right angle.

She had the right angle. What she didn't calculate was re-entry in the middle of one of Ukraine's legendary autumn storms. Did she look at the weather app before she made this flight? No. It was a beautiful day in England, and it didn't occur to her that two thousand miles away the weather could be a little bit different. A stupid Alizah mistake.

It was a northerly, a nasty gale. As she descended, Alizah could see the grey boil of clouds beneath her, and she sighed. She'd be soaking wet by the time she found House.

The descent was rough, but that didn't bother Alizah. She loved it. If she weren't so ashamed of her old life, she would whisper that diving through a thunderstorm was the ultimate turn-on.

There was no drug that came close to the exhilarating joy of mainlining the raging power of a storm, and this was quite a storm. White water rafting? Parachuting? Free-jumping? Those sports were as weak as water compared to flying through screaming air as hard as rock, dodging balls of plasma, and surfing on the sheer power of the sky and earth as they exchanged energy. Alizah had become an adrenaline junkie and happily free-based on her new poison of choice – pure power.

The further she descended, the worse the storm grew until visibility was almost nil, and except for the flashes of lightning, the air around her was thick and black. To the howling winds, she was just another piece of random debris and of no more consequence than the gnats they also swept away. A ball of plasma cracked next to her, and Alizah looked up and in front of her. Where did that come from? *Bloody 'ell!*

A wall. A concrete wall in the middle of the sky.

She shot straight up as hard and fast as she could, but she wasn't quite good enough. As adapted as her body was becoming to this new life she had miraculously lucked into, the g-forces of the corkscrew turn and ascent still made her black out for a good ten seconds. Her foot caught the top of the wall as she blew over, and there was a flash of pain, then gale-force winds caught her and blew her where they wanted. Like that first day with the lords she tumbled and tossed in the wind, totally helpless, and her life was in the hands of the gods.

Jack

Jack looked in the Breakfast Room window. No Alizah. He looked in the kitchen window. No Alizah. She wasn't in her bedroom, and there was no sign of her on the lawns or in the barns and paddocks. He tapped on the front door with his beak and impatiently waited for the front desk to answer. One of the great disadvantages of being a raven was the lack of hands with opposable thumbs. He couldn't turn a doorknob.

As always, whoever was manning the desk that day opened the door, looked right over him, and then almost closed the door back in his face and so they forced the raven to caw to get their attention. Most undignified.

"Lord Jack! My apologies! How can I help you?" The receptionist was a human today, a pleasant-looking Oriental lady holding a crochet hook and a very ugly baby blanket she was working on. A pity she wasn't an elf, but he'd deal with it.

"I'm looking for Lord Alizah. Do you know where she is?"

She frowned. "Lord Alizah is on the log as being with you, sir."

And all the air was sucked out of Jack's lungs. He knew in an instant. She'd gone a-roaming. By herself.

"She's not with me. Track her."

The oriental lady was quick. She might not have had any taste in choosing her crochet wool, but she certainly knew her job. She whipped out her tablet, Jack hopped up on her desk, and they searched for Alizah's phone on the tracking app. The app pinged some unknown satellite, which pinged down to her phone, and the map on the tablet spun wildly before settling down. The pin for the phone showed up on the map in a blank green area that told them nothing, so the receptionist zoomed out.

Alizah was in Ukraine! Fucking Ukraine!

Jack was beside himself. He was so angry he couldn't speak, but the receptionist was fast and didn't need to wait for orders. She immediately put out an all-call and an emergency alert. Within minutes, security personnel in Ukraine were out looking for the wayward lord.

Jack didn't wait to find out what they found. He would deal with her in person.

An elf ported Jack to Dover, where he flew across the Channel. Once in Calais, another elf started the port chain that ended with House in eastern Ukraine. He was in the lord's living room in fifty-three minutes.

Caddy was sitting on the sofa with her laptop, and when Jack popped in, she looked up at the raven, and the expression on her face told him all he needed to know.

Alizah

The wind pushed her to the ground about ten miles from The Wall – on the wrong side. Alizah knew she was on the wrong side; she could smell the wrongness of it. She could smell orcs.

When the elf was removing some of her tats, he asked her who wrote on her body like this, and she told him she'd had an old boyfriend who trained to be a tattooist, and he practised on her. But he smelled bad, so she broke up with him. The elf looked up and frowned. The next day, her elf trainer came to her and gave her a little jar with a piece of cloth inside. Smell this, she said. It was horrible. Rank. Foetid. And it smelled just like the boyfriend who was such a crazy fucker she pushed his name right out of her brain. That's the smell of an orc, the trainer said. Don't forget it. Alizah didn't know how she ever could.

The place where she landed reeked of orc.

She could barely walk on her sprained or broken ankle, so she huddled under some bushes and held on, afraid that the wind would push her even further east.

I have really fucked up.

She had to rest. If she flew up, she didn't know if she could fight the wind, and gods, what would happen to her if she went further east? She was in Russia. She was in Lord Lester's land, and she knew all about him, too. He would mess with her mind, and she didn't have too much mind to mess with. And then he would kill her.

A light sparkled through the bushes, and when she parted the dying leaves, she saw a low building with an outdoor utility lamp. It wasn't much more than a shed with a corrugated plastic roof and concrete block half walls with an open front. A cow shed? Whatever it was, it was somewhat sheltered, and it had a roof which would keep her from floating away. And it didn't seem to have any people in it.

Cautiously, she crawled forward, praying she was right and no people were in there. She had her elf knife in her boot, but Alizah had no idea how to use it.

The building was a three-sided ramshackle pig shed. Inside were four sows lying on their sides and about a million piglets. There were no people. Alizah crawled into a dark corner and onto a pile of old straw and pigshit to rest and wait for the wind to die down.

She had to get back on the other side before she was missed, and Jack came looking for her. Alizah knew he would search for her, and she knew he'd fly over The Wall to find her. He'd flown over The Wall before, and she couldn't let that happen again. He wouldn't let her stay lost, and if Lester had her, then he'd get Jack. It made her whimper just thinking about it.

Jack loved her.

He would come to save her, and she had to get out of there before he crossed The Wall. He was just a bird. The orcs would kill him and eat him.

Kyrylo and Jack

Kyrylo sat in the Patria with Alizah's phone in his hand and argued with Jack.

Alizah's phone had fallen out of her pocket and lodged high up in a fork in a tree, and it took them a while to find it. It fell just inside the wide no-man's-zone that bordered the Ukraine side of The Wall, with the northerly winds blowing over a section of The Wall that ran east-west.

Every man and elf available combed their side of the wall, but Jack thought – and Kyrylo agreed – that Lord Alizah had probably blown over the wall. Kyrylo couldn't stop Jack from flying over to find her, but he wanted to do this with a bit more thought. Jack didn't want to think; he wanted to *go*. If he weren't locked in this damn claustrophobic truck with Kyrylo, he'd already be long gone.

"Listen, man! If you go now, you won't find her in this shit, and you'll end up being blown to Moscow. Let us put a tracker on you, if nothing else, and give this wind another hour. It's going to die down. The weather guys say it will."

"*Let me out*," the raven hissed. His eye glowed bright blue. "They could have her."

"And then what are you going to do? If they have her, we have to mount a rescue. If she's holed up, she'll fly back as soon as she's able, and we'll need you to look for her and guide her in. If you go looking for her in this wind, you'll just exhaust yourself, and you won't do her or us any good when we really need you." Kyrylo paused, but Jack wasn't buying what he was selling.

"Brother," and Kyrylo's voice broke, "I know what you're going through now. I know."

"*Let me out!*"

"Can we at least put a tracker on you? It'll be here in ten minutes. You'll need us if she is hurt. It will track you, and you can talk to us. Voice activated."

Jack hesitated, and Kyrylo let out the breath he hadn't known he was holding. He won that round.

"Ten minutes. And then I fly."

Olina

Olina didn't mind slopping the pigs, even in this weather. It got her out of the damn house and away from Sasha. The shed was even a bit warmer than the house, despite having an open side. Pigs generate a lot of heat.

She walked in and took her time feeding her piggies, chatting with the huge sows and cooing over the piglets. It wasn't like she was eager to get back to Sasha. The wind howled outside and whistled through the tin roof, and no one could hear her talk to her pigs.

She needed to be careful nowadays. If the wrong person heard her talk to the pigs, they'd say she was a witch or something, and it would take a lot of bribes to get out of that mess. Not to mention, she knew in her heart that Sasha would rather see her burned as a witch than pay a priest a bribe. It's not that he was looking to get rid of her; he was just that cheap, and women were easy to replace.

The pigs needed clean straw, so she scraped a pile of old straw and shit into her shovel and turned to throw … and Olina saw her.

Crouched in the corner was a terrified demon. Olina knew this was a demon because her eyes glowed bright green. She also knew the demon was scared shitless because Olina recognised terror, as well. God knows she'd seen enough of it.

The demon was crouched in a corner, and unless you looked for her pale face, she was invisible in the dark. She was wearing those witch clothes just like the posters in the church. The priest said every Sunday that if one of their imps or anyone from the west came over the wall, they were to call the police right away. There would be a big reward.

But if anyone helped them in any way, the KGB priests would build a big pyre in front of the church and traitor demon-lovers would be burnt as the devil's minions. They weren't joking. She'd seen it. As miserable as her life was, Olina didn't fancy dying. Her fondest hope was to outlive Sasha and visit his grave every Sunday so she could spit on it.

If she ran to Sasha and told him there was a demon in the pigsty, he'd turn this demon in – if the drunken bastard could catch her. And he'd drink all the reward money.

The demon was breathing heavily. She was scared. And she was a mess. Stuff blew in over The Wall all the time, and this one probably blew over in the storm. Demons could fly, couldn't they?

Olina made up her mind. She said, "*У вас есть тридцать минут, чтобы уйти.*" The demon shook her head. She didn't understand. Alizah was too panicked to translate the Russian to Elvish.

Carefully putting the shovel down and slowly, slowly turning her wrist to the demon, Olina tapped her watch. The demon blinked.

She held out her ten fingers and fluttered them three times. Then she pointed to her watch again. "*тридцать минут.*" Then she pointed out the door.

Olina turned and finished cleaning the pigs' old straw and putting fresh bedding down, always watching the demon out of the corner of her eye. She stopped to listen; the wind was dying down.

"*...пятнадцать минут*". She tapped her watch, and this time the demon nodded. She understood. She gingerly rose and hobbled to the door, still breathing heavily. Olina could see that this one wouldn't be walking anywhere. The rain was coming straight down now, not sideways.

The demon looked back at Olina and gave her a wan smile, and bowed her head to her. "Ta, love," she said. And then, right in front of Olina's eyes, she floated up to the sky and disappeared into the rain and low clouds. Like an angel.

Olina waited ten minutes and then threw down the shovel and ran shouting to the house. "SASHA! SASHA!" But when she finally woke her drunk husband up and they ran back to the shed, no one was there. He was too slow.

Sasha called the police. They came screaming in and said that, yes, a demon had been there. They could smell her, they said. They didn't blame Olina for running away as soon as she saw the devil. Olina was just a woman; it was only to be expected. Sasha was given a small reward for calling the authorities so quickly, and he only had to hand half of it over to their priest.

Three days later, after all the excitement was over, Olina went to feed the pigs, and in the dark corner where the demon-woman hid stood an imp, a perfectly formed soldier about a metre tall. He bowed, then disappeared in a shower of gold sparks– just like that! But he left behind a nice big pouch of British gold bullion coins. A fortune!

Olina didn't tell Sasha.

Alizah

Alizah sat high up a tree, resting. Her ankle screamed, but not as loudly as it did when she tried to walk on it. She could see The Wall – the wrong side of The Wall – off in the distance. Even through the mist and rain, its massive ramparts couldn't be hidden.

She needed to gather enough strength to fly high enough to get over it, and normally it would be a doddle, but today the flight over it might as well have been the Bataan Death March. She was exhausted from the long trip, fighting the wind, and the terror and pain of being on the wrong side.

When the beaten-down farm woman walked into the pig barn, Alizah was scared speechless. But when the woman stopped and stared at Alizah cowering in the corner, the lord sensed a kindred soul. They weren't that different. They were both just two broken women barely managing to survive. The only difference was that Alizah had found an escape and a future, and it was the Russian woman, with nothing ahead and everything to lose, who gave that future back to Alizah.

The tree swayed in the wind and lost some dessicated brown leaves to the storm, but she still had enough cover to keep her from being seen from the ground. Off in the distance, she could see Russian army trucks patrolling their side of the wall, but they seldom stopped. When the soldiers got out to pee and smoke, even though they were far away, Alizah could see they didn't seem too bothered. Over the years, when she lived on the streets, she watched a lot of coppers, and she could tell when one was looking for a dealer or when they were just wandering on patrol. These soldiers weren't looking for her or anyone else.

The rain faded to a mist, and off in the distance, she could see the ragged end of the storm clouds and the late afternoon sun shining behind them. A flock of crows flew over her, and scattered in the flock were a few large ravens.

The ravens made her think of Jack and, oh, she could have cried. She missed him so much, and she knew he would be looking for her by now. The ravens passed overhead, and she knew they weren't Jack. She could always tell Jack from the ordinary ravens; he was far bigger and, well, he was Jack. She didn't even have to see the blue eye to know it was him.

Alizah kept her eyes on the west and towards The Wall. She didn't see the ravens wheel around in a big, lazy circle and head back the way they came.

She decided to wait a bit because the constant patrols worried her. The forest shadows were lengthening, and it would get dark about five o'clock now. If she waited another hour or so for the sun to go down, she wouldn't be silhouetted against the sky.

Dusk came, but with dusk, there was a different burst of activity with the patrols. All of a sudden, they weren't so casual; the soldiers didn't dismount to pee and smoke. They looked at the sky now, and she could see the lights of their vehicles reflecting off The Wall. Then a truck-mounted searchlight drove up. They were looking for something on The Wall.

"ALIZAH!"

She screamed and jumped, almost falling off her branch. It was Jack! She was so happy! And then she burst into tears.

"Jack! Blimey –" and she clung to her branch and sobbed her heart out.

"Alizah, darling, you need to calm down." He lit on a branch near her. "We have to get out of here."

"I'm so sorry, I didn't –" She sobbed again, "I'm sorry –"

"Don't worry about anything. You need to be brave. We have to go." Jack tilted his head so he could see her out of his good eye. It glowed bright blue, something Alizah very rarely saw. He must be very angry with her.

"Can you fly?"

She gulped a great shuddering breath and nodded. Now that Jack was here, she could fly.

"We're going to have to get altitude, but not as high as you were today. You have to stay with me. Do you understand? Stay with me." She nodded.

"Good girl. Ready? Steady! Go!" and off they flew. He pumped with his wings, gaining height, and she stayed right with him.

He didn't fly directly to The Wall, but banked so that he came at it about half a mile to the north. She could see there were fewer patrols on the ground there. This was where he wanted to cross.

Something spotted them. Maybe it was a visual spotter, or maybe they showed up on some radar, but they were seen. There was a scattering of gunfire from the patrols below, and Alizah saw the tracer bullets as they aimed their chain guns at the two lords. But they were high now, and the Russians' aim was bad, and she and Jack raced to The Wall. It suddenly loomed in front, and its grey mass was both a barrier to freedom and the finish line.

It was so close now.

The helicopter came out of nowhere. Diving at them from above, the Hind sped towards the two flyers, raking them with its mounted machine guns. A bullet grazed Alizah's face, but not enough to even slow her down. She and Jack screamed over the wall with all they had, but the Hind closed in, recalibrated its aim, and –

It exploded.

There wasn't anything left after the explosion. Nothing. A Hind Mi-24 has titanium rotor blades that are resistant to 12.7 mm rounds. The cockpit is protected by ballistic-resistant windscreens and a titanium-armoured tub. The rest is heavily armoured. None of that helped this helicopter.

Jack and Alizah plummeted down and landed hard in no-man's-land. The minute they hit the ground, elves ported them to safety.

Kyrylo stood on top of The Wall and watched the disintegrated Hind's ashes fall to the Russian earth below like a thousand sparklers.

"I've always wanted to do that," he said to Bram.

"Yeah, Boss. I can see why. It's very pretty."

They ported home.

Kyrylo

Kyrylo sat on the front porch on one of the big rockers, watching the sunset and smoking a cigar. Caddy wouldn't let him smoke inside. She said it was rude to House, and, of course, she was right.

Autumn was here, and it was getting cold out now, but he had a good coat on, and Caddy was sitting on his lap, so really, he was nice and warm.

"You are hot," he said and kissed her cheek. She giggled.

"Oh, that's what all the boys say."

"Oh, yes, that, too."

Alizah and Jack

Inside, in House's spare bedroom, Alizah had finally fallen asleep. She cried and cried and couldn't stop apologising to Jack and absolutely every elf or human or lord she encountered for being so stupid and causing everyone so much grief and putting everyone in danger as they worked at rescuing her.

She cried because they loved her.

She told Jack everything that happened and how worried she was when she realised how badly she had screwed up and how angry she was sure he would be. Because, as she said, "You love me, and you wouldn't let me stay there. I knew you wouldn't, and I was so afraid you would come for me and the orcs would get you. And then what would I do? Who could I love like you? I'd be alone again – forever."

He must have told her a million times he wasn't angry with her, not any more at least. It took a long time to convince her he didn't hate her, and that yes, he was very mad, and then he was worried, but now he was fine. Disaster was averted.

Sleep finally found her. The healers patched up the bullet wound on her face and said the scar would fade to nothing in a few days. If it had been a millimetre to the left, it would have taken out her eye, and the only way to fix that would be the cauldron. The fractured ankle would take a few more days, but it would soon be fine, too.

Now all they had to do was get more food in her. She was fine-boned and thin on the best of days, but now she was shockingly emaciated after using up every bit of her fat and reserves.

Jack nested in the armchair, dozing, his good eye opening with the smallest of slits every ten minutes or so to see if she was still sleeping. To make sure she was still there.

When Alizah's breathing became deep and regular, he got up and went to the kitchen. House or the elves would have something cooked for him, and he would have a bite and then go find that head healer, Dr Mandy. Jack had a question, and he wanted her opinion.

Lester

Lester was apoplectic. A farmer had reported that a "demon" was found hiding in his pigsty. The report was investigated by the local police and found to be credible. His orcs had visited the site and could smell him.

Their report was sent to Moscow, and there it sat unread for hours. By the time it was read and the general in charge of the area put the border patrol on alert, the demon was on his way back to The Wall – flying! It was a fucking flying lord. A flyer!

Lester hadn't seen a flyer for over three millennia. They were incredibly rare. A HIND was put on patrol on their side of the wall as soon as the alert went out. When the border guards saw the lord flying, they told the HIND, and the copter went tearing over there and, by some miracle, spotted the lord just as he reached the wall.

And then that damn Kyrylo blew the helicopter to smithereens. It didn't just explode, it disintegrated into dust. He must have been waiting on top of the wall for that flying lord to return to the West.

Helicopters were hard to replace. Very hard now that Russia has been oppressed by more than a decade of sanctions. The West still had the best toys, the best tech, the best everything, and they weren't selling any of it to Russia. The greedy bastards certainly held a grudge.

But what was worse than losing the lord and the helicopter was what this all meant.

Lord Kyrylo was sending in probes to Russia. They were doing what Lester had been doing all along and looking for weak spots. And that meant they were out to assassinate Lester.

Lester could hardly breathe. He wasn't that strong in his abilities. In the end, he was just a run-of-the-mill lord, and when he was honest with himself, he didn't even rate "mediocre". He wasn't part of the elite Elemental club, nothing near it. He won his fights by stealth and trickery, not by the strength of his ability. Lester couldn't even levitate things. Kyrylo was an Elemental. He was amazingly powerful, and that bitch lord of his was pretty strong, too.

Lester never did figure out how she got out of the prison cell he put her in.

He heard all about New York even though that wasn't one of his operations. She boiled the bastard to death, and that took real power. He wondered if she was an Elemental, too.

So Lester, the Tsar of All the Russias, had an Elemental lord trying to kill him. Maybe two. He had never fought an Elemental, and the prospect scared him shitless.

Lester and Lena

Lester went to Lena to complain to her about her cursed father. If Kyrylo was out to kill him, then he needed Lena more than ever. She was a human shield that Kyrylo might – might – hesitate to kill, and she knew how her dear daddy's mind worked. She might help Lester find a weak spot to exploit.

But the woman was not feeling well. She was throwing up, and one thing Lester could not abide was a sick human around him. Since he couldn't kill her, he left.

The doctor told Lena that she could have what she wanted, but not until tomorrow. The pharmacy was closed now. Then he called up the general in charge of the medical department, who told Lester she was looking for a morning-after pill. She thought she was pregnant.

Lena was sitting at a table in her lounge, working on a thousand-piece puzzle of kittens. Lester walked in, and she looked up to give him a kiss, and he slapped her so hard she went flying off the chair.

Then he kicked her. What he really wanted to do was kick her in the stomach, but he couldn't do that, so he dumped the table. As she frantically tried to crawl away through the scattered pieces of kittens, he picked her up by her hair and held her ear near his mouth. He had to pause because he was breathing so hard he couldn't talk.

"Don't you ever do that again. Don't you ever try to abort *MY* child, you fucking bitch."

"I thought you didn't want any kids. I thought you'd be happy," she sobbed, and Lester saw the fear in her eyes. It was enough.

"You didn't ask, did you?" He dropped her. She was heavy. "Is it mine?"

Lena nodded, scared. People here kept saying that you can't lie to this lord, and she knew better than to try. She told the truth. She also knew how to talk to Lester.

"Yes, it's yours. How could I fuck anyone else after you? You screw me a lot. I have lots of orgasms. I guess I was more fertile than I thought."

Lester thought about this. He was a stud; he knew that. She certainly seemed to enjoy him; how could she not? And he believed the ancient lie that a human woman must climax if she is to drop an egg. The lord was almost four thousand years old and was barely literate. Women's plumbing was not something he ever thought about.

And then he blinked. Lena was the daughter of an Elemental. A woman of good blood. *His* bitch. And now she was going to whelp *his* child.

He looked at the sow crawling on the floor. His child would be the grandchild of an Elemental and sired by a lord. His child could be a lord. The bloodlines were there. With Lena, he could create his own cadre of lords. He could breed his own power base.

With something like regret, Lester thought about all the female lords he had killed over the years. He should have kept them and created a dynasty, which he would forever be the head of. If he had kept them, he might not be in the trouble he was now.

He bent over Lena and picked her up, and hugged her. She was as stiff as a board, terrified he was going to hit her again. This was going to take some talking to smooth over, but this was what he was good at.

"Love, you make me so angry. It's your fault I beat you. Why do you do this? Why do you make things so hard? I love you so much, and then you do something that makes me so angry, I lose my temper."

He stroked her face and looked into her eyes. "Of course, I want this baby. It's *our* baby. It will be as beautiful as you."

"You–you don't want me to get fat. I just want to do what you want."

"Of course, you do, love. But being a pig at dinner is one thing; growing a miracle in your belly is another." He kissed her forehead. She was bleeding from a cut lip, and her mouth was disgusting.

"Please don't make me so angry again. Don't provoke me. I love you, you know that. I love you more than you know, more than you deserve."

Her back relaxed, and he smiled to himself. It was working. He was really so good at this.

He started kneading her ass, his little signal to her. "Come on, let's go make up. You have to promise me that you won't do anything, nothing, without asking me. Don't make me hit you again. I really hate that." He kissed her again. "We have to work together as a team. You have to show you love me as much as I love you."

Lena smiled at the Tsar. Everything was back as it should be. She liked being Tsarina and wouldn't change that for the world. If he wanted this brat, she would make it. It's not like it would be more work for her. That's what nannies were for.

"I promise. I'm sorry– I thought–"

"You thought wrong. Let me do the thinking. " He cupped her butt and rubbed against her.

"Let's go make up."

Jack

Two days after he and Alizah returned to Suffolk, Jack went back to see Healer Mandy in person in Ukraine, porting and flying the same route he took when he sped east to find Alizah. It made him feel better to see her in person; this was too important for a video call. He had asked her earlier what she could do for him, and she said she'd think about it.

The doctor's office was a pleasant one, as doctors' offices go. There weren't any weird charts of body parts and STD warnings on the wall like in the human's NHS office. The chairs weren't plastic, and the desk was a pretty Louis XIV confection that held nothing on its gleaming surface but a pad of paper and a computer terminal.

Jack sat on the chair in front of the desk and tried not to dig his claws into the padded leather seat. Dr Mandy, the senior elf healer, looked at her blank pad of paper and tapped at it with her pen, frowning.

"There's a risk, you know."

Jack nodded. There was always a risk. Everything was a risk. Breathing was a risk.

Dr Mandy leaned forward. "What if it doesn't turn out the way you want? Have you thought of that? I'm not talking about dying, I'm talking about," and she looked at the big raven keenly, "disappointment."

Jack tilted his head. "There are worse things than disappointment. I'm disappointed now, and I muddle along. When I was a man, I wasn't exactly a god. I'll be happy with my old imperfections. I don't think I'm expecting too much."

"I'm not just talking about a crooked nose or an unfortunate mole. I'm saying that you could come out as some other kind of bird or some half-bird, half-man combination like Neptune. Only Neptune has his half-and-halves to live with and make a community. If you come out half raven, half human, you won't be able to shape-change at will like Neptune, and you'll lose the community you already have, the ravens."

Jack had thought of this. He was very old and knew about the risks of the cauldron from his life in Before Times. He had heard of the satyrs, minotaurs, gryphons, and other half-and-halves that emerged from it. Most of the time, the cauldron worked. Occasionally, it didn't, with disastrous results.

"You've been a raven for 3,500 long, long years, Lord Jack. That's a lot of muscle memory. Your body thinks it's a raven now. Your mind will have to think it's a man again. Not just the memory of what you looked like. You'll have to think you're a man and want to *be* a man. When Lord Cadence went into the cauldron, she had only been an octopus for a little over a day. In her mind, she was unquestionably a woman with two legs, not eight. She knew what she was and what she should look like."

"I understand, Healer Mandy. I am ready for this. I have a clear idea of what I am and what I will be."

She nodded. Lords commanded the impossible, and elves obeyed when they could. And this impossibility was what Lord Jack wanted. Mandy would do it.

"Have you told anyone about this yet? Have you told Lord Alizah?"

"Not yet. I wanted to talk to you first."

"Talk to everyone, and if you still want to do it, give me a call. Think long and hard about what your body looked like before you changed. If you start dreaming you have wings or the way your beak looks, you're not ready, and you're risking chimaera. "

Jack nodded.

"I will visualise, Healer Mandy." He tilted his head. "I wouldn't mind being a bit taller this time around."

Mandy laughed. "Keep it in mind, Lord Jack."

Jack and Alizah

That afternoon, during flying practise, Jack told Alizah he was going to the doctor for a little procedure.

She was practising floating in one place, which was harder than it looked. Hovering like a hummingbird meant constant compensation against variations in wind, temperature, and even the gravitational mass of objects that passed by.

She lost concentration and slowly turned upside down.

"What kind of procedure? What's wrong with you?"

Jack fluffed his feathers and shifted from one foot to the other.

"Nothing is *wrong* with me. Think of it as plastic surgery. I'm going in for some improvements."

Alizah was immediately suspicious. Jack was being evasive, and that meant something was wrong.

"What needs improving? You're perfect," she bounced gently, still upside down. "You're not tellin' me porkies, but you're not being honest, either. I can tell, y'know."

He sighed; there was no getting around it.

"I'm going to turn back into a man, like I was."

Alizah dropped like a rock. Luckily, the damp grass was soft. She sat up, rubbing her head.

"Back to a *man*! You used to be a *man*?"

Jack was surprised. How could she not have known?

"Of course, I used to be a man. I wasn't born a raven. I shape-changed into a raven. Now I want to morph back. The doctor is going to help me."

She crouched on her hands and knees until she was eye-to-eye with the big bird. Her green eyes glowed, and her face was scrunched up like she was going to cry.

"*No*. Don't do it."

Jack was mortified. Alizah's objection was the last thing he anticipated.

Or maybe, if he was honest with himself, he did worry about her saying no. Maybe that's why he didn't want to tell her. Still, it was disconcerting to hear she liked him better as a bird over being a man.

"Why not? I was born a man. I became a raven out of necessity, to save myself. I stayed a raven to stay alive when lords were hunted, but now I feel safe enough to be a true man-lord again."

Big tears ran down her face as Alizah sat up, shaking her head. "If you become a man, you'll leave me." Then she really let go into sobs.

All Jack could do was fluff up his feathers and caw. If he were a man, he could run to her and hold her and tell her not to be silly, but he couldn't do that because he was a damn overgrown, meat-eating black chicken.

"Alizah! I wouldn't leave you! Why would you think such a thing? I'll still be Jack. I'll just have arms instead of wings!"

"You'll leave me because you're a man, and all men want to do is run off and fuck women. I'm an old, ugly, stupid dopehead, and you're going to leave me."

"Alizah! The only woman I want to fuck is you!" Shit. He said it. How crass was that?

She stopped crying.

"Really?"

Jack was embarrassed. If he could've blushed, he would've, but he couldn't because he was a bird.

He tried to regain some dignity. "Alizah, you and I are dear friends. If I stayed a bird, that's all we could ever be." He scratched the ground.

"You're not an old, ugly dopehead. Every day, you're growing into a healthy lord, and when you're at full health, to anyone looking, you'll be neither young nor old, and they'll certainly think you're beautiful. You're beautiful to me, just as you are now. You'll have your pick of men when you start going back out in public. And there will be new lords coming. There's Sam."

"Sam is married."

"He'll outlive her, Alizah. She'll be gone soon. How many hens have I outlived?"

Jack looked in the middle distance, towards nothing but a bleak future.

"You'll grow and change. And I'll still be a bird. A pet." He didn't sigh, but he could have. "You're changing, Alizah. I have to change, too. Nothing ever stays the same, and we have to accept that."

Alizah sniffled and wiped her eyes.

"Promise me you won't leave me when you become a man again. *Promise!*"

"I promise I won't leave you, Alizah."

Alizah gulped and blew out a long, shuddering sigh, deflated. Jack said he wouldn't leave her. She didn't believe him; they always left in the end. But at least he said it.

"When does this operation thing happen?"

"Anytime I want. Maybe I'll go in tomorrow. There's no point in dragging it out."

"Have you told Caddy and Kyrylo yet?"

"No, I will, but they're not the important ones, and they won't change my mind. You're the only one who's important, Alizah."

"Can I change your mind?"

"No."

Alizah sighed again and accepted the inevitable. She started to float a bit. Just a few inches from the ground.

"Okay, I'll go with you and wait. Where is this going to happen? Is there a waiting room?"

Jack shook his head and explained everything to her about the process. Well, not every little thing. There were details he thought he'd save for later. Like the risks. There was no point in getting her all worried again. She was floating now, and the wind was carrying her back to the house, and he had to fly to catch up.

"When I'm a man, I'm going to tie a string to your foot and tow you around like a balloon!"

Alizah laughed and floated a bit higher.

Jack

The cauldron was set up in an unused drawing room in Aelfeham House. To Alizah, it looked like a big metal hot tub.

She was pretty laid back about the entire process as she watched the pot being set up. It was the expected result that unnerved her. She was okay when Dr Mandy gave her instructions via video phone about how to talk to Jack while he was asleep and not to touch the water he would simmer in.

Anyway, she was pretty calm until Ms Caddy and Kyrylo came by to give Jack their best wishes and have a last drink with him before he went in. Suddenly, their solemn faces and tearful hugs made her wonder if Jack had told her everything.

The cauldron was filled with water that trembled with a simmer so gentle it was almost invisible. Alizah stood opposite Jack, who was perched on the lip of the huge pot, and she tightly held on to Ms Caddy's hand. Kyrylo stood behind, a hand on their shoulders.

A nurse elf gave Jack a pill, and he immediately started to go to sleep. His eye started to close. It fluttered. Then it popped open.

"Good night, everyone. I'll see you on the other side."

"Good night, Jack," they all replied. No one said *good luck*.

He started to sway.

"I love you, Alizah."

"I love you, Jack," but she was too slow. He had already fallen into the pot.

Alizah ran to the cauldron and looked over the side. Earlier, she was told not to touch and contaminate the water, so she didn't reach in, but she could see him, eye tightly shut and lying at the bottom, bubbles already forming over his entire bird body where feathers trapped the air. Dr Mandy's nurse threw in something that looked like herbs, and the liquid thickened to a golden custard, and that was that.

A glossy black flight feather was on the floor, and Alizah picked it up.

Now she just had to wait.

Alizah

Kyrylo had told Alizah what he did when Caddy was in the cauldron, and while he didn't understand why he was talking to a pot, it made perfect sense to Alizah. They were talking someone down, like they were high and it was a bad trip. They were connecting them to the real world.

She only left the cauldron to go to the toilet and to shower. She ate and slept next to it. There was always an elf nurse sitting there, too, and Dr Mandy checked in to see how Alizah was doing at least twice a day. The healer had remote access to all of the cauldron's particulars through her computer, so really, she was watching the entire time. If Mandy needed to add something to the goop simmering in the cauldron, she told the nurses what to d,o and they followed her instructions exactly.

Once Alizah was curious about the bubbles, and she floated over the big pot. The nurse yelled at her to float her ass back over the floor. She was NOT to float over the pot and lose a hair or cry a tear or sneeze into Jack's goo. Chastened, she didn't try that again.

So she sat in a big, overstuffed chair and listened to the gentle plop-plop of the simmering goo and waited. She talked to Jack until she was hoarse. She told him about her old life, sure in the knowledge he wasn't going to remember a thing she said. She haltingly read the newspapers aloud, and she talked about the weather. She gossiped and spread rumours and offered her own muddled interpretation of what was going on with orcs and Russia and whatever else she could think of. Every day, she told Jack she missed him terribly.

On day five, a big egg floated to the top of the goo. Dr Mandy told Alizah to expect that, but it was still a shock when it happened. It was a big fucking egg, and it wasn't hard, it was kind of rubbery. If she looked very closely, sometimes she could see the faint outlines of body parts. A foot, an elbow, the top of a head, the curve of a spine.

A man was in there.

On day ten, the cauldron exploded.

Alizah sat, as she did every day, in her comfortable chair with her feet up on a footstool, flipping through dance videos on TikTok. Without any warning, the custardy goo that Jack lived in began to boil. As soon as the nurse saw the temperature spike and the thick glop bursting with huge bubbles, she hustled Alizah out of the room, calling for her colleagues. Just as Alizah left the room, the entire contents of the cauldron exploded, leaving a thick, opaque golden slime covering every possible surface of the sitting room.

The nurse gave Alizah a massive shove and slammed the door behind her, and all she could do was stand there in the hall and wring her hands. She was told that this would happen, so she wasn't entirely surprised. Dr Mandy had said that all births were sticky and violent and so not to worry about that, but to see it for herself shook her up. What if Jack got hurt? What if he were drowning in custard? What would that goo do to his feathers?

An elf popped in and led Alizah to the Breakfast Room, where she waited for news. Every few minutes, the nurse elf assigned to Alizah would pop out to go to the cauldron and then pop back in and tell Alizah not to worry, everything was going fine. Then she would pop out again to repeat the cycle. Every time she popped back in, she was a little bit messier and gooier and a bit more out of breath.

Finally, about an hour later, she said Jack was okay and sleeping up in a bedroom and that if the lord wanted to see him, she could, but not to touch him or try to wake him up. Of course, all Alizah wanted in the world was to see Jack, and they raced to the bedroom.

And there he was.

Alizah crept forward and looked. There he lay, a waxy, pale, puffy man with no hair at all, as still as a corpse on the snowy white sheets. His hands were down at his side, and he barely breathed. But breathing, he was. His lashless eyes were closed. He was asleep.

Slowly, her hands went to cover her mouth, and her pale green eyes filled with tears. Somehow, the man's face looked like the raven Jack. Somehow, as puffy and round-edged as this new Jack's face was, she could see the angles of the raven's head. Maybe it was the rather large hatchet nose or the set of the eyes, but this was Jack. Man-Jack.

The cauldron worked.

She sat down to wait.

Jack

Jack woke up, and Alizah was there. He looked confused and groggy, but he smiled at her when he saw her. And when she said, "Hiya, Jack," he weakly nodded.

He had two eyes! They were a flat pale blue with black rings around the irises, but they were both there, and they both seemed to be working.

He didn't say anything at all, just looked around with that puzzled expression on his face. The nurse came in with a bowl of soup, and Alizah was allowed to feed him. It took a bit of coaxing to get the first spoon in, but whenever she spoke, he stopped and looked at her and smiled. Then the smile would turn into a goofy grin, and it's hard to eat if you're grinning.

When the last of the soup disappeared down his throat, he shut his eyes and fell back to sleep. Alizah's hands were shaking so hard when she handed back the empty bowl to the nurse that the spoon rattled. Then she went out to the hall and had a good cry.

Alizah fed him every two hours, and the nurses kept him clean and dry. She was going to feed him throughout the night, but the nurses wouldn't have any of that. The lord needed to sleep, so they shooed her out of the room exactly at ten and wouldn't let her back in until she was finished with her own breakfast at eight.

In two days, the puffiness was gone, probably because Jack peed out all of the water. He pissed a huge amount of water and weird, black poo, but no one seemed worried about it. Dr Mandy said his internal systems were starting their work and adjusting to the real world. By the end of day two, he was much brighter mentally and he started making some noises.

It was funny, the raven Jack was extremely articulate and spoke a lot. Sometimes too much! But the man Jack had problems. He stuttered and seemed to have problems connecting the sounds he made to words. Dr Mandy just said something about neural pathways resetting, and since she wasn't bothered, Alizah wasn't going to be bothered, either. It would all smooth out in good time.

By the end of the third day, Jack was sitting up in bed and his hair was starting to grow back. Alizah could see the glint of the peach fuzz as it emerged. His hair was going to be white, like Caddy and Kyrylo's. For some reason, she thought he'd have black hair, black like a raven, but then, he was very old.

Dr Mandy was quite firm that Alizah couldn't touch Jack in any way until she gave the go-ahead.

"They aren't like real babies. Cauldron-babies are reformed and reborn in about a week, and everything like skin, bones, and internal organs is tissue-thin and fragile. Think of him as a bubble that can pop at the slightest touch. Every day, he'll get stronger and sturdier, but it'll take time and he'll have to process a lot of food. By the end of the second week, he'll be walking. Maybe earlier. We'll see how it goes.

"But in the meantime, keep your hands to yourself even if he makes the first move. You would feel badly – and I would be very angry – if there was a setback or broken bone because one of you got a bit ahead of yourself."

Alizah promised to follow the rules. She was very, very careful not to touch him when she fed him. By the end of the first week, he was speaking much better and one day, when she was feeding him the inevitable bowl of soup, he reached up and touched her hand. It was the lightest of touches, but she panicked and flew to the other side of the room.

"Jack! No touching! What if I hurt you?"

He scowled and stuttered, but his meaning was clear.

"I'm ff-fine. Y-you didn't touch me. I touched y-you. How c-can you hurt me?"

"I don't know, but I'm not going to find out."

She floated above him and fed him with her feet, almost touching the ceiling and from as far away as her arms could reach. He would have to leap up to touch her.

This made him laugh, and he was okay. Besides, Alizah didn't know it, but he could look up her shirt. That was interesting.

The next day, Jack insisted on using the toilet by himself, and when Alizah came to help with the breakfast soup, the menu changed to porridge, eggs and heartier food. He also managed some shaky steps to a small table set up in the bedroom and he had his first meal as a proper adult man. Alizah still cut up his meat and helped him with buttering toast and that sort of thing, but he was moving forward and everyone was happy. That afternoon, the nurses ended the round-the-clock care and instead only came in when called.

They told Jack to go to the drawing room and watch TV from the sofa because it was a bit of a walk to the room, and sitting up was "good for his core", whatever that meant. It was there that he kissed her.

Alizah was fussing over his place on the couch, making sure he was comfortable and re-arranging the pillows that the nurses had carefully placed there, when she bent over him, and it was then that he put two fingers on her jawbone and turned her head slightly, and he kissed her.

It was a long, slow, tender kiss, as light as a whisper. And Jack smelled so good. Every now and then, Alizah got a whiff of Kyrylo and that put thoughts in her head. But Jack – Jack was starting to smell like a man now, and whatever he had in his sweat put the other lords to shame. She floated on that kiss.

When the kiss ended, and it ended much too soon, and her feet touched the ground again, Alizah was flustered and bright red.

"If you kiss me like that outside, I'd better be tied down. You'll have to chase me to China."

Jack leaned back and smiled. "I'll chase you t-to the moon."

The next day, Jack started practising his abilities. When he was a raven, he couldn't do much other than be a raven. Before he morphed, he didn't need wings to fly, and he could move things. Alizah was naturally a better flyer than he ever was, but then, in Before Times, he didn't see the need to practise and stretch his ability. When everything went to shit, it was too late to work at getting stronger. It was all he could do to stay alive.

For her part, Alizah couldn't move anything other than herself. She tried, but it just wasn't in her.

When she came for breakfast, Jack levitated a bit of toast to her plate, very pleased that he could still do that. By the afternoon, he was moving things around as if the intervening 3,500 years were a dream and right before dinner, he put on real clothes and went outside to see if he could still fly. He could and made a very wobbly circle around the lawns, but his magic worked the way it should.

There was only one piece of equipment he still had to try out, and Dr Mandy hadn't given the green light on that, but he was patient. He was more worried about Alizah's psychological state than he was about his own physical well-being. She'd lived a rough life, and he wasn't going to add to any trauma. Jack heard more during his time in the cauldron than she realised.

And so it went, day by day, with Jack growing a little stronger and both becoming a little more sure of where they stood with each other.

After about two weeks, Dr Mandy signed off on Jack and released him as a patient.

While they both knew they could have sex, they didn't. Alizah was terrified of breaking Jack's bones, and Jack was terrified of breaking Alizah. If she didn't want that kind of intimacy, he wasn't going to force the issue. There was too much bad sex in her past; he wasn't going to add to it. When she was ready, he would be there.

Wendell

Life returned to normal in Lowestoft. Wendell rose at four-thirty every day and jogged to Fen Park, where, rain or shine, he had his five in the morning exercises and close combat training.

It was normal, but different now. Before the trip to New York, he worked hard and was respected for that and only that. Amongst themselves, the elf soldiers admired his ability to take a beating, but that's where it ended. They didn't respect the human stripling. Most didn't like humans, period. There was too much Before Times history of warring humans and orcs working together to slaughter elves to forgive and forget. Too, too much history, too many family members murdered, and some could never bring themselves to talk to their pet humans. But the soldiers were also too professional for any animosity to come out in the open. They were told to work with Wendall, not marry him.

Wendell knew.

They didn't understand what Lord Cadence was thinking of when she asked Victor to make this soft, serious boy a Ranger. They didn't even know what a Ranger was supposed to be.

When they asked him directly what the shit a Ranger was, all they got back was a fuzzy mish-mash of "wood lore expert, loner, survivalist."

But lords command, elves do, and so they whipped him into shape, taught him some basic hand-to-hand, sword, and knife skills, and in the afternoons, he took bizarre lessons on political systems, psychology, sociology, and, gods help the poor sod, etiquette, dancing, and how to dress himself. It was weird.

Then he was trotted out to be a go-fer and give Victor a break from teaching, and ended up killing the first orc he met, in hand-to-hand combat no less! *And* then he rescued a new lord and got him through orc country and into the hands of security. *And* while doing that, he incapacitated *three* more orcs.

There were elf warriors who didn't have four hand-to-hands with orcs notched on their knives, and yet here was this kid, whom *they* had trained, batting orcs away like flies. When the Lowestoft soldiers visited the Safe Haven pubs, where the warriors from different clans hung out, they were quite insufferable.

A Ranger, it seemed, was a freelance warrior working secretly and alone amongst the humans to help the elves. James Bond worked for MI5. Wendall Bunn worked for elves. Same job, different employer signing his paycheque.

About two months after the Lowestoft security team returned to their home base, Victor told Wendell to meet him in the conference room. The room was empty, and Victor sat at the huge table with an envelope in front of him.

Without comment, he pushed it to Wendell. The front of the envelope had Wendell's name and "% The Rum Lot, London Road South, Lowestoft" in girlish loopy handwriting. The back had LeeAnne's name and return address. It was still sealed, but Wendell had no doubt it had been opened and read by everyone who felt a need to see it. Elves had no sense of privacy.

Victor frowned. "Did you ask her to write to you?"

"No, sir. I certainly did not."

"Well, she did." Victor glowered. "She should be sending your post to your house, not here. We don't have time to be playing central sorting office here in the shop, and I don't have time to hand deliver letters to you."

"Yes, sir."

"So when you write her back, make sure she knows that."

"Yes, sir."

Wendell put the letter in his jacket pocket and turned to leave.

"Oh, and Bunn! You are no longer on duty with that job. That mission has been completed."

"Yes, sir."

Wendell sat on his childhood bed at home and opened the letter. Leanne wrote a short, polite, rather stilted thank-you note for saving her life and best wishes for his career as a Ranger. There was nothing personal in it. No entreaties to set up a chat group on WhatsApp. It was as if she knew other people would be reading the note.

For a long time, he looked at the heavy Crown Mill Bond note paper. Then he answered it.

Jack and Alizah

The new Jack was unnerving. He was still the same old Jack if she shut her eyes and listened to him, and he was still her true friend. But, but, but….

Alizah could honestly say she had no real friends in her old life; the drugs and the itinerant nature of street living prevented that. There were plenty of people around her who came and went in an unending train of use and abuse, but she certainly wouldn't call them friends. They didn't hang around her because they liked her; they hung around for what they could get out of her. As she aged and sickened, there was less and less benefit to them. She was just an old addict with a monthly benefits check who was only useful on benefits day and a stinky, addled, needy pain in the arse the other twenty-nine days a month. In the last ten years, she couldn't even sell her body for a fiver. No one wanted it.

At Aelfeham House, she found friends. Jack was just one, the most important one in the end, but she also had the elves, the human staff, and Caddy and Kyrylo. They all liked her and would talk and laugh with her. They were all kind. They dried her out and kept her sober. They asked for nothing other than that she be as kind to them in return.

They loved her flying! They wanted her to practise and get better at it. Once she allowed herself to open that box in her mind where she kept the Curse caged, she didn't need the drugs. She stopped, cold turkey, and that was the end of it.

If anyone asked, she'd tell them she could happily live in Aelfeham House forever.

Jack was a true friend. He loved her even when she was silly. He wasn't afraid of her Curse; he was even proud of it! He didn't steal her benefits money. He didn't steal her stuff to pawn to feed his own habits. He didn't demand BJs in return for a fix and a place to sleep it off.

He was a bird, but what of it? Alizah didn't need a man; she needed a friend, and Jack was perfect as he was.

But this new Jack, Man-Jack, was a different beast. He was still her best friend, but now he wasn't quite so neutral a being. Ravens didn't have penises, but this new Jack did, and Alizah knew what that meant. If she didn't give him some release, he would find someone who would. Oh, he'd still be her friend, but it wouldn't be the same. She'd be sharing him, and she didn't want to do that, not at all.

Without knowing the term, Alizah the lord had bonded to Jack the lord even before he became a man, and there never would be anyone else for her. The thought that he would leave and fall in love with someone else made her cry just thinking about it.

She had vast experience in ten-minute increments with men and a few women in back alleys in return for a tenner, but she had no experience at all with making love. She didn't even know where to start.

What if he looked at her naked and saw her as she really was?

What if she bedded him and he didn't like it?

What if he didn't love her *that way*?

Already an addict and living on the streets before her first sexual experience, Alizah was like the vast majority of hookers in that the actual act was just a meat processing job. Sex used a few inches of her body in order to milk the cow, and she felt nothing at best and only pain when they beat her. A few times in her life, she fell in with a boyfriend and if they were sober enough to care, they might take more than a few minutes to play with her and give her a kiss, which felt nice. But she hung around with other addicts, and most couldn't even get it up if they wanted to. The drugs took the place of everything, including sex and certainly intimacy. Alizah would bet nuns and priests fooled around more than the typical addict.

Between Jack's new man scent driving her crazy and being weighed down with fear of losing him because of her own inadequacies, Alizah couldn't stop thinking about sex. The problem was that the more she thought about it, the less sexy she felt and the more afraid of losing him she became.

Tuân and the Old Man

Tuân lived on the wrong side of the Binh Di River in Vietnam with his three younger brothers and sisters, his Mom and Dad, and the Old Man. In front of the house was the river and a small dock. The back had a vegetable garden that ended with a fence, and on the other side of the fence was Cambodia.

They lived what could only be described as "poor but happy" lives, which was something rich people said when the poor didn't complain in front of them.

He and his brother and sisters all went to school. The Old Man insisted on it and somehow always came up with the school fees, even when Mom and Dad would rather the money be spent on something else, like fixing a leaky roof and other minor luxuries like eating.

If they went to school hungry, the Old Man said that at least they wouldn't be sleeping and wasting his money. He just went out fishing for a few hours longer, if they needed something to eat. It wasn't like Mom and Dad didn't work hard; they did, it just wasn't always enough to support three kids and an old man with no pension.

But to the Old Man, Tuân's education was important, so the boy tried his best and was very successful in school, such as it was. He was considered clever, and he spoke English and Chinese perfectly in addition to his native Vietnamese, so there were cautious hopes he could get into a modest university and find a career that would lift up the whole family.

The only hitch to that reasonable and happy plan was Tuân himself. He didn't look Vietnamese, and that mattered a lot in a homogeneous society, especially one that lived outside the big cities and tourist areas. Tuân stuck out. He had frizzy rust-coloured hair and bright blue eyes. Aside from that, in a black and white photograph, his face shape and slight build perfectly matched his father's. He was just so damned colourful!

In school, he was teased unmercifully, and more than once, the Old Man or Dad would meet him after school to make sure he got home safely. After a few years, the bullying faded away, but lately it flared back up again. When Tuân came home one day with a bloody nose and told the Old Man the kids at school called him "dead fish" because he smelled like one, the Old Man was more upset than usual. Just finish out the term, he said. Then you'll be out of that school, and I'll find you another.

Tuân had no idea how the old guy expected to do that or even where he thought Tuân could go. It wasn't like they were swimming in money to pay for university tuition.

The Old Man, though, was full of surprises.

One day, he walked into the house and gave Tuân a bag. In it was a brand new pair of shorts, a Slayer t-shirt (Tuân had no idea who Slayer was, but the t-shirt was cool), some Crocs, and a backpack. He was told to pack underwear for a week and a couple of his best t-shirts, shorts and that they were going to Ho Chi Minh City. And that's all he would say.

Mom was really upset at the Old Man's vagueness. Why? Who are you going to see? Where will you stay? She peppered the Old Man with questions, and he just grinned and said, "You'll see. It's a surprise." Dad was more phlegmatic. The boy would be leaving home sooner or later, and the old guy loved Tuân best and wouldn't let him come to any harm. He probably has some university scheme cooked up. It was just like the Old Man to keep it a secret.

So one morning, they boarded a bus and made the exhausting trip to Ho Chi Minh City, where they stayed overnight in a dirt-cheap hostel. The next morning, they hired a taxi, and no one was more surprised than Tuân when the Old Man said, "Tan Son Nhat, please. International flights terminal."

That's when Tuân got upset. Was the Old Man going crazy? In the last week, he'd been pulled around like a doll, and now he reached the end of his rope. Wasn't this *his* life? Didn't he have a right to know what was going on?

The Old Man was calm in the face of Tuân's meltdown. Secretly, he expected Tuân to lose it much sooner, but the boy was patient and trusted him, which made him feel all the more pressure to get this right.

"Do you trust me?" he asked.

"Yes, but –"

"Then let me do what I have to do. I'm going to get you into a good school."

"At the *airport*?"

"No, stupid boy, in England. We have to go to the airport to catch our flight." The Old Man looked out of the window of the cab, grinning like a demon.

Tuân's jaw dropped. *England!* ENGLAND!

"Thanks for telling me."

The Old Man did have the grace to look a bit sheepish. "I didn't know if I could come up with the money for this until the last minute. If I told you, you'd tell your parents. They wouldn't want me to spend this kind of money on a trip, and Sen would scream if she found out we were going so far away. She's going to be very angry with me." He shrugged, "Not that it'd change my mind, but it would have caused a lot of unhappiness and we would've had to sit through her freaking out for days, maybe months."

"England! Where did you get the money for tickets to England?"

The Old Man shrugged. "The same place I always get money when we need it. I do jobs for people." And he looked out the window; Tuân knew the conversation on *that* topic was closed.

The airport was chaotic, but only to Tuân, who'd never been in one before. The Old Man, on the other hand, seemed perfectly at ease. He didn't have any problems at all and was in a fine, good mood, telling Tuân to watch and learn because one day he'd go through airports by himself. They went to the ticket counter, and the Old Man pulled his and Tuân's passports and visas out of his backpack; he presented everything they needed for the international flight. The old man and the boy breezed through security, and after an hour of sitting in the waiting area and watching travellers bustle to and fro, they boarded an Air Vietnam airliner for a direct fourteen-hour flight to Heathrow.

The only problem they had in the air was a flight attendant who served them dinner and started retching. After that meal, they didn't see her again, so that was okay.

When they landed at Heathrow, it was very early in the morning. The Old Man was a bit more hesitant because, he said, he had never been to England before and they had to figure out the Tube. It was here they started to speak English instead of Vietnamese, and after a few minutes of adjustment, Tuân had no problems understanding Brits, despite the accent. The Old Man had enough money on him to pay for the Tube to central London and for a bite to eat, but that was it. How he was going to pay for a hotel, Tuân didn't know.

But he knew where he was going, despite jet lag. He had an old-fashioned paper map since neither of them had a phone, and he did fine with it. By eleven o'clock, they were sitting on a park bench outside of a very, very fancy mansion, and the Old Man dug deep in his backpack and handed Tuân an envelope. "Take this to the door," he said, "Hand it to whoever opens it, and tell them we're waiting here."

Tuân looked at the envelope, then back at the Old Man, and sighed. There was no point in putting up a fuss now, not when they've come so far.

So he did as he was told.

He went to the door, rang the intercom button, and in his best American-accented English said that he had a message and they were waiting outside on the bench for an answer. A voice asked him to please put the message in the post slot.

Mission accomplished, he walked back and took his place on the bench, and they waited, drinking Cokes and sharing a can of Pringles.

"How long do you think this will take?"

"I've no idea. An hour? A day? A week?"

It took about ten minutes, then an elf popped out about a foot in front of them, took a good look at both and then popped away without saying a word.

"SHIT! Did you see –?"

The Old Man nodded. He saw. He blew out a long, slow breath and looked at the sky.

He flashed a grin at Tuân as if he saw elves every day, but his hands were shaking, and the Pringles can rattled.

Tuân knew about the elves. Who didn't? Even the backwaters of Vietnam watched news about the Lord's visit to New York and the assassination attempt, and elves was on TV for over a year now. *Mrenh kongveal* were a part of Cambodian stories, and the Vietnamese had their own spirits, so there was a lively discussion at school about which group the elves of Europe fell into.

And here was one who came out in response to something the Old Man had written. Tuân didn't know whether to be more impressed by the elf or the man sitting next to him on the bench, who had summoned him. The Old Man was always something of a mystery, but this was an entirely new level.

Suddenly, about ten armed guards trotted out the front door and between them walked the King and Queen of the Fairies. She raced ahead, and the men and women ran to keep up. In her hand, she clutched a battered navy blue passport, and she cried, "How did you get –"

Then she stopped as if she had been punched in the stomach and put her hand to her mouth.

The Old Man stood up and grinned.

"Hi, Mom!"

2000, Caddy and Ricky

Ricky was seventy-two when he retired after forty-one years of sitting in his cubicle at Lackland AFB in San Antonio. He had a very, very good civil service pension, and Caddy had her teacher's pension, so they had absolutely no money worries. Not that anyone would ask, but they hadn't worried about money for decades.

They lived in the same tiny ranch house on the north-west side of San Antonio that she and Ricky bought back in the early '60s. Back then, the house was hidden way out in the country where, as Ricky used to say, it was so far out they had to pipe in light. Over the years, San Antonio doubled in size, and now the modest forty acres of useless mesquite scrub and caliche they bought for almost nothing were surrounded by some very posh houses.

In '78, Ricky inherited a modest amount of cash from his dad, and since they didn't need anything, he invested it in the stock market for the kids. Maybe, he thought, they could use it to buy a car or something. With his usual thoroughness, he studied how to buy stocks and created a few spreadsheets and did some thinking about possibilities. He set up an account with a broker, and every month he put most of Caddy's teaching money into tech stocks. First, it was Intel, then over time, he changed to Apple and Microsoft. Investing was a light hobby, a different way to think of strategy, and he was good at it.

They became very, very rich. The only evidence of unusual prosperity that any of her colleagues in the school noticed was that Caddy stopped shopping at Walmart and changed to Target. The only change Ricky's workmates noticed was that he bought a used Cadillac instead of a Ford pickup.

Then their boys died. They wouldn't be buying any houses or cars, and the deposits in the Bank of Mom and Dad simply sat there, earning dividends, and the automatic allotment from Caddy's paycheck deposited every month went to buy more stock.

In 1999, when she was forty-five, Lizzie married a Brit named Gareth who worked in the oil and gas industry in Houston. In 2000, they moved to, of all places, Lowestoft, where he worked in an office designing rigs for the North Sea oil fields.

Caddy and Ricky lived in Texas with nothing to do, piles of money, and no kids nearby or grandkids in the offing. Lizzie was all they had. So when Ricky tentatively suggested they move to Lowestoft, Caddy was shocked because Ricky hated change, but after thinking about it, she didn't see any reason not to.

She hadn't been back to the town for almost fifty years. She didn't go back for her father's funeral; indeed, she didn't even find out he had died until two years later when an addled uncle sent her a Christmas card and mentioned it. She had no contact with her mother or her brothers, and everyone seemed satisfied with that arrangement.

They flew in for an exploratory visit with Lizzie and ended up buying a big ramshackle terrace house on London Road South, not at all far from the first flat Caddy had shared with Reggie so many years ago. Ricky was happy with it and paid cash with no complaint, so Caddy was happy.

Caddy's mum, Dora, lived in a care home in Oulton Broad. At ninety-nine years old, Dora had some form of dementia and never said a word to anyone about wanting to see her daughter. Caddy made no plans to visit her, but Lizzie was determined that she should go see the old woman "for closure". Caddy went simply to satisfy Lizzie, not for herself, because Caddy couldn't think of a more nonsensical idea than "closure".

Caddy never forgot that day and always rolled her eyes when she bothered to think of it.

"Closure". There was no such thing as "closure". That was pop psychology crap written by people who obviously had never felt real grief, hate, or love. All three emotions can fade, but only with time, not through cheap words or theatrical hugs. As long as there is memory, there is no closure. Closure only came with your own death and the memory-erasing Void.

She and Lizzie walked into a brightly lit conservatory that smelled of pee, stale coffee, and disinfectant. A row of ancient women in wheelchairs sat lined up in front of the window, all in various stages of slumping and sleeping. Glenn Miller played in the background.

The carer pointed out the one who was Dora, and Caddy walked up to her, clutching her purse in front of her like a shield, her knuckles white. Dora looked up, frowned, and then waved a manicured hand in front of her face, and Caddy thought for a minute she wanted to shake hands. But no, she was pointing.

"Caddy? Is that Caddy?"

Tears came to Lizzie's eyes. This was going to be beautiful.

"Hiya, Mum."

"Caddy? Good Lord, girl, you've gotten fat."

And then she went back to sleep.

There was no such thing as closure.

Conary

Caddy sat in the sitting room of the guest suite in the Elf Nation embassy and stared at her long-lost son, Conary. Conary, who at age eighteen had walked out of their house in a drug-induced haze and disappeared, only to be declared dead four years later.

Conary.

Sitting in front of her was the same Conary who had slammed the door on her so many years ago. Conary, who obviously was not dead and had never been dead, but who now had decided to reappear and pop in for a visit with his mum.

Kyrylo sat next to her, holding her hand tightly, worried to death that she was going into shock or suffering some sort of mental breakdown. Anyone could see Conary's resurrection was as traumatic as his death. There had been no closure with Conary.

Tuân, Conary's grandson and Caddy's great-grandson, sat across from them in something like a stupor, only his eyes moving as they darted from person to person, desperately trying to make sense of what he was hearing. The Queen of the Fairies, Lord Cadence, was his great-grandmother. The Old Man was his grandfather and Lord Cadence's son.

Across from his mother sat Conary, who seemed rather calm, considering. He held a cup of tea in his hand, wearing the tourist uniform of a t-shirt and shorts, his tanned legs crossed, and looking around the room with open curiosity. He just finished telling the lords who he was, who the boy was, and their relationship. This was all news to the young man, too, who also stared at Conary in shock.

"Why?" That was all Caddy could choke out.

"Well, Mom, Tuân here needs to go to a good school. He's –"

"No. Why didn't you contact us years ago? Why did you disappear? Why?"

Conary placed the teacup and saucer carefully on the table next to him, sighed, and looked at his hands.

"I was ashamed. I guess that's it in a nutshell. At first, I was ashamed of who I had become. I was ashamed of how I had treated you and Dad. Then I was ashamed of what I was doing to get by. Then later, when all that bad stuff eventually became part of my past, too much time had gone by, and I was ashamed for not trying harder. I was dead to you, and it was better for all of us if I stayed dead. That's what I thought."

Conary looked at Caddy. "I'm an old man now, Mom. What I thought was the best thing to do when I was nineteen or twenty was, looking back, pretty selfish, self-centred thinking. You flew a long way to look for me, and I was still being selfish. Thinking about myself and my shame came first."

"I always thought you were around when I was in Bangkok. I never saw you, but I felt you watching." Caddy's voice shook.

"Yeah, I watched you twice. The second time you sat in a phone cafe and did one of your puzzles. I guess you were waiting for a call to come in. Dad called you. I could tell from your end of the conversation. You told him not to cry, that you would go back to Texas, that you couldn't find me. You cried, too." Conary sighed from deep inside and stared into his teacup. "I was so ashamed I had caused you so much grief and expense. To come to Bangkok and spend that kind of money, risking your life going to dangerous places, looking for your druggie son –" Conary looked away again, and his jaw trembled.

"So you sent me ashes –"

"Yeah, to put a final period to my life story. To allow everyone to move on. Closure. It seemed a good idea at the time."

"But time went by. Why didn't –"

This time, Conary smiled, and in that smile, Kyrylo could see the family resemblance.

"Well, as time went by, I matured a bit. I was living in Vietnam, married, and had a couple of kids. Sen is my daughter, and Tuân is her son. I lived way deep in the country; backwater doesn't begin to describe the way it was back then. I was going to ground because of business associates who thought I should keep working for them, and I didn't want to, so I disappeared. I became invisible. When I finally worked up the nerve to contact you and Dad, you had moved! You left with no forwarding address, and my letters came back! I didn't have the money to go look for you or pay someone to do it; I had to take care of my wife and kids first. So I let it go. After all, I was dead."

"I was here in Lowestoft. So were Lizzie and your Dad."

"I didn't know that. You never said a word about going there for a visit in all of my life, and certainly nothing about moving there. I never thought Dad would ever leave the country. Actually, I thought you were in Florida."

"Florida?"

"In the States, that's where retirees go to die, right?"

Caddy didn't know what to say to that. Florida!

"So, how did you find me now?"

"Jeez, Mum! You're a worldwide celeb! The Queen of the Fairies!" Conary laughed. "Can you imagine what it was like to be in the deepest, darkest jungles of Vietnam and look up at a TV in my local bar and see the Queen of the Fairies meeting the King of England, and her name is Cadence Aeldor? How many Cadence Aeldors live in the world now? Only you, I bet. It's not like your name is Jane Smith."

He continued. "When I picked myself off the floor, so much – so much – started to make sense. I read everything I could about elves and lords and such. You were always a lord, weren't you? You never told us. Did Dad know?"

"I didn't know myself until the elves told me I was a lord. So no, Ricky never knew." Caddy looked at Kyrylo. "Kyrylo didn't know either for a long time. We just knew that the older we got, the odder we became, but not what it really meant. We're still learning."

She looked back at Conary. "We have a lot to talk about when it comes to being a lord, you and me and Tuân, but now I need to know what changed your mind. Something changed your mind and made you come to me."

"Tuân. He's having some problems. The same problems I had at school with bullies and such. People were saying he smelled funny, and they beat him up." Conary looked at the boy fondly. "He's a good boy and needs to go to college or something, so I'm here with my begging bowl to see what you're willing to do for him."

Caddy nodded. As soon as she saw him, she knew it was Conary. And she knew the boy and her son were both lords.

"You and Tuân will get everything you need. We have a lot to talk about."

Tuân

The ceiling was very tall and had a chandelier in the middle and elaborate plaster cornices where the ceiling met the walls. The bedroom was massive, probably as big as four rooms in Tuân's home, maybe as big as the whole house. No one shared it with him. He was alone.

Tuân lay in the huge bed, stared at the chandelier, and thought about what he had heard.

The old man who had lived with them all of his life as a boarder was really his grandpa. Tuân wasn't surprised. He had a mirror and could see the white man parts of his own body and face, and there weren't many white men in their branch of the delta. But it was still a shock.

His mom had never once mentioned that his blue eyes were like her father's or that his kinky red hair was down to normal inheritance.

Conary/Grandpa/Old Man always had a deep tan, so his whiteness didn't stand out as much as it could have. And he shaved his head, so his hair didn't give anything away, but he couldn't hide his blue eyes. But now that Tuân thought about it, he did; the Old Man wore sunglasses all the time when they were out in public.

Being old, he had wrinkles just like every other grandpa. He spoke perfect, unaccented Vietnamese, which helped hide him in a crowd. And he kept to himself. There were no women, no carousing in bars, no male friends to go fishing with. None of the neighbours cared that he was there, and no one noticed he was different. He was invisible.

And he was the son of Lord Cadence, a magical person according to the news reports, of unknown and unimaginable power and wealth.

And the Old Man had risked everything to bring his grandson here. If Lord Cadence hadn't recognised him or accepted him, if she had hated him for what he had done, then this entire trip would've been a disaster.

Tuân was pretty sure that Lord Cadence would send him to a school. Probably a good one. And he was pretty sure she would pay for the Old Man's flight back to Vietnam so his family wouldn't be bankrupted by that. Tuân would offer to pay it all back, of course. That would only be right.

His last thoughts before he went to sleep were how much he loved the old guy, even as weird as he was. He was true family.

Caddy

Caddy lay on her back and stared at the ceiling. Kyrylo lay on his stomach facing away from her, his hand rubbing her belly, not because he wanted to start anything frisky but as a comfort for her. He was there.

Conary was back from the dead. She still couldn't get over it.

He was Conary but not Conary. The Conary she knew had been eighteen years old and was a sweet, quiet boy who listened to music in his room, read history, and suffered bullying in silence, not wanting to worry his parents. Then there had been druggie Conary – the spaced-out, surly addict. And then there was dead Conary, the invisible hole torn in the hearts of his parents.

Today's Conary was an old man who had lived a full life, but one as a fugitive hiding from gods knew who. Probably drug dealers or Mafia types. A man with a dead wife and three kids of his own, who had their own families.

Caddy had three grandkids! All adults, all with lives that would soon be horribly disrupted. All with wants and needs that would need to be managed.

She had nine great-grandchildren!

It was beyond belief.

Tuân was the only one with blue or green eyes, according to Conary. All the rest had the dark brown/black eyes of the native Vietnamese.

Conary was old but very fit for his mid-seventies. He had been using his magic even if he didn't realise it, and that had kept him younger than his years. He looked to any stranger to be about sixty.

At nineteen, Tuân was too young, as far as Caddy knew, to be able to use his ability. He probably didn't even know what it was much less practise and use it. He was at the dangerous age when orcs could smell him, but he couldn't defend himself against them. And as a young man, he couldn't and shouldn't be kept in a gilded cage at home. He had to get out in the world, but he would need training, and he would need bodyguards.

Tomorrow will be very busy. She turned and spooned up against Kyrylo and went to sleep.

Conary

Conary didn't stare at the ceiling; he was exhausted. Emotionally and physically drained. He slept the minute his head hit the overstuffed pillow.

He did a lot of smiling and had a light and breezy air about him, but that was a facade he had perfected decades ago. Look confident, act as if everything is going well, crack some jokes, and get yourself through whatever trauma that needs to be managed.

Inside, he was screaming in fear. Pain. Regret.

But it was going to turn out okay, he thought. Underneath the fairy queen surface, Mom was still Mom. She loved him despite his weirdness – because it turned out she was even weirder.

She forgave him for all the lies, or at least he hoped she did. Conary didn't know if she would ever forgive him for breaking Dad's heart. He couldn't forgive himself. That's why every day he tried to be the best dad and grandpa he could be. It was payback for being such a god-awful son.

Now he had more to pay back for not being around when the rest of his family died. He figured Dad had died when the news kept talking about this Lord Kyrylo, who was Mom's new man. Ricky would be over one hundred himself! Conary hadn't known that Lizzie and John were dead. That was a hard one to process now.

He hadn't known that when he sent his parents those fake ashes, they were still mourning their John. That bit of torture he had inflicted on his parents would take a lot of atoning.

Sam

Sam sat in the fancy house that was now the training school for newly found lords and had breakfast with Vera. She was fading fast now, and no one bothered with putting *The Addams Family* on the TV for her because she was now past caring. The doctors told him that her Alzheimer's was shutting down her body, and he had to make decisions on how far they should go. Feeding tubes? What if her heart stops? Resuscitation? What happens when she can no longer swallow water?

Getting old sucked.

Being the loved one left behind sucked, too.

She had all the nurses and elves that she could possibly need to keep her clean and comfortable. Her care was first-rate, and for that, Sam was profoundly grateful. But first-rate or not, she was a human, and there was only so much the elves could do. The human doctors and specialists could do even less.

Sam was going to let her go. No special measures were to be taken; just keep her comfortable and let her slip away. It was the hardest decision he had ever made, and he sat with the pen in his hand a long time before he signed the Do Not Resuscitate paperwork. He knew it was the right choice and the one Vera would want him to make, but still – it tore him up.

She no longer knew who Sam was, or anyone else, for that matter. When she was awake, she just stared into space, her eyes watching some mysterious and private internal movie. Occasionally her lips moved, but no words came out. Mostly, she slept.

Sam shared breakfast and lunch with her and dinner with his elf mentor, Jared or with Jack and Alizah. During the day, he waited for Vera to die.

Caddy and Kyrylo were in London, and Sam knew about the sudden reappearance of Caddy's long-lost son, but frankly, he didn't care. There was just too much drama in his own life for him to be interested in what was going on with people he didn't know.

The elves and the RumLot people bent over backwards to make Sam comfortable. He had good rooms, and a lot of his personal items were on their way to the UK on the RumLot jets. His work tools would be there in a few days, and he already had good rock ready to carve and a fine studio to do it in. That was part of his training, to see how his abilities were going to be used in manipulating stone and to stretch those abilities to get stronger.

The stonemason was learning a lot about this bizarre world he was now a part of. He learned about orcs for one thing. Sam knew them as stinkers, but everyone called them orcs, and that's what he did now. But he knew in his head he'd always use stinker.

After learning more about them, their part in the elf and lord genocide, and how even today the ones who didn't know they were orcs still became sick or enraged by the smell of a lord or elf, Sam started to understand how close he and Vera had been to being discovered and probably killed by the orcs. If Ranger Bunn hadn't followed them into the subway when he pushed Vera in her wheelchair while running away from the orcs, they probably would've killed them then and there. He and Vera would have been just another senseless, random New York City homicide.

So, as well as everything else, the elves taught him some basic human-type self-defence like judo. Mostly, though, his self-defence would be his magical abilities, and the elves were very interested in his rock throwing and levitating, so that was an area he worked on every day.

Alizah and Jack were good company, and Sam enjoyed being around them. If Alizah wasn't so smitten with Jack, Sam could see himself enjoying Alizah's company more. It felt traitorous at this point to think of Vera being gone and Sam moving on with his life, but it was hard not to. The real Vera, the Vera he had loved so passionately, had left years ago; Sam was just babysitting the shell that remained. She'd be at peace soon, and Sam didn't like being alone.

He had been alone too long.

Caddy

She woke up nauseated and barely made it to the toilet in time to spit up nothing but mucus and yellow bile. After a few good heaves that brought tears to her eyes, Caddy sat up and caught her breath, and the nausea dissipated a bit.

If she weren't so old, she would have thought she was pregnant, but she didn't have a womb. That hysterectomy for the botched diagnosis of ovarian cancer had taken care of that. The doctor had been a jerk, and his diagnosis proved to be wrong, but that didn't put her womb and ovaries back. So she lived with a nasty scar, a year of life disruption, and then forgot about it. At least she never suffered through menopause.

So this morning's bout of nausea was a bit disconcerting. She hadn't had the flu for years, not even COVID.

Caddy sighed; well, maybe she was due for a good bout of some flu. She washed her face and told Kyrylo she was tired and wanted to sleep in another hour or so, and he was sympathetic.

How could she not be tired after yesterday?

Jack and Alizah

When female lords did what female lords were made to do, which was get busy and create the pheromones that allowed the elf women to ovulate, then all of the Elf Nation was very happy. In Before Times, there had been enough lords bonking each other that Scent production and distribution weren't an issue. All a clan needed was to provide a bit of food, a nice place to live, and an occasional porting for a female lord and then lure in someone of either sex to give her a pheromone-producing climax, and, Bob's your uncle, job done. Ten months later, elf babies. Everybody knew their place, did their job, and the world spun on.

Now, in this new and dangerous world, they had one Scent-producing female. One. And there were now hundreds of thousands of elves scattered across the European continent, with more waking up every day.

Amongst themselves, elves were rock-solid sure that Alizah and Jack would do their duty sooner or later. They doted on each other! If Alizah needed more time to get used to this new Jack, then so be it. In the big scheme of things, a few months was nothing to an elf when you live three thousand years.

So they talked about the couple incessantly. With the obsession of a Suffolk sheep farmer hiring a good ram for the ewe's winter tupping, they looked at the lord's health, relative randiness, and watched for every tiny sign that things were moving along in the right direction. If Jack kissed Alizah on the cheek or she held his hand a little longer than needed, it was noted in the pubs of Safe Haven, and oddsmakers changed the numbers written on chalkboards hanging next to every pub bar. Loving a little flutter, they gambled on the date, location, and even the preferred position of Jack and Alizah's first encounter.

Having another working female lord would take the strain off Lord Cadence, too. The elves well remembered how sad she had been when a well-meaning clan leader mailed her the vibrator after she broke up with Neptune, and everyone thought she'd be alone forever. Or the email from that idiot clan leader that made Kyrylo so snappy when he was asked to do his duty and screw the newly re-birthed Ms Caddy before he thought she was ready.

Elves had no sense of privacy or boundaries when it came to Scent production, not any more than a farmer hesitated discussing breeding a cow while standing right in front of the heifer in question. But they quickly learned that these human-birthed lords didn't like having their sex lives observed or discussed. It was, as Lord Kyrylo said, "cheeky".

So they were very careful about what they said outside of the confines of Safe Haven.

It didn't stop them from making an occasional mistake, though, and letting an ill-considered comment slip out.

Conary and Tuân

Kyrylo, Jack, Alizah, Conary, and Tuân sat in a private sitting room deep inside the embassy and practised porting. Everything Conary and Tuân knew about elves and lords had been learned from public sources, and they were finding out two things – first, much of what they had read and seen on the news was nonsense, and second, that the elves and lords were very powerful indeed.

They watched Alizah float to the ceiling and Kyrylo juggle a ball of plasma. They heard about Sam and learned about House. Jack gave them an overview of Before Times and what it was like to live with all four tribes back then. And the elves! Just watching the elves go about their daily business was a revelation. The more they learned, the more they understood how little they knew.

Conary and Tuân were told they were lords by everyone from Ms Caddy on down, elf and lord. The elves insisted on calling them "Lord Conary" and "Lord Tuân," and the other lords smiled and shrugged and said Yeah, no doubt you're a lord. But neither believed them for a minute.

They could do none of the things they saw these lords do. The two men couldn't move a grain of sand with their minds, they couldn't do anything magical, their eyes didn't glow, and their ears weren't pointed. Conary pointed all this out to Kyrylo and said that just calling them lords didn't make them one.

"How do you know?" Tuân demanded answers from the real lords. He was sure they were making fun of them, that this was all some elaborate and rather cruel practical joke.

Kyrylo looked a bit confused. How *did* he know? Was it the way their eyes glittered blue when they were tired or emotional? Was it their smell? He just knew.
Jack was the one who convinced the two new men.

"So you don't believe us. Will you believe each other? Conary, can you smell orcs?"

Conary wrinkled his nose at the memory and shrugged. "Sure, who can't?"

"Everyone human can't. Or I should say only a lord or an elf can smell an orc. Humans can't smell an orc. Surely you've been around one and could smell them and noticed you were the only one who could. And they knew you were different by your smell."

Conary thought for a minute about his orc encounters in the past and looked at Tuân. "Boy, have you ever smelled an orc and you were the only one who did?" Tuân nodded. Recognising the smell of trouble was a survival skill.

Tuân also thought back to his school and how bullies made fun of his body odour when he knew he was clean, and other people said there was no odour. People he now knew were orcs could smell him.

Then Jack asked them to look into each other's eyes and think of orcs. Conary just rolled his; this was all getting a bit touchy-feely for him. What was next, trust falls? But they did, just to play along with Jack, whom they liked and didn't want to offend.

Conary stared deep into Tuân's eyes, and Tuân stared back just as intently, and they both thought of orcs. Immediately, Tuân stepped back, scared, and Conary's expression changed from mild annoyance to startled. "Grandpa! Your eyes glowed! They really glowed!"

"So did yours!"

Conary looked at Jack, who just nodded.

"You two are lords. You'll just have to get used to the idea. It's what you are."

Alizah giggled from her mooring point on the chandelier, floating above them all. "Now that you know, you'll change fast. You'll learn. I learned, and you know what? Being a lord is lots of fun. Much better than being a human."

It was too much to absorb, and Kyrylo called time on the porting lessons, saying they all needed some lunch. That was one truth everyone could agree with. The lesson was finished for the day, and Conary and Tuân spent the rest of the afternoon thinking about lords and what it would mean if they were one of those magical creatures, too. It was scary.

Caddy

Three days of nausea and vomiting were enough. She had to do something.

Kyrylo was scheduled to go to Estonia to look over some defences on The Wall and do a tour of a newly created RumLot outpost. Elf soldiers were being integrated with existing NATO and Estonian military units as defensive units. A parallel guard of elves and RumLot security personnel was set up to augment existing military units guarding the border. Their role was purely defensive, and while individual elves didn't have the mobility of a human army because of *terrior*, tactics were developed to take advantage of their unique abilities.

Caddy didn't want K to change his mind about going just because of her upset tummy, so she put on a show and cheerfully waved goodbye when he ported out, but it was all she could do to stop heaving.

In the meantime, she needed a doctor. So after Kyrylo left, Caddy asked Norma to get someone in to talk to her about her stomach and prescribe something to stop the damn barfing.

Elf doctors made house calls, and Caddy's healer popped in directly to her sitting room and took a good look at the lord. His name was Bart, and he was short even for an elf, stocky, and looked exactly like a Nast Santa Claus. This healer was new to her, but then she had never needed an elf doctor in Lowestoft.

"Goodness." He held her wrist and took her pulse, "Your heart is racing! Only to be expected, I suppose, if you aren't feeling well and in your condition." Healer Bart was quite cheerful about it. "It's probably 'white coat hypertension' because you're talking to a healer. We do make people nervous!"

"I'm not nervous. I'm nauseated." Caddy was impatient. "I just want to know why and if there is anything I can take for it." She fumbled with the button on her cuff and almost called the housekeeper elf for help, but she got the stupid thing in halfway.

The "jolly old elf" beamed at her. "Oh, I can give you some herbs for your stomach. Make a nice tea, and you'll be as right as rain in no time. But you can expect this to all settle down in another month or so when the foetus passes. Morning sickness is perfectly normal at this stage."

Caddy looked up, the button forgotten. "Morning sickness? What do you mean – morning sickness? I thought you only got that when you were pregnant."

"Well, you're pregnant, of course. Didn't you know?" Bart looked shocked. "Didn't you feel the egg drop?"

"Egg drop! I'm not a chicken! I don't even have ovaries. No womb either! What the hell are you talking about?"

Bart sat back on the couch, frowned, and tented his stubby fingers. "Lord Cadence, you most certainly have a womb and ovaries. I'm very sure that when you came out of the cauldron, you were fully intact. I have nothing in your records to say they've been removed since then."

Caddy's jaw dropped. "Oh shit –" It had never occurred to her that when she came out of the cauldron in her recovered form, the hysterectomy she had had back in her fifties would be reversed along with three capped teeth and various scars she had accumulated over the years. It just never crossed her mind that over sixty years later, she would be fertile again. But, of course, she would. She was a fully rebirthed lord now. Her body was brand new.

"I've never had a period –"

"Well, of course not. You're a lord, not a human. Human females have menstruation every month. You drop an egg once a year or so. It sits in your womb for three days, and if it's not fertilised, it's simply reabsorbed into your body. You should have felt it drop."

Now in full flow, he continued, "Of course, the odds of this particular egg being fertilised are pretty low. If Lord Kyrylo is the father, then you'll probably abort it. If Lord Neptune is the father, you'll probably keep it. But you won't know –"

He nattered on, but Caddy didn't hear – couldn't hear – him. She was pregnant. It would be Kyrylo's, of course. Probably conceived during the cruise. She couldn't remember feeling anything weird in her body. Egg drop? She wouldn't have had a clue. She probably thought it was constipation.

She suddenly jerked back awake –

"What do you mean, '*If Lord Kyrylo is the father, then you'll probably abort it*' ?"

"Lord Kyrylo is still mostly human; he hasn't fully physically changed to a lord. That takes either time or the cauldron, so you are carrying a mixed child. You'll abort a child that is genetically a human the first time you use your abilities to their full extent. It won't be able to live in a body that makes magic." Bart chuckled. "It's nature's way of sorting out a defective foetus. It's not as if you *want* a human baby!"

Caddy had never lost her temper with an elf before. Never. But she lost her temper with this one.

Bart didn't know what hit him. One minute he was sitting on the couch chuckling, and the next minute his feet were dangling, and the lord had him hoisted by his shirt. Her glowing, furious eyes were an inch from his.

"*I will decide what I want.* Now you listen to me. You will say NOTHING to anyone about this!" She shook him, and he nodded. "NOTHING. I don't want Kyrylo to hear about my pregnancy from some clan leader in Estonia deciding to be the first to congratulate him. DO YOU UNDERSTAND!" She shook him again.

"Yes! Yes! I won't tell *anyone* –" he squeaked, terrified. This lord was going to kill him; he just knew it. He was only 987. He still had a full life ahead of him.

"You leave your herbs with me. Not the housekeeper. And if anyone so much as whispers about this, I will know, and I will know who blabbed."

"Yes, ma'am!"

"Go." She dropped him, and he ported out before he hit the floor.

Lord Cadence Aeldor, the leader of the Elf Nation, stood alone in her sitting room in her terrace house in Lowestoft, swaying with shock and then slowly sank to the floor and howled, her heart breaking.

She was going to lose a baby she hadn't known she was going to have and now desperately wanted. And she would be the one to kill it because she was who she was.

Kyrylo

Kyrylo was in Estonia on a tour of a weapons depot examining a CV90 that was being adapted to RumLot Security Forces specs when he stopped and listened. The man talking about the safety features of the killing machine saw the lord jerk up and look around, and he paused mid-sentence. The lord's eye was glowing, and as he cocked his head, his pointed ears twitched.

Something was wrong. Something was wrong with Caddy.

The feeling faded, and he turned to his human PA and asked him to check on Lord Cadence and let him know if he was needed back in England. Then he returned to the demonstration, but now he was distracted.

Something was wrong.

Caddy

Caddy sent everyone home. She didn't want anyone, elf or human, in the house with her while she sat in her old familiar kitchen, drank the herbal tea, and tried to make sense of what she had learned.

She was pregnant, probably a month along. She was now a full lord, having fully ripened from human to lord. Her baby's father was Kyrylo, who was still carrying a lot of human genetic material, so that made the child an unknown percentage of human. If she used her abilities "to their full extent," she would kill it.

She used her abilities every day. Caddy looked at her tea. She probably should have boiled the water in a kettle instead of just thinking it hot. Obviously, that wasn't enough to miscarry because she had been unwittingly doing things like that all along. What was the "full extent"? Where was the line?

She drank the tea and then went for a walk. She needed to clear her head.

Kyrylo

The PA leaned over and whispered to Kyrylo.

"Lord Cadence is not answering her phone; it's turned off. And she is not in her house or office. She's sent her staff home. We are tracking her now."

Kyrlyo stood up, interrupting a presentation on warehouse capacity, and apologised for leaving so abruptly, but there was an emergency elsewhere he had to get to. He promised to come back as soon as he could for the rest of the briefing and thanked them all again.

He ported directly from the meeting in Estonia to Calais, where he had to sit for ten agonising minutes for his helicopter back to the UK to get fired up. During the wait, he looked at his phone and tracked Caddy down. Unknown to anyone but Kyrylo, her engagement ring had a tracker in it, and he found her right away. She was sitting on a bench in Kensington Gardens at the boating pond.

He sent an elf soldier to watch with strict orders not to bother her. Out on the parking lot, a couple of RumLot security guards pulled up and sat in their Range Rover to watch the lord. Caddy never saw any of them. She didn't move, staring blankly into the inky waters of the boating pond.

Caddy and Kyrylo

Forty-five minutes and a dozen portals later, Kyrylo stood in Kensington Gardens looking at the forlorn, still figure of his fiancée sitting on the park bench, looking at the reflections of the sky in the green-black water of the boating pond.

His heart sank; even from the back, she looked so sad.

Kyrylo slipped in as silently as a ghost and sat down next to her, and put his arm around her shoulders. She didn't look up but put her head in her hands and shuddered.

"What's wrong, Caddy?"

Nothing.

"*Zaychik*, you have to tell me what's wrong. Remember that time you got so mad at me for not telling you what was bothering me –"

"I'm pregnant." She shuddered again, "And the doctor tells me I'm going to kill it."

When Kyrylo had been hit by the IED, he was knocked out, and when he woke up in the hospital and took that first look in the mirror, he felt like this. The air was smashed out of his lungs. His world had tilted and then reordered, and now everything was different.

Caddy, his world, was now sobbing in his arms, and there was nothing he could do.

"Oh, *Zaychik* –"

He hugged her as she sobbed and kissed her hair while his mind raced. It had never occurred to him that at their great ages she could get pregnant. They had never used any sort of birth control and would have laughed at the suggestion. They both were still thinking in human terms, not in "forever as lords" terms. Past the sex act and the by-product of Scent for the elves, how lords reproduced and their unique biology was simply not something either Kyrylo or Caddy ever thought about.

"*Zaychik*, you have to tell me exactly what's going on. Why did you call a doctor?"

And she told him, in between sobs, what had happened.

"Did you talk to Dr Mandy?" No, because there was no need. She thought she had the flu. Who needs to talk to the head doctor if you just need some milk of magnesia?

That was all Kyrylo needed to know.

"We're going back right now to the house and call Dr Mandy. Right now. I have questions."

He signalled the elf he had put on guard, and they were ported back to the house, even though it was only two blocks away. Then he yelled for the housekeepers who popped back in instantly and had them bring Caddy some tea while he called Dr Mandy. Immediately, he was directed to her voicemail. She was on holiday.

Too bad. Lords commanded, and elves obeyed, and she was tracked down in the Safe Haven at the Elf-tastic Water Park and hustled back to her office still in her swimsuit. Within minutes, she was on a Zoom call with the lords. Mandy sat dripping in her pretty office and looked at her screen. The lords were sitting together on the couch in their sitting room and looked very, very upset.

After she heard Caddy's story, she was very, very upset herself with Healer Bart. Majorly pissed. He would never talk to one of *her* patients again and certainly not to any lords! What a cock-up! She draped a flamingo-printed beach towel around her shoulders, playing for time, and let her thoughts get in some sort of order.

"Technically, what Healer Bart said was true, if massively undiplomatic. But he also left out, or Ms Caddy didn't hear, some info."

She shook some water out of her ears.

"Ms Caddy is indeed a full lord genetically now. That's what happens in the cauldron. You're taken apart and put back together again according to your true nature. She could have put herself back together from being an octopus, but she was badly wounded and didn't have the strength, which is why Neptune said she needed the cauldron, and he was right about that. But she didn't come back as her old body, the one born with human DNA, but as her true self, as a lord. That meant she had all previously missing parts back, and her DNA is now that of a lord, not a human."

Dr Mandy sighed. "I will take some blame here in that it never occurred to me that you would see that your hysterectomy scar was gone, but not realise that the inside parts had come back at the same time. And lord female biology regarding ovulation should have been explained. It's something lords would tell each other in Before Times, and, of course, you didn't have aunties and such to tell you the lord facts of life.

"It's true, too, that Lord Kyrylo is still quite a bit human. He will naturally shed his human DNA the way we all shed our hair and skin, but it will take a while. About fifteen more years, I think. In the big scheme of things, that's a very short time, but again – maybe someone needed to say that aloud.

"And it's true that a human foetus in a lord's womb won't survive if the lord stretches her abilities. It's simply too hot inside her. But using your abilities very lightly, where you aren't releasing a lot of body heat and your whole body isn't glowing, that won't kill the foetus.

"What Healer Bart didn't say is that there is also a chance this baby is not human at all. Lord Kyrylo is well on his way to being a full lord. It's possible some of his sperm is already there. We don't know. If this is a baby lord, it doesn't matter how much heat Ms Caddy produces; it will be fine. Vigorous use of your abilities will make it even stronger."

Kyrylo gripped Caddy's hand. "Can we find that out? So she knows what she can do and can't do?"

"Well, the baby is still there, and it's a month on. So has she used her abilities lately? Has she stretched herself in the last month?"

Caddy thought about it. She hadn't done anything in the last month she'd call "stretching". They weren't waking elves up now while they were busy with travelling and diplomatic stuff. And then Conary came.

But Kyrylo thought differently. "Doesn't it depend on when exactly she became pregnant? I mean, she sang for Neptune; that was a stretch for her. Then she had a few days off – about five or six – and then she popped that terrorist, and I know she was hot enough to burn Joan's hand when she pushed Caddy into the limo."

Mandy nodded. "If Ms Caddy became pregnant before both of those things, I say she is certainly carrying a lord and not to worry about miscarrying. If she got pregnant after we just don't know, and we have no way of finding out. The only way to find out is to do something that will make her use her abilities to their fullest."

"Then I just won't do anything for the next eight or nine months. That seems to be the solution." It was all Caddy could think of.

Mandy smiled sadly and shook her head. "Anything is possible, Ms Caddy, but carrying a human baby to term is going to be very, very hard on you. You're a lord. Your body will reject a foreign body. The bigger it grows, the sicker you will get. You'll make yourself very sick, and you'll still lose a human baby."

Caddy looked at her hands. "I have no choice but to carry it to term. I can't have an abortion because what if this baby is a proper lord? You say we don't know yet. When will I know that? When will I know what it is?"

"You'll know if it's a human or a lord when you first look into its eyes."

They all sat in silence, wrapped in their own thoughts.

"Thank you, Dr Mandy, I'm sorry we interrupted your holiday. Let us stew on this for a while."

Mandy nodded and said to give her a call anytime, and the screen went black.

Kyrylo pulled Caddy onto his lap and rocked her. Neither said a word.

Later that night, when they crawled into bed, exhausted from the emotional upheavals of the day, Kyrylo put his hand on Caddy's belly as they spooned in the bed and said, "I never did say, in all this mess today, that I hope this baby stays with us. If it does, we'll be blessed, and I'll be very happy. If this isn't meant to be, then we'll recover together."

She turned to kiss him and they fell asleep together, each with a hand on her belly.

Sam

As Caddy and Kyrylo dreamed of a new life, Sam was saying goodbye to Vera.

An elf knocked once on his door and immediately popped in next to Sam's bed where he was sleeping. They had the theory but not the practice of privacy and door knocking, and didn't always get it right.

Sam didn't mind when he opened his eyes and saw a tiny matronly woman standing next to his bed, shaking his shoulder.

"It's time, Lord Sam." She peered at him with sympathetic eyes, and Sam knew she didn't mean "for breakfast". Sam pulled on jeans and a t-shirt and ported to Vera's room.

There she lay, his beloved wife of fifty years, on her back with her hands at her sides. For a brief moment, he thought she was already dead, but she wasn't. He looked very closely, and he could see her chest move and hear her faint breath rattle through blue lips. Her hands were blue. Her closed eyes were bruised, matte-black circles. Vera was shutting down.

Sam sat next to the bed and spoke to her. He had no idea what he said, but he remembered it as something along the lines of he loved her, and it was okay for her to go now. Her job in this world was over, and she was a good wife. The best.

I love you, Vera.

Her eyes flew open; one hand raised a few inches. And then it was over.

A priest from the local Catholic Church came in and gave her the last rites. He'd been contacted weeks ago and had agreed to do this. But tonight was the first time he had ever ported, and he was a bit shaky from the experience. The padre did well, Sam thought. Considering.

The funeral was very nice, and Sam was quite pleased with it. Classy, even. He could have whatever he wanted if he just asked. Shit, the elves would have built Vera a Viking longboat and shoved her out to sea in a flaming pyre if he had asked, but no, that wasn't Vera. So Sam asked for a normal cremation. When he was given the option of a standard British cremation or an elf version, he opted for the elf one. Only he decided that one day was enough instead of the elven three. He thought Vera would like that, and so that's exactly what he got.

They built a massive pyre on the back lawn, and she was laid out in a beautifully made woven straw box. Then a priest came and did whatever it was priests do at funerals, and after that, Sam lit the pyre, and it went up in a flash. Everyone, masses of folk, came and sat around and chatted quietly and tended the fire. All of the lords were there, RumLot guards and Ranger Bunn, and more elves than Sam could ever count. Everyone came to Sam and wished him peace.

By the next morning, there was nothing but a small pile of ashes, which the elves scattered in the rose beds.

Caddy

In theory, no one at Vera's funeral knew that Caddy was pregnant. She hadn't told anyone, and the only people – in theory – who knew were Healers Bart and Mandy and her Kyrylo. But at the funeral, a couple of keen-eyed elf matrons spotted Caddy's condition right away. They were old for elves and had been around lords in the Before Times. They took one look at Caddy and knew.

When Caddy went on the mission to New York, no elves had gone with them. When she came back, she was with mostly humans and younger elves who staffed the embassy, Aelfeham House, and the Lowestoft house and offices. The younger elves might have noticed or smelled something odd, but never made the connection. There weren't very many of the ancient elves who had survived the massacres before going into hibernation, and the ones who had worked entirely for their elf clans as elders and leaders.

When one of the old women walked up and bowed to the lord and had a word on behalf of her clan, she could smell it. The lord smelled pregnant. She smelled fruity and ripe, like windfall apples.

Since they hadn't been told to be quiet, they happily gossiped, and by the next day, all of the elves and a good number of the humans on staff knew that Lord Cadence was expecting.

Ellen, Caddy, and Kyrylo

It was after breakfast, and Caddy and Kyrylo were in their Lowestoft sitting room. Caddy was working her morning crossword, and Kyrylo was on his tablet answering his overnight pile of emails when Ellen burst in, all a-flutter.

"WHY DIDN'T YOU TELL ME!" She was near tears; she was so happy. "I had to find out from Sally in the mailroom!"

Kyrylo snapped his tablet shut and looked at Ellen with real annoyance, "With this house, we have no secrets." He was so angry that he spoke in Ukrainian word order.

Ellen looked into Caddy's sad eyes and suddenly thought, Oh. Shit.

"I assume you're talking about my pregnancy."

Ellen looked back and forth between the two lords.

"I–yes. I heard you were pregnant –" She sat down, really worried now. "Is that wrong?"

"No, it's not wrong. I'm pregnant." Caddy looked down at her crossword and doodled a small, careful circle in the corner. "We don't know for how much longer, though, so we didn't want to make a big announcement in public." She looked up at Ellen, outwardly calm. "At the moment, the odds are not good."

"People gossip too much." And with that, Kyrylo snatched up his tablet and stalked off to the kitchen, where he could get some work done.

"Oh, blimey, Caddy – I'm so sorry. I came here thinking you would be over the moon, and I've put my foot in it. I didn't want to make you feel bad."

Caddy nodded. "I must make a decision soon, and it's a hard one. Kyrylo and I haven't really talked it out yet."

"Oh, shit." Ellen teared up. "Oh, shit. I don't know what to say. If you'd rather not talk –"

"I'll always talk to you, Ellen. It helps me focus, and you're a good friend. None better." Caddy looked down at the puzzle again as if her answer was hidden in there. Maybe it was.

She started slowly, "The baby will be either a human or a lord. We don't know what it is. If it's human, the next time I do serious magic, I'll probably miscarry. If it's a lord, everything will be fine, and I'll start buying baby clothes. If I don't do serious magic, and it's human, it will live longer and *might* go to term, but my health will be seriously compromised. I could be sacrificing –" she waved her hand, " – all this for no good outcome.

"To the elves, this is an easy decision – do some heavy-duty magic, and if it's human, let it go early in the pregnancy, and I keep my health. If I do my magic and it survives, then it's a lord like me, and everyone is relieved. But Ellen – " and Caddy leaned forward, " – what if it's *human* and could have lived, and I killed it?" She leaned back and looked at her puzzle again. "Can I kill my baby for the greater good?"

Ellen gasped. She couldn't imagine her life without her sweet baby Matt. Would she have aborted him if it meant she could keep working to save the Elf Nation? For Caddy to have to choose between her unborn child and staying healthy to lead an entire nation, Ellen couldn't wrap her head around that.

So instead she asked, "You don't know if it's a human or a lord?"

"No, there's no lord/human pregnancy test you can buy at Boots."

Then Caddy explained that they had no idea when the baby was conceived and if it had already survived the two serious magic bouts during the New York tour, or if it was conceived afterwards. Knowing that would make all the difference in the world.

Ellen's mind was racing.

"You didn't have a period? You can't date from your last cycle?"

Caddy relayed her newly acquired knowledge of female lord anatomy and that she was supposed to feel it when her egg dropped, but had had no idea at the time.

She looked at Caddy blankly, grabbed her phone, and frantically started swiping.

"Kyrylo! KYRYLO! Did you two fuck on the first night on the *Queen Catherine*?"

"Ellen!"

"I'm serious. Look at my notes for that day." She turned on her phone and started to scroll down.

"There are three pages of notes! What the hell am I looking at?"

Ellen snatched the phone back.

"Here – *C w/gut pain during dinner. Couldn't eat dessert. Dr?*"

"You keep notes of my indigestion and what I eat? What's next, my farts?"

"Yes, it's my job. And I know that for you to skip dessert, it had to be a damn big pain – so could that have been your egg drop? Did you two get frisky later on? In a missionary way?"

Kyrylo threw his hands up. "Now woman is asking about positions."

But Caddy brightened up. "Yes, yes, we did. The next morning, too. That's the night we got engaged. We were pretty happy with life then."
She turned to Kyrylo. "If we made the baby that night, then there were two strong magic episodes after that. Do you think we're okay?"

Realisation slowly dawned on Kyrylo, and he grinned. "Maybe, *Zaychik* – maybe."

Caddy looked up at him, afraid to hope. "Maybe."

Sam and Conary

At night, the terrace was deserted, and Sam liked it that way. He had made it a habit this last week, when he couldn't sleep, to go sit on the cushioned garden sofa with a six-pack of Bud, light up the fire pit, and see how many beers he could drink before he fell asleep. It was getting cold now, but with a coat, the fire, and the beer, he was warm enough.

There was something nice about sitting under the stars, even if the weather in the UK was overcast most of the time. He knew the stars were there, and sometimes they peeked out and winked at him.

Tonight, though, he had company, which was a pity, but there was nothing he could do about it. Conary came out and, without a word, sat down on the chair on the other side. He had his own Saigonese "333", and popped the cap and took a swig.

They sat in silence, which started off as awkward and then, without saying a word, the beer did its work, and they relaxed into "companionable".

"This is a weird place." Conary made the observation to no one in particular.

Sam nodded. It certainly was.

"Could be worse."

Conary nodded. It certainly could.

"No orcs. At least you can sit here and have a beer and not look over your shoulder all the time. I stopped going to bars. Too much hassle." Conary grinned. "Got tired of going home with a black eye. Not my idea of what a beer and a bump should be."

"Fuckin' stinkers. Hate'm. I could put up with them fine if they left me alone, but no-ooo –"

They both agreed that orcs were a pain in the ass, so the conversation moved from orcs to sports (neither were interested in sports, so that was a bonding moment right there) to their self-defence lessons and how they were too old for that shit, and then, tentatively, right before they got too drunk to make sense, to what it was like living in a human world and discovering you were not one of them.

Both woke up with headaches the next day, but it was worth it. Instead of eating by himself, Sam started coming to the community table, and Conary was pleased to have another adult to talk to.

Caddy and Kyrylo

Kyrylo was almost asleep when Caddy nudged him.

"I've been thinking." She sat up and hugged her knees.

"Mmm-mmm"

"The next awakening is scheduled for next week, right?"

Kyrylo turned and looked at the ceiling. No sleep for now. "I've cancelled them all."

She closed her eyes. "I think I should do it. What do you think?"

"You don't have to. That's why I cancelled them. You can wait."

"I talked to Mandy again – " And Kyrylo nodded. So had he. He knew what was coming.

" – and she says my odds of carrying a human baby to term are almost nil and that the bigger the baby gets, the more likely I'm going to have a bad allergic reaction to the foreign body inside me. So my options are to keep going and eventually have a bad reaction that will do me no good, or terminate, or do some major magic and let the chips fall where they may."

"Yes, she told me that, too."

"So, I don't have much of a choice."

"No," he sighed. "Most of the options are bad, but you *could* have one good outcome. You could stretch yourself, raise your body temperature, and the baby will miscarry. But if it's a lord, it will live and might be stronger for it."

"How will you feel if it's human? I would have killed it."

Kyrylo rubbed her back. He could feel the bones in her spine. She wasn't eating well.

"If it's a human, I will be sad, but it's more important that you live to do your job, which is for us all. If you die – " And he had to stop for a minute.

"Anyway, I was thinking about that. During the Russian War, many Ukrainian families sacrificed their loved ones for the greater good. Some sent their loved ones off to war voluntarily, but most had no choice. No one, not a single family I met, was happy to send their loved one into danger, maybe to die. When I was an officer and saw people say goodbye to a son or daughter, I was pretty cold about it. I didn't like it when one of my soldiers died because that was a failure on my part, but in the end, death is a part of war. I didn't have the same perspective because, as the Americans say, I had no skin in the game. I took other people's children to war, and some were sacrificed for the good of all. For a free nation. The right choices are often the hardest."

He sighed. "I think it's the right decision, but that doesn't make it an easy one." He rubbed her back. "It's hard, *Zaychik*. I will be there for you. No second guesses later."

"It could be a lord, and all of this agonising is moot."

"Gods, I hope so, but I am prepared for any outcome."

She nodded and lay back down. The decision was made. "Please reschedule. All of them that you cancelled. And make the first one as soon as possible. Let's get this over with."

He kissed her and left to get his tablet. There was no point in waiting, and he couldn't sleep anyway. Orders would be waiting in various inboxes as soon as people arrived at work.

Conary and Tuân

At breakfast, the Aelfeham House elves gave Conary and Tuân a note that they were to visit with Lord Cadence at ten instead of a morning lesson, and at the appointed time, they found themselves sitting in Caddy's RumLot office drinking tea and eating tea cakes and sausage rolls.

Conary still couldn't get over the fact that the alien-looking creature called Lord Cadence was, in fact, good ol' Caddy, his mother, a middle-class housewife and grade-school music teacher from San Antonio. He remembered Mom as being depressingly ordinary in every way – actually rather frumpy if he were honest about it. So, how she grew into this fairy queen – well, it was quite a transformation. Yeah, she'd been a bit weird back then, but not *this* weird.

He had known his parents were odd, which was part of his problem growing up, when all he wanted in the world was to be an average kid and disappear into the crowd like the kids who seemed so self-confident and happy at school. But the Aeldors weren't average, and neither was he. And while their oddness didn't seem to bother either of his parents in the least bit, it bothered him a lot.

When he was growing up, he and John and Lizzie would joke that their last name should be Munster like the comedy monster family on TV. The Munster family were a very nice family with a cousin who lived with them who looked normal, but they thought she was the weird one. John and Lizzie, the normal ones, could make friends and laugh about their unusual parents. Conary found he needed drugs to deal with teenage social situations. By the time he realised he didn't, it was too late to make up with his family. Too much water had gone under the bridge, and he had his own young family to bring up.

Mom was not mom anymore; she was Caddy to him and Tuân, and this Caddy was still a bit formal. They were strangers to each other, and while she loved them both, it was the love of distance, the ghost love of memory. He supposed that was just to be expected. He wasn't eighteen any more, and she wasn't human. The water under their bridge had widened to a gulf that would take some time to cross.

Caddy took a sip of her tea and looked at her lord kin. They had so much to learn and so little time to learn it.

"Conary, what have you told your family in Vietnam about being here? I know you've been talking to them. Are they okay?"

He shrugged. "I told them that we are getting Tuân settled in school, which is true. I said I knew a benefactor who was paying for everything as a favour to me, which is also true, I guess."
She looked at Tuân. "Same story?"

The young man nodded, his mouth full of sausage roll.

"Good. Now that you've been here for a while and seen the set-up and learnt some of our history, I hope you can understand a couple of important points."

She leaned forward, her green eyes intense. "We are extremely blessed to be aligned with elves. But we are also cursed with people who want to kill us. Orcs, Lester, who is a lord, and humans who want to eliminate us are everywhere, and while we have relative safety in elven areas, outside of those areas, life is very dangerous. We can't guarantee the safety of your relatives in Vietnam because we have no presence there. So you mustn't tell *anyone*, ANYONE, that you have kin there. You mustn't tell them what you are doing here. I cannot protect them." She looked at Tuân in particular. "Do you understand?"

Tuân nodded, his eyes wide.

"I think that Conary has had some experience with keeping his private life separate from his business life, so I'm not going to tell him what to do, but I'm concerned about you, Tuân, because you're so young."

She looked at Conary, who nodded, impassive.

"So, we can't protect you everywhere you go, and we can't stick you in a gold-plated jail to keep you safe. But we can train you to keep yourselves safe and to recognise the dangers out there so you can avoid them.

"We'll support your family as much as we can financially. For now, it will have to be subtle, but we have ways, so you don't have to worry about that. They will not suffer at all because you are here. They will actually be much better off. So when you hear that, for instance, your mother has a new job that pays very well, just say "Great, Mom!" and move on. If your Dad has a winning lottery ticket –" Caddy shrugged. "Financially, there's a lot we can do remotely, and we'll do it."

She turned to Tuân again. "So you came here to get an education. What field were you planning on going into? Do you have a burning desire to be a doctor, or accountant or something?"

Tuân shook his head. "I just want to be able to help my family and have a good life. I haven't thought past that. I figured my first years in uni would be general subjects anyway."

Caddy smiled; she had thought as much. He was nineteen and hadn't landed on a passion.

"Then this is what I want you to do, if you are willing. I want you to be a Ranger. We have one in training now, and he'll guide you. I plan to find another two or three to start soon. You will be the only lord in training, but I think it will stand you in good stead until you figure out your passion – and your abilities. You'll be useful to us, and you'll be free to roam the world."

"What's a Ranger?"

"Think James Bond on steroids." Caddy grinned. "You will do assignments for the Elf Nation where elves can't go. You will learn how to defend yourself against anything, and you will always have the backup of other Rangers, so you won't be alone. It will require a lot of self-discipline, imagination, and you'll have to like a bit of adventure. Do you think you can handle that?"

Tuân nodded, his blue eyes as big as saucers. James Bond on steroids?

"Conary, do you have anything to say about that?"

Conary shrugged. He brought Tuân here to better himself and to learn. He trusted his mother to take care of the boy, and from what he was learning, they both would need to be able to defend themselves.

"The boy can do what he wants; I've done my bit now. It's time for him to make his own decisions."

Caddy smiled and called in Victor and Wendell, who were waiting outside.

"Tuân, this is Victor, your instructor. You will do everything he says. He has total authority over you. He hates his job and will torture you. But you will come out of his training rolling your eyes at that pussy James Bond. This is Wendell Bunn. He's been in training for a while now and has learned to crawl, and we are quite proud of his progress. He will be your mentor, at least through the beginning stages." Caddy waved her hand and grinned. "Head off now, boys. Have fun! Oh – and Victor –"

"Yes, ma'am, don't hurt them too much. I remember, Lord Cadence."

"Good."

The door closed, and Caddy turned to Conary.

"Okay, now you need to tell me what you want to do. Stay here and learn about being a lord, or go back to Vietnam? This is not a prison; you can come and go as you please."

Conary looked at his mother, trying to figure out what she was thinking. He couldn't.

"I'm in my seventies now, Mom. It's a bit late for me –"

"Conary, you will live forever if we can keep the orcs off of you. Your life has barely begun."

"I know lords live a long time –" He frowned. "But forever?"

"How old do you think Jack is? He's almost four *thousand* years old."

"You mean literally? I thought he was just making a joke."

"Literally. Neptune is an untold number of years old. He could go back a hundred thousand years. He's forgotten."

Conary was stunned. He was learning new things about lords and elves every day, and he learned in his classes that lords live a long time – but no one had put a number to "long".

"The more you use your powers and the more you stay with the elves, your human side will fade, and your lord side will dominate. It's like going through puberty, in a way. One day you're a child and the hormones kick in, and two years later you're a man who shaves. I've changed. Kyrylo is changing. We're moving along that road. You'll be changing, too."

"Gee, Mom, this reminds me of 'the talk' when I was fourteen, and Dad caught me jerking off to Playboy."

Caddy laughed, a deep belly laugh like she had when her children were kids.

"I was well over one hundred when I first realised I could move things with my mind, but I think I made my great age because I had been using my abilities without realising it, so I was very slowly changing for years. Now Kyrylo is about your age. He knew he could move things, and started thinking he was going crazy. When I came along, I was already waking up elves, and I sent an elf to him to help him train, and he very quickly figured out what his talent was. He has worked incredibly hard at it, and now he's very, very strong. Look at his ears;

he's changing. The more he practises, the faster his human side dissipates. He practises a lot. "

She took a sip of tea.

"So, Conary – what do you do? I know you're a lord; I can see it in your eyes. The elves know you're a lord. Have you found a special ability? "

"No, I can't do anything–not that I know of."

"Then that is your mission, to figure that out. Once you figure it out, your life path will be determined. Some lords can't do much; others are very strong. Kyrylo is what the elves call an Elemental, a top-tier lord. He can manipulate pure energy, the elements. Others, like Alizah, can do one thing, and that's it. Alizah can fly, but she can't make anything else fly, not that we know of. She's a basic lord."

"What are you, Mom?"

She looked at Conary and tilted her head.

"I'm an Elemental, Conary. I can manipulate anything with waves. Mostly light and sound. I can throw my power into something else; it's not just inside of me. I can also move things, and I can shape-change."

Conary looked out of the fake window in Caddy's office. There were fake birds out there sitting in a fake tree.

"I'm living in a Marvel comic book."

"Yep, that's pretty much it. So what do you want to do? Do you have an idea, or do you want to go home and think about it? Any decision can be changed. After all, you have forever to work out any problems and to explore new paths – as long as the orcs and the humans don't get you first."

He looked at his teacup, a pretty thing, but so fragile. Mishandled, it would crack. Dropped, and it would break. Properly taken care of, it would last forever.

"I think I would like to learn to be a lord, a proper one."

Caddy blinked, relief filling her eyes with tears. She didn't know what she would have done if Conary had said Thanks, but no thanks, I'll just go back home. Probably nothing. What could she have done?

"I'll send you a mentor. Treat him well, and he'll take good care of you."

Tuân

It was decided to turn the Royal Hotel across from the Rum Lot Bauble Shop into a Ranger barracks. Wendell moved out of his parents' house and took one of the flats to their great relief because his mother wanted to turn his bedroom into a sewing room. Tuân was given a flat, and the others were set aside for the new recruits.

Tuân started with the five am exercises at Fen Park, and like Wendell, went home every night exhausted and sore.

"I thought Ms Caddy –"

"LORD CADENCE TO YOU, SHITHEAD!" yelled Victor.

" – Lord Cadence was joking when she said we would be tortured."

Wendell looked sympathetic, but not for too long. Take your eyes off those elves and you'd soon find them on the floor. The eyes, not the elves. "It's painful, but it works."

And so it went. Tuân took his lessons in hand-to-hand, knife work, and was eventually taken to the gun range and taught all of the weapons skills. He, too, had sociology, psychology, business, politics and government, and even etiquette and dance training.

And he learned about elves.

From the start, they were friendlier to him than they were to Wendell, maybe because Tuân wasn't as huge as the other Ranger at only 165 cm, but mostly because he was a lord, so they didn't consider him human. And, of course, his great-grandmother was Lord Cadence. That helped. Nonetheless, they trained him just as hard as they trained the human and beat up the young lord every day like clockwork. Lord Tuân wasn't going to go out in the world and get eaten by an orc, not if they could help it. That would be embarrassing.

A few weeks later, Luke from Ukraine, the same Luke who first met Caddy in that Patria when she went a-roaming, was added to the team. Lord Cadence wanted the best young people and the right personalities for Ranger training, but she also wanted a couple of females, too, and told HR to keep their eyes open for good prospects.

Caddy and Kyrylo

A few days after Caddy and Kyrylo's midnight decision to resume their scheduled elf awakenings, Caddy found herself in a barley field in Estonia about ten miles from The Wall.

She walked through the dry stubble listening for sleeping elves. Looking at the satellite photos of likely areas, she picked out this field, and she was seldom wrong when she made her choice. Some places just *looked* better than others; she couldn't put her finger on the reason why. She wished she could.

The field was huge, and it took about twenty minutes of stopping, listening, and starting up again before she found the best place. There were a lot of elves sleeping deep under the earth, and she could hear their murmurs and sighs and even a couple of snores. They were dreaming of her.

Around her, in a large, rough circle, were about a hundred members of the RumLot Security border guard, all in their field uniforms. In an outer circle, ringing the RumLot soldiers were hand-picked members of the Estonian military. Nearby sat an anti-missile battery and the helicopters that brought the lords and some of the senior military members, along with the trucks and gear needed to move the soldiers around. Off in the distance, unannounced roadblocks kept everyone local away, along with the elf-parazzi. Overhead, she heard the buzz of drones.

It was a far, far cry from the early days when Caddy had gone out with Ellen and Rashim under the cover of night to wake ten or twenty elves and pray to whoever was listening that no errant humans or orcs stumbled in on them.

She found her spot and looked at Kyrylo, who nodded, and then he and Jameson trotted around the circle, double-checking each of the soldiers and fussing with their exact position. At this point, the RumLot personnel all had several awakenings under their belt and knew what to do. The Estonians were raw and needed to be watched so they didn't forget their mission, and they were there to keep out anyone who decided to crash the party.

When the men were done with their final check, Kyrylo jogged back to the middle with Caddy. Unlike the dozens of other times they had done this rebirthing ceremony, this time he stopped in front of her.

"Are you okay?" She nodded, and he lifted her hand and kissed it. "I love you." "I love you, too." Then he took his usual position behind her, and she took a deep breath and started to play. Only Jameson noticed the change in routine.

She played with passion as she always did. As many times as she did a re-awakening, she never approached it as a job or got tired of playing to her elves. How could she? To bring them back to this dangerous world was a supreme act of trust on their part and a huge honour for her. Maybe one day a new lord would appear who would know how to wake them, but for now, it was just Caddy.

The concert was always in two parts. The first part was to rouse the hibernating elves enough to get them to listen to her.

Wake! Wake! I'm here! Listen –

And the second part was deep and rhythmic and led them, from wherever the elves slept in between this world and the next, to this ancestral piece of earth, their home. Making these subsonic, deep, long waves was the hard part, and where Caddy glowed until the soldiers couldn't see her at all.
She was a mass of boiling, vibrating, green light. The ground vibrated, and they could feel the sound waves she aimed deep in the earth shaking up their legs and making their teeth rattle.

Come to me! I'm waiting. Come, Come, COME TO ME!

Just as the lords never got bored, the soldiers never got bored, either. They heard the otherworldly song, they saw the brilliant light show of the lord, they felt the earth under their feet heave and strain, and they waited like Olympic runners waiting for the starting gun to begin the race of their lives.

Then the last note faded away, and Caddy, still glowing and drenched in sweat and swaying on unsteady legs, stopped, tilted her head, and listened. The field was deathly quiet. Everyone held their breath.

She pointed with her bow, and the soldiers who watched that sector raced towards her and were met with a fountain of exploding dirt and barley stubble as the elf eggs violently erupted from the Earth.

Then the rest of the ploughed Estonian field boiled and exploded. The RumLot soldiers leapt forward to frantically slice open the egg sacs, free the confused, naked elves from their egg prisons, and throw them high into the sky, where they instantly ported to Safe Haven. Jameson, Kyrylo, and a few seniors ran around the perimeter hunting for elves who erupted outside of the circle, and they showed a few of the Estonian soldiers how to slit the egg sacs and throw the elves up. But the vast majority rebirthed inside the circle.

In less than an hour, it was all done, and the field, now muddy with amniotic fluid and rapidly dissolving egg sacs, resumed its autumn nap. When the last elf was reborn, Caddy gave her triumphant cry, her signal of victory to all of the humans, and they had their reward – a moment of pure joy.

Kyrylo ran to Caddy, swept her up in his arms, and carried her to the helicopter, which would take them to the nearest elf colony where she could start the port chain to House.

"Are you okay?" He was worried, and she heard it in his voice.

Caddy thought for a minute. She felt pretty good. He didn't need to carry her anywhere, but hey, if he was feeling gallant...

"Yeah, I'm fine. Very hungry though. Starved!" She looked up at him and smiled dreamily. Kyrylo was sure she was going to say that she loved him; she had that look. But he was wrong.

"Do you think we could stop at a McDonald's?"

They didn't find a McDonald's on their flightpath, but the local Estonian army soldiers told them of a Hesburger nearby, and Caddy was quite happy with that. Even better!

Since the drive-thru didn't take choppers, the three helicopters landed in a nearby park, and the King and Queen of the Fairies, as well as a couple dozen guards, senior Estonian Army officers, and the RumLot Security descended on a very, very surprised afternoon shift of Hesburger employees.

Caddy was halfway through her third pear milkshake and fourth MegaBurger when she felt it.

The baby was not any bigger than a small grape now, and she didn't expect anything dramatic if she miscarried. Dr Mandy had told her not to even expect a blood spot. Her body would simply reabsorb the foetus, and she would no longer be pregnant. Elves would smell the change in her when she returned to normal, and the old matrons would see it in her eyes.

But this was different. Caddy sat bolt upright, and her face flushed as her hormones surged. She felt a wave of good. Settled. The overriding anxiety and fear she had felt since she learnt she was pregnant simply disappeared. The baby was happy, swimming in the mommy cauldron. She and the baby were going to be all right.

Kyrylo was watching her like a hawk and noticed her red face right away. She got up and went to the toilet only because she didn't want to tell him in front of the boisterous soldiers. He followed her in as she knew he would.

So it was in the women's toilet of Hesburger that Lord Kyrylo learned that everything in his life was perfect, and he was going to be a father.

Lester

On the other side of the Wall, baby breeding was also going along at pace, and Tsar Lord Lester was quite happy with how things were moving along. Without any elves to guide him, he had no worries at all; his human doctors would take care of Lena or die trying.

Literally.

If anything happened to her, Lester would kill them, and they knew it. Most of the staff who tended to Lena assiduously avoided upper-story windows lest they go flying out of them in a fit of Tsarist rage.

So with Lester, ignorance was bliss, and since Lena didn't miscarry or seem particularly bothered by the pregnancy, he was unconcerned with the technical aspects of lord reproduction. He didn't know that the baby Lena was gestating needed to be of the same tribe as Lena herself.

Lena was starting to show, and Lester could see she was nesting, which he thought was very amusing. She gathered a pack of women around her, a court of ladies-in-waiting, and they all looked like her. Same blonde hair, same Slavic cheekbones and straight nose, same height. Sometimes Lester got them mixed up, but if he saw them standing next to Lena, she was always the prettiest. Lena wasn't stupid.

One night, Lester was feeling a little needy, as in "I need a screw," and walked into Lena's bedroom. There in her bed were two Lenas. In the dark, he couldn't tell who was who, so he simply copulated with the first one he came across and then flopped down between them and went to sleep.

RealLena just glanced at the Tsar bouncing up and down on the other Lena, shrugged, and rolled over. That's when Lester found out that Lena's particular twist was that she liked making love to herself, which was the function of the alternative Lenas, which didn't bother him at all. After some thought, he could see the advantages and started visiting her room more often because he never knew which Lena he would find in there.

Adem

When Caddy first walked into the old outhouse and woke him up, Adem was asleep. Which was not unusual. He had been asleep for well over fifty years, and he was oversleeping anyway.

He hadn't seen or heard a lord on his ground for over 3,500 years, and yet here one was, a woman of great power, pushing a bicycle into the outhouse, huffing and puffing from the exertion because, for some reason, she didn't use her abilities to help her.

Maybe she was being cautious about attracting orcs, so that was wise. Adem couldn't have been more astonished than if he were a human watching magic for the first time. Oh, he knew there were lords around, but not *here*. Not in his patch of Earth.

He could feel other lords so faintly they were like ghosts; their spirits were the lightest of breezes that touched his consciousness if he happened to be awake. They would brush against him as soft as butterflies and then immediately fade away to either hide or die. Mostly, they died.

But this lord-woman, she wasn't a soft wisp of air. She exploded into his silence with lively vigour that was as exhausting to Adem as it was welcome. She was *alive* – and she was quite cheerful about being alive. She was looking for a place to stay, not a place to hide, and oh, did he want her to stay with him.

When she went outside to look around and squat in the snow to pee, he looked over the kit she left behind, and with a little effort figured out her tent. Making a proper toilet would take a few hours, and he wouldn't work while she was in the outhouse, but that would be the next task. Without elves to keep the place clean and manage the slop buckets, which was his job if she was going to be tempted to stay. She wouldn't stay if she weren't comfortable, clean, and fed.

The lord came in, her green eyes glittering when she saw the tent up. Adem knew she was listening for him, but he was very quiet, deathly afraid he might frighten her off. Nonetheless, she wasn't afraid and didn't run away. Later that night, she thanked him for what he did and gave him the gift of a song. Adem was so happy he cried. She was content to stay, she *talked* to him, and she was *polite*! After that, he couldn't do enough for her.

He would do anything to keep her. Anything.

Her name was Lord Cadence Aeldor, and she talked to him every day. She called him House because Adem was mute, so he couldn't tell her his name, and by the time he figured out a way to communicate with her, he didn't bother. "House" was perfectly fine with him.

Adem was very old – well over ten thousand years old – but he could be off by a few thousand years or so. He slept a lot, and that makes one lose track of time. He was born a man-shaped lord just like all the others of that tribe. He was powerful but not attracted to women, and because of that, the elves didn't find much use for him despite his power. He couldn't help them with Scent production, and his ability wasn't anything they thought they could use for protection from marauding orcs and humans. So while he was a powerful Elemental, he wasn't fed and kept healthy by elves. He and the elf tribe lived in peace, but not together, much the way Neptune and the land elves lived.

His ability was to alter space, and one way he altered space was to diffuse into things, which took a lot of energy but wasn't really practical. He didn't become those things, but could live inside the empty spaces between the atoms of things like trees, boulders, or a kitchen chair. Some would say he could turn into a ghost and back again. He could diffuse into a tree, for instance, and then what? He was a sentient spirit living inside a tree. Big deal. He wasn't much better at being a tree than the ones that grew from seed. Elves didn't need a tree with opinions, especially one that would drop a branch on their head if they tried to cut it down.

Before Gaia went insane, Adem roamed the world visiting friends who were bonded and had elves who fed and took care of them. In the parlance of the time, he was a rakefire, one who overstays their welcome, the person who lingers late and keeps the fire going even though their host wants them to leave. He was the original couch surfer – an entertaining and very talkative visitor who would hang around until his hosts started dropping broad hints about his next visit, and wouldn't Saul, who lived in the next town, really love to see you now, Adem? He would diffuse every now and then to keep up his skills and maintain his health as a lord. He slept a lot.

His other ability, which was also totally useless, was to make an in-between place, a bubble, outside of space and time. It sounded pretty powerful on the face of it, but who wanted to live in or even visit a sterile bubble? No one. Bubbles were a dead space, creepy and boring at the same time, and there was no point to them. They were, like his meaner acquaintances said about Adem, a waste of space.

About three thousand years ago, he had made a big bubble just to see if he still could. Its creation took so much energy that his starving body locked up, and an elf took pity on him and fed him. So Adem gave him the bubble to thank him. It was all he had to give. The elf ported to it, which was very brave of him, and returned quite happy with the trade, and after that, elves would feed him whenever he asked, so they must have found some value in it.

Diffusing, which was a way of leaving his present space and becoming part of another space, was a lot like morphing and had its dangers. His problem was that by diffusing into something like a rock, he was still sentient, but he lost his cellular memory and the ingredients that made up a mammalian being. Changing back from something inanimate to something that was sixty per cent water and forty per cent living cells, like a man, was very, very difficult, not to mention painful. He only did it once. So he diffused to living beings with no brains or souls, like plants. That didn't solve the elf problem, though. They didn't have any use for a lord who could integrate into a tree, even a big one.

When Gaia went insane, Adem was sleeping. He slept through the explosion that killed almost all the lords and through the first waves of chaos that followed. When he woke up, the world had changed and certainly not for the better. He was horrified. His friends were all dead, and the elves were being slaughtered as fast as the orcs and humans could wipe them out.

He immediately understood that if he went into his man form, he would be hunted down and killed just like his lord friends. He had no way of defending himself; his warrior skills were non-existent. Adem could sleep for five hundred years or so, but when he woke, who would feed him if the elves were exterminated? He would have to feed himself, and he didn't know how.

The elves, the ones who were left, could go into hibernation, but only for a few years. Then their egg sacs would rot, and they would die just like any untended egg in the wild. They couldn't go into the big bubble he had made because of *terrior*. *Terrior* had been their life, and now it was their death.

Watching them die – it was horrible and heart-rending. Adem couldn't do it. He couldn't stand still and watch them be killed one by one. They needed a place to hide to wait out this horror, this insane world.

Adem made a bubble deep in the earth at the very top layer of the asthenosphere where the elves could escape to and hide, outside of time and space, but still stay in their *terrior*. It took everything he had in him to do it. He told a few clans how to port there and to come back when they felt the call, and then he diffused into a being that could hide from the marauding orcs, feed itself from the very earth, and had the mass he would need to survive as a sentient being. He became a fungus.

Five hundred years later, he woke up and checked out the world. He had grown as he slept, as his starving fungal body fed deeply from the very ground he was sleeping in. His mycelium had spread over four square miles, and he weighed over 43 tons; it was a lot of mass and much too much organic matter to turn back into a man. As it was, he didn't see any elves at all and very few humans. The world of humans and orcs had gone to sleep with him, burning itself out in a blaze of chaos and hate, and now they were suffering from the hangover.

Adem heard a few lords' heartbeats, but so, so far away, and with his huge fungal bulk, there was no way to go find them if he could find them at all. So he went back to sleep, determined to go on a diet, and recalibrated his food intake. It left him grumpy, but really, his weight was out of control.

A thousand years later, he woke up again, and yet again, no elves. Upset, he listened hard and thought he could hear them deep underground, but no. No real evidence of any elves. He didn't realise they were asleep in his in-between bubble, waiting for a call. When he told his local clan to go to the bubble, he didn't know that they also went to the Safe Haven, to what they now called the bubble he had made so long ago. From there, they told all the clans left in the world where to hide. So Adem had inadvertently saved all the tribes, not just his nearby clan. But when he had told them to come up when they felt the call, he had meant that figuratively. However, elves being elves took him literally. He meant "when the urge strikes you," and they heard "when you (literally) hear someone calling for you." When he woke up the second time, they were still asleep, waiting for the cosmic alarm clock to ring.

This time, there were more humans about, and they seemed saner, but not enough for him to bother to stay awake. Since he was still too big, he went back to sleep. He had lost a little weight, though, so that was good.

In 1941, he woke again. Now there were humans all over the land his fungus body lived in. They ploughed the top layers of the earth and built houses and roads. There were wars, and their bombs made huge craters. They used chemicals on the earth to fertilise and chemicals to kill plants – and each other. Not that any of that bothered the fungus; it just worked around any disturbance. But while he was smaller now, he wasn't small enough to turn back into a man shape. But he was going in the right direction. He decided to wake up again in fifty years and hit the snooze button on his internal alarm clock.

When Caddy came by, he had overslept.

Adem was still much too big to turn back into a man, and a fungus can't talk, but it can inhabit wood and make itself into a hard enough mass that he could move and do things. He knew where man-made things were buried in the earth, and his fungal fingers could move them quite quickly to the ex-latrine he was living in. If he had let Caddy see him work, she would have seen a mass of toadstools and mushrooms exploding up from the ground, forming around whatever it was Adem was making, and then, within minutes, dying off and getting reabsorbed into the earth and leaving something behind she could use. He built an entire house for her that way.

Then, just a few days after she arrived, she woke up elves. If Adem thought she was a miracle before, now she was a god. When he saw his first elf, he cried all day.

He loved, loved, loved Caddy. Not in a sexual way – he didn't lean in that direction – but as a mother/sister/friend, she had no peer. When Kyrylo came along, he was ecstatic for her. Anything that made his Caddy happy made him happy.

He still couldn't talk, but he could move a wooden spoon around as a surrogate. It seemed friendlier and cleaner than a fungus, but he could have used anything organic that could hold a spore, really. Spoon could have just as easily been Chopstick or Ruler.

The diet was out the window because he needed the energy to do things, and he now had a way to talk to people that didn't need a man-like mouth. Besides, he really liked being useful and building things, and he didn't think he could do that as a man-lord. After being told for millennia he had no utility and was pretty much a waste of space, he was now important to a community, and his new family, his clan, loved him.

He might still be a fungus, but he was one very happy mushroom.

Sam and Conary

Sam and Conary, and Terrence, the elf trainer assigned to Conary, were hanging out in Sam's studio drinking beer and practising their abilities. Sam could move any kind of rock, but he had trouble with other substances. At first, he couldn't move anything at all, but after some encouragement from their elf trainers, he made a toothpick roll across a table. With that proof of concept, he buckled down and began rolling toothpicks, although he still thought it was a useless skill.

Conary, on the other hand, couldn't move diddly squat. Grains of sand? Feathers? Puffs of air? All stayed stubbornly in place. Like Alizah, he couldn't move anything. Unlike Alizah, he didn't have a compensating ability he could show off. It was very discouraging.

Done with practice, Sam returned to his carving and left Conary at the table, staring glumly at the pile of feathers. The only thing that made them move was his breath. Terrence, the elf trainer, decided to try another tack.

"I heard you worked for some pretty rough people at one time."

Conary looked up, wary. He didn't like to talk about those years.

"I had some difficult employers, that's true."

"Drug dealers, mafia types. Who was the worst? The Japanese or the Chinese?"

He thought about it. The nationality made no difference. Drug dealers were all sociopaths. If they cared about people, they wouldn't be drug dealers.

"The Chinese, probably. The Japanese Yakuza were tough, but to them, it was all just business. You could predict them. The Chinese weren't always so predictable."

"So were there orcs around, too? I guess there must be Chinese orcs like there are with every other human race."

"Probably. I didn't know about orcs then, of course, but looking back I could smell some –"

"Stinkers," interrupted Sam.

Terrence ignored him. "So did they do anything that really, really scared you?"

Conary laughed. "Fuck, yeah! All the time!"

"So, how did you handle it? Did you talk to them? Run away?"

"I found that if I just went super still and let them rant, they would eventually just walk away. I guess I just bored them to death."

A slow smile from Terrence, and he took a sip of his beer.

"Show me."

Nonplussed, Conary didn't know what to do. How do you show someone that you're boring? But, hey, he was game. It was better than trying to move feathers with his mind. So he sat down and imagined the time Crazy Joe had a meltdown over a missing shipment and threatened to cut off his ears and stuff them up his ass. He slowed his breathing and went to his calm place, inside. The room went quiet and a bit hazy, and like the time with Crazy Joe, Terrence seemed to recede into the distance. He could hear Sam tap-tapping on the stone, but –

Sam stopped carving, "Hey? Where'd he go?" He looked around. "Did you port him?"

Terrence grinned and put down his beer with a loud thump. "Come back, Conary!"

Conary woke up with a jerk. "Oh, sorry, I must have dozed off."

"You weren't there!" Sam was flabbergasted. One minute the man had been sitting there drinking his beer, and then the next minute he was not – and now he was back.

Terrence just kept grinning.

Jack

Jack was not quite sure how to go about this seduction thing. He hadn't done anything like this before. For 3,500 years, every twenty or thirty years or so, like clockwork, he'd spot a likely hen, bring her a piece of carrion, and ask her if she'd like to fuck. The hen would look at him, make a snap judgment on his ability to father and care for a nest of eggs, and say yes or no.

Almost always, it was yes because for a raven, he was pretty big and impressive. Since ravens didn't have penises, the mating act itself was not much more than a flutter and a smear and was over in five seconds. It was all very easy, and he didn't have to try too hard or look very far for companionship. All he had to do was make sure they weren't related.

Alizah was not a hen. She was not impressed by gifts of roadkill. She didn't give a flip about his fitness to tend to a nest, and while he was now slightly above average height for a human, he was skinny and fine-boned. Not exactly an impressive specimen in the hunk department.

She was, Jack thought, getting more open to the idea of sharing his bed, but it was slow going, and he was getting impatient. He would make some tentative move, a kiss on the cheek maybe, and she would laugh it off or move her head at the last minute and giggle, and that would be it. She never told him to get lost, she never got mad at the attention and often seemed to like it, but too big a move made her nervous. For the life of Jack, he couldn't figure out why. She gave all the signals that she loved him, and he was certainly bonded tight to her, but, but, but –

But what was really getting under Jack's skin was the subtle attention Sam was beginning to pay her. She didn't see it, or at least she acted like she didn't see it, but Jack certainly could. Vera hadn't been gone a month, but then she hadn't been a wife to him for a long, long time, and Sam had done his mourning for her years ago. He liked women, and in their tight circle, the only female lord available was Alizah. Any of the men could go and find a human lover; Conary and Sam had done it in the past. But humans died, and neither of them wanted to go through that again. The lords wanted their kind.

Sam would bring Alizah a Coke when they sat down for lunch as a group instead of waiting for the elf housekeepers to do it. He'd smile and joke with her, and that all seemed rather normal, but if she went across the room or stopped to chat with someone else, he watched her. He was getting a bit testy with Jack, too, and Jack knew what that meant. Jack was quite familiar with dominance posturing. You don't live 3,500 years in flocks of ravens without understanding dominance and pecking order.

So he needed to get Alizah firmly bedded and bonded before she started to understand what Sam was up to and before Jack walked up and punched Sam in the nose.

Kyrylo and Jack

Kyrylo was in the embassy in London, meeting with a couple of generals and defence contractors who were doing interesting things with micro-drones, when he received a text from Jack asking if he could meet him at the Trowel and Hammer in Lowestoft; he had a question and wanted to talk to K in person.

Jack wasn't a pub guy, so Kyrylo was pretty sure he didn't just want someone to share a beer with, so with a quick rearranging of his schedule, he told Jack he'd see him there at three.

At three in the afternoon on a damp and dreary autumn day, the pub was empty. Kyrylo walked in and ordered a lager at the bar, but it took a minute for him to see Jack in the dark, deserted pub, sitting in the back by the window, lost in thought.

"So, my friend, what's up?"

Jack sighed and then looked around to make sure no one could hear him, then sighed again.

"I need advice, and you're the best man I know to give it. Personal advice."

Kyrylo nodded, took a sip of his lager, and sat back, and in the back of his mind, he had the stock three phrases lined up – "Women are crazy sometimes; no figuring them out." "Have you talked to a doctor?" and the classic "Jack, it happens to all men every now and then."

"I need to know how to seduce a woman."

To Kyrylo's great credit, he didn't spit out his Adnam's Kobold all over the table. Instead, he took a thoughtful sip and gave the only answer he knew.

"I think you're asking the wrong guy. I don't have a clue."

"Well, you seduced Caddy! And you've been married before. And someone told me you had a couple of girlfriends years and years ago, so you have *some* practice at it." Jack looked glumly into his glass. "In Before Times, there were a couple of women lords I knew who weren't attached, and it was just a matter of asking them up front. They either would or wouldn't, depending on their mood. Mostly, they wouldn't. The only humans I messed with were barmaids who did it for a coin or two. Then, when I was a raven, it was the same thing with the hens. You just asked if they wanted fertile eggs, and they said yes or no, mostly yes. I never had to actually – you know – set out my stall."

It began to rain outside, and Kyrylo could hear it gently splashing on the window. No one bothered to turn on the lights in the pub. He cleared his throat. "Well, I didn't actually seduce Caddy." He turned red, grateful for the gloom. "She seduced me. I was the one who didn't want to –"

Jack looked up, shocked.

"And Katya was more than willing to jump into bed with me. She was husband hunting."

"What do you mean you didn't want to?"

Kyrylo cleared his throat again. "I've deep scars all up and down my left side. I'm missing an eye and a finger. Katya said it was all very disgusting. I was with a couple of women, once each, and they found my body – unnerving. After that, I just gave up. I didn't have anything to do with women for thirty-seven years, until Caddy came along."

Jack looked at K intently, nodding. It had never occurred to him that confident, he-man Kyrylo had ever had a woman say no to him. Even Jack had never had a thirty-seven-year dry spell.

"Caddy gave me every hint that she was interested, and the more she smiled and batted her eyes, the more I avoided her even though I didn't want to. She thought it was her, that she was too old or ugly or something, but it was always me. I think near the end, she was getting fed up with me."

"Maybe I should be talking to her then."

Chuckling, Kyrylo agreed.

"So what happened? How did she get you to change your mind?"

"A bottle of wine, a picnic on a blanket on a hot day in absolute privacy. Totally relaxed. No elves, no humans, no nothing for miles around. We just, you know, started, and once we started we couldn't stop." Kyrylo smiled at Jack sympathetically. "Caddy gave me a chance. Several chances. That first time was a disaster, and, without going into details, my fault again. But by that evening, everything was great, and it's been great ever since."

He sipped his lager, thinking about that day.

"The original plan was to go to Odesa with a large group of people, but it ended up just the two of us. Neither of us intended to make the big leap there, but that's what happened. You need to find your own Odesa where you aren't competing with all the background clutter, and Alizah can focus on you. Get her relaxed and happy, and think less about what you want and a bit more about making her glad to be with you. Caddy wanted to go to Odesa and visit a music shop there. What would Alizah like to do?"

"I don't know, but I'll figure that out." Jack raised his glass. "Thanks!"

"You're welcome, although you really did come to the wrong person for advice on women. I'm hopeless."

Jack

Norma was checking over the monthly sales figures for The Rum Lot Bauble Shop and saw that there was another run on fairy decorations in the shop. For the life of her, she *did not* understand why humans loved the nasty little creatures, but they did, and while elves thought it was weird, they still sold them. Tons of them. She was deciding whether to increase the stock when Jack called.

"Hiya, Jack!"

"Hello, Norma." Then he paused so long Norma wondered if the line had gone dead.

"Norma, I've a question."

The elf nodded even though this was a voice call, and he couldn't see her. She figured he had a question; otherwise, he wouldn't be calling.

"When I was a raven, I would fly around London sometimes, and I noticed that humans lived on the tops of some of the tallest buildings. Their houses up there are called penthouses, I believe."

"Tis true, Jack, those are penthouses. I've seen them in movies, but of course I've never been in one. I don't go above the second floor. Makes me queasy. "

"Yes. Well. I want to know if you can rent one or if there are hotels that have penthouses. I want to use one for a couple of days during the next thunderstorm. As high as can be found."

"What do you plan to do in a penthouse during a thunderstorm? Fly a kite?"

The line went silent again, and Norma shook the phone. Maybe it had a fault or something.

"I thought Alizah might like it."

"Oh, I don't thin – " Norma snapped her mouth shut. The penny dropped. Glory be! Jack was going to try to get busy with Alizah.

"Ohhhhh – Yes, I think that she probably would." And now Norma was all business. "Jack, you just let me handle this. I'll set it all up." She started tapping on her tablet. "The tallest building is the Shard, and there are penthouses on the top floors, so let me do some digging. So you and Alizah would like to do a bit of storm watching, have a nice dinner, maybe? That sort of thing?"

Jack sounded relieved. Yes, he would like to do some storm watching, and dinner would be good if it could be arranged.

"You leave it with me. Not a problem." And Norma hung up the phone gently. Jack didn't see her fist pump and do the happy elf dance in her chair.

Luke

Luke loved being a Ranger. He loved the specialness of it, the rocking uniform, the camaraderie, the constantly changing and challenging lessons. He was never bored, and every day he knew this was where he was meant to be.

He even loved working out with the Warrior elves at Fen Park every morning. Unlike Wendell, who started his time as a Ranger out of shape and ignorant of soldiering, Luke came into the program several steps ahead of his friend. He had served in the Ukrainian Border Guard for two years and was an accomplished drone operator, so even that light military experience was miles ahead of what Wendell had. At least he knew how to put on a uniform and salute. He was also a founding employee of Kyrylo's RumLot Security Service. One of his first assignments, which he screwed up, was tailing Kyrylo and Caddie on their holiday to Odesa. He had been part of the security detail in New York and had acquitted himself very well.

But very short guys do get picked on, and Luke was only 157cm when the average male Ukrainian was a good 20cm taller. Caddy didn't know it, but her shy, sweet Luke was pugnacious. He had been in a lot of fights when he was a kid, and while gymnastics was fun, judo won battles.

So he walked into Ranger training already in good physical shape, along with some history that the Warrior elves respected, and it helped that from the beginning, they had to sweat a bit to beat him up. Oh, they still ground him to a pulp, but he made them work at it.

He loved living in Lowestoft. No one minded that he had a heavy Ukrainian accent. And Lowestoft teemed with elves! There were elves everywhere, working and living openly. They didn't stay hidden from orc incursions like they did in the border areas of Ukraine.

He thought the women elves were beautiful, every last one of them, and there was one who worked the front counter of The Rum Lot shop who had a sharp twinkle to her eye that only made her prettier. She was very tall for an elf, blonde, and built in a way that would make a healthy man sweat if he looked too long, so Luke didn't. She was an elf, and they didn't have anything to do with humans. Period.

About once or twice a week, he would go to the shop, which was directly across from his assigned flat on London Road South and have classes in the big conference room in the back. Since it was just across the street, there was no need to bother an elf to port him there, so he would go behind the sales counter and on through the service door hidden in the back stockroom.

He would wave and say hi as he passed by, and she would smile and say hi back, and that was it for a long time. Then one day the rain just poured down, and he didn't bother with an umbrella for a mere 15-metre dash. When he ran in, soaked to the skin, she fussed at him for dripping on her floor. So the next time he came in, he brought her a doughnut from the bakery, and soon they were having short conversations about the weather and how busy the shop was as he passed through. Her name was Sian.

Then came the day he walked in, and she was kneeling on the desk, the computer screen turned around as she tried to replace one of the wires that had gotten loose. Luke bent down and looked under the terminal and found the correct opening. As he plugged it in, he looked at her, and, dear God, he looked right down her costume's shirt. She was dressed in one of those faux Oktoberfest-y, Christmas-y elfy things, and from his angle, he could tell she didn't bother with a bra. He looked up and saw that she knew he was looking, and Luke turned the same colour as the red in her striped elf stockings. He flipped the terminal back and ran off as fast as his legs would carry him. Sian laughed and laughed.

After that, Sian became a bit flirtier, and Luke got a bit friendlier, and then Tony noticed what was going on. He took Sian aside and told her to knock it off, that it wasn't fair to the human to lead him on. Then he privately told Luke to knock it off, that it wasn't fair to the elf to lead her on, and that cooled things down for a while.

Luke walked in for his Wednesday lesson, and at the counter, Sian sat putting price tags on little resin fairies.

"I have no idea why you humans like these things. What's the attraction?" She held up the little winged figure, puzzled.

"Oh, I don't know. There's no accounting for taste, I guess. Humans think they're pretty the way elves are considered pretty. I know several human women who have fairies tattooed on them, on their legs and arms."

Sian sniffed. "I'd rather have an orc tattooed on my ass than have a fairy tattooed on my leg. Really."

Luke howled with laughter. He couldn't imagine the beautiful Sian with an orc tattooed on her butt. Well, he could, which was one reason it struck him as so funny. Tony popped out and frowned, and Luke went on to his class, wiping his eyes.

That was the last time he saw Sian. When he walked in the next Friday, a much more matronly woman was behind the counter.

Jack and Alizah

The storm promised to be a very bad one, or if you were a weather watcher, a very good one. It was going to barrel up from the south, and the worst winds could hit up to 70 mph. Everyone was urged to stay off the roads and hunker down at home. It was perfect.

Norma booked the Shard penthouse for three days during the storm. Jack and Alizah would be ported to the lobby and simply had to take the elevator to the top. Everything was ready. All Jack had to do was get Alizah to agree to go.

Alizah was sitting in the Breakfast Room watching the Met Office reports when Jack came in, and since no one was around, he gave her a kiss on the cheek, which earned him a smile. He whispered, "I have a surprise for you."

She spun around. "OOohhh. A surprise! What is it?"

"If I tell you it won't be a surprise. I'm going to take you out, and we're going to have a little fun. Go put something nice on; we can't do this in work clothes."

A black cloud crossed her face. "Is it posh? Are we going to a function?"

Jack smiled. "Functions aren't fun! But I don't want to look like RumLot Security. I want to blend in so no one notices us. You'll see." He leaned down to whisper again. "Trust me."

And so, of course, Alizah did what he wanted and went to her bedroom to find something "nice". One of the housekeepers brought her a very pretty slip of a dress made out of heavy silk, and she thought, "I look dead sexy in this!" And that lifted her mood considerably. When she went back to the Breakfast Room, Jack was already dressed in a white shirt and tie and a proper posh suit.

"You look beautiful. You really do." He admired her from all angles, making Alizah giggle.

Then, before she could ask any questions or even tell him how nice he looked, Jack had them ported to the lobby of the Shard, where the Shangri-La hotel had its reception area. The lobby was rather busy, and the snap of the port startled a few of the guests standing by the marble counter, and Alizah could see why he wanted her to dress up a bit. She would have felt out of place in her everyday flying gear with all the snooty people.

Everyone – workers and guests – stared at the two lords. "Blending in" was not an option. The porting wasn't hidden at all, and Jack's lord's ears were unmistakable, but Jack wasn't bothered. He knew at least two of the milling guests were undercover RumLot Security, so there wasn't any chance of a random orc getting snotty with them. He walked confidently to the desk to get the key code to the penthouse. The nice lady behind the desk was very efficient and helpful, and her hands only shook a little as she completed the reservation paperwork. The only hesitation came when she asked him his last name. Jack just raised an eyebrow and smiled. "I don't have a last name. I'm Lord Jack, and that's about it." Alizah worried that the lady would give Jack a hard time, but she just smiled back and handed Jack the key card.

"What are we going, Jack? Is the surprise a party?"

He didn't say anything, only smiled and winked. Then he took her hand and led her to the elevator and pressed a button. They shot up forty floors, changed elevators, then shot up another thirty floors to the top.

Then Jack grinned, and it was a mischievous grin. "Are you ready?" He opened a door to a small lobby, and through the lobby, Alizah could see a magnificent room with two-story-tall windows overlooking sprawling, sparkling London. In the distance, they could see the thunderclouds boiling up for a massive storm.

Alizah ran to the window – actually she flew to the window – drawn by the view and hypnotised by the raging storm. "Oh, Jack, it's gorgeous! Look at it!" She floated in the window, mesmerised by the storm, and then she looked down at Jack. "Is this the surprise? Are you showing me the storm?"

He nodded. "We can stay as long as we want. I thought you would like to see the storm roll through, and we could just sit and watch it and have some lunch." He pointed to a table set out with a cold buffet, salads, and cakes. "Just the two of us, no elves, no waiters, or anyone to worry about."

She looked back at the storm, and then back down to Jack, and suddenly dropped down and gave him a passionate kiss on the mouth, something she had never done before. Startled, but not so startled he forgot to kiss back, when Jack came up for air, he grinned at her.

"I'm glad you like it!"

"This is the nicest thing anyone has ever done for me!" She floated up against him and kissed him again, only with more thought. Thunder rumbled in the distance.

Pulling her in tight against his body, Jack's hands roamed all over her, and the silk of her dress felt like she had on nothing at all. Alizah looked up, and she saw his eyes glow. That created a heat in the pit of her stomach that she wasn't expecting. A very nice heat.

It started to rain, and the room suddenly darkened as the first thundercloud rolled over the Shard.

The heady, narcotic Jack perfume made her dizzy. Alizah's breathing became ragged.

Jack picked her up, and she was sure he was going to take her to a bedroom, but he didn't. He took her out to a balcony, and as soon as he opened the door, the rain and a furious wind lashed down on them and made Alizah scream; she loved it.

The wind whipped at them, and if Jack hadn't held on to her so firmly, Alizah would have surely blown away. But she felt the steely strength in his arms, and that strength meant safety, security, and for Alizah, pure, unadulterated, unfiltered lust. Her mouth found his, and as it did, he shoved her against the balcony rail and took her right there in a driving gale, teetering dangerously seventy stories above London, and she climaxed so hard and fast she thought she was going to split in two.

When he was done, he brought her back to him, holding her tight against the wind in a sheltered corner of the balcony. She could feel the racing thump of his heart against her cheek, and his chest heaved as his body demanded oxygen. Her lungs were screaming for air, she was soaked to the skin in freezing sheets of rain, and her entire body shuddered and shook. Alizâh felt wonderful.

"Jack?"

"Mmmm –" He nuzzled in her hair.

"Do you think –"

"Yes, let's go in now." And he kissed her ear.

"No, do you think –"

"I asked them to put out sausage rolls for you –"

"Jack! Do you think we can do this again?"

Jack laughed. "Give me a half hour, love."

Jack was quite smug as he lay with Alizâh in the huge penthouse bed, playing with her curly hair. She was asleep. This seduction business, he thought, wasn't that hard if you put some thought into it.

When he got back to the house, he would buy Kyrylo a box of cigars and tell him that he and Alizâh had found their Odesa.

Lord Cadence and the Rangers

The email was very polite, but the contents were not. Caddy looked at the clock. It was five in the morning, and she was in Ukraine, which put her two hours ahead of Lowestoft. She was always up at the crack of dawn, much to everyone's dismay, when she was on a tear about something. And today she was definitely on a tear. She was furious.

First, a call to Victor. She wanted Wendell, Luke, and Tuân in the conference room in full uniform in half an hour. She would speak to them. Yes, she knew it was their day off. Half an hour.

In exactly half an hour, the men were in the conference room in the Rum Lot back offices, in full uniform, having been none-so-gently jerked out of bed by Victor and his senior elves. All three looked pretty rough around the edges. Tuân was particularly greenish.

Lord Cadence Aeldor appeared on the screen, her hot eyes brightly glowing and her face as cold as ice.

"Gentlemen, why are you sitting?"

The three jumped up so fast that one of their chairs fell back. They faced her the way they were supposed to, at parade rest, eyes forward.

"Gentlemen, I received an email this morning. It is a report of some activities your group engaged in last night. The report says that the three Rangers went to Norwich and had a very good time in the strip clubs, where they got roaring drunk. And one, a Mr Luke, went out –" Here Caddy looked at her tablet again. " – and banged on the door of a tattoo parlour at two in the morning saying he wanted a tattoo of an orc on his ass."

Victor looked at the floor. The three Rangers blinked but were otherwise impassive. They were well-trained.

"Wisely, the tattoo parlour would not open for three visibly inebriated young men, and so a soldier elf from the Norwich clan rounded you three up and opened a port hole to get the group back to Lowestoft. It seems that one of you was very rude to him, saying that he would go back when he was good and ready. The elf had to shove him into the port, and the other two Rangers dragged him through."

Caddy looked up; if possible, she was even colder.

"Then, in the third chain of the port, the rude person somehow lagged behind the other two and threw up in Mrs Sandra of the Fenn clan's living room. She was *quite* upset. Finally, all three finished the port, which should have only taken about a minute and instead took over ten and made it back to their comfortable beds in Lowestoft, where they proceeded to pass out."

Tuân blurted, "Ms Ca – Lord Cadence – it was me who threw up. I'm reall –"

"Tuân, I have not asked you to speak."

"Yes, Ma'am"

"Now I am going to be perfectly clear, and I don't want to hear a word back from any of you. There is nothing for you to say.

"First, I am deeply, deeply disappointed in all three of you. I am embarrassed that I must apologise to various elves and Mrs Fenn in particular for your behaviour. I understand that young people have to let off steam, and I understand everyone makes mistakes, but I do not understand how you can let each other down like this.

"Wendell, you have been in Ranger training the longest and are the senior in this group. You *know* what an orc is. You have fought them. And yet you went out and exposed your two brothers to real danger. Tuân is a lord. He will attract orcs by his smell. No matter what he thinks, he is totally defenceless at this time. You know that. So when you got drunk, in a part of town and in a strip club where you know orcs hang out, you allowed yourself and your brothers to be a target, and targets don't get second chances in our world. Having fun is one thing, being a sloppy drunk is quite another. You showed a lack of self-discipline and forethought.

"Luke, you haven't been here long, but you are an experienced soldier and the oldest. I won't repeat what I just told Wendell, but hear me, every single word applies to you, too. I expected better of you. You have shown a lack of self-discipline that is very, very disappointing.

"Tuân, you are a lord. I realise this is a new concept for you, but you need to get this through your head right now. You have responsibilities to these men and to every elf who helps you. You are an orc magnet. They can smell you, and they will attack."

Caddy leaned forward, and her voice shook.

"Tuân, these men will die for you. But that means so little to you that you were willing to put their lives at risk so you could go on a little toot in a strip club. You did not look out for your brothers last night. You put them in danger, and if something happened to them, you could do *nothing* to save them. You have the danger of being a lord but NO abilities, and you won't have any abilities for decades. We lords live lives of great privilege and great responsibility. You showed no responsibility."

Tuân blinked. He wasn't going to cry in front of the guys, but oh, gods, he felt awful.

"To all three of you, this is my second part. I will *not* put up with *any* disrespect towards MY elves. None. I will kick all three of you out to the kerb if I ever hear of any of you giving any elf a hard time again. How much energy do you think it takes to bend space and time for *ten minutes* so they can port three drunken yahoos back home? Does a person who gives up part of their home in the middle of the night to be a train lobby for you drunken louts deserve to have barf all over their living room floor? They have kids living there!

"Porting is a privilege that none of you have earned. Elves do this for you, especially for you humans, out of the goodness of their hearts. That includes washing up after you, feeding you, making your beds, and doing your laundry. And cleaning up your vomit. I have half a mind to stop all of that, as you three don't appreciate the huge privilege it is to be associated with the Elf Nation. You can't even show common courtesy.

"I'm going to turn you three over to Victor, who will conduct any retraining as he sees fit. My part is done, and as far as I'm concerned, this incident is over.

"You are all still Rangers, but –" And Lord Cadence paused. "I will not receive another email like this again."

"Yes, Lord Cadence," they said in unison. The screen went dark.

Victor walked to the front of the room and glowered at the three Rangers, his hands on his hips. Wendell could almost see the steam rising from his shoulders.

"Fen Park. PT clothes. Ten minutes."

And that was just the start of the pain.

Kyrylo and Caddy

Kyrylo leaned against the door jam, eating a bowl of breakfast kasha and watching Caddy dress down the Rangers.

"Man, I hope you don't ever yell at me like that! I think they were all going to start crying."

Caddy turned to him and shrugged. It wasn't a pleasant part of the job, but it had to be done. It was over now.

"They needed to be taken down a peg or it would get out of hand. When new people come in, they will hear from Wendell and Luke what happens if they get loopy. They're good boys; they will take this lesson to heart.

"Now you tell me, K – you used to be a feckless young man – why on Earth would anyone get a picture of an orc tattooed on their ass? Why?"

"*Zaychik*, I don't know. Maybe he doesn't want to sit on a picture of his mom."

"Sometimes I don't understand men. "

The Rangers

Later that week, when the muscle pain from Victor's retraining was fading away and very early one misty morning, Wendell glanced up during hand-to-hand practise and saw Lord Cadence standing off to the side watching them. She bent over to say something to Victor. He knew better than to give her more than a glance and turned back to business. When he looked up again, she was gone.

Luke was demonstrating a judo move to Tuân, and Wendell walked over and told them to keep their eyes and ears open. Something was up.

Wendell wasn't too worried about any aftereffects of their Norwich spree, so if Ms Caddy was around, it wasn't because of that. She was tough, but she was fair, and if she was going to kick anyone out of Ranger training, she would have done it that day. It was a lesson learned.

A week after their memorable night out, everything was back to normal. The Rangers had completed – better to say endured – their deserved punishment and apologised profusely to every elf involved and a few extra. Mrs Fen was sent a huge bouquet and personal, hand-written apologies. They were teased unmercifully by the Warrior elves who thought the whole incident was hysterically funny, and every one of them shared their own story of getting stupid drunk and what they did and how they were punished. If anything, the Warrior elves liked the humans a bit better for screwing up. One morning, the Rangers jogged to morning formation, and all the soldiers stood up, turned their backs to the Rangers, dropped their trousers, and mooned them. On the ass of each of them was a (temporary) tattoo of an orc.

Morning PT ended, and instead of meeting everyone at the pub for their mid-morning meal and pint, the Rangers were told to get their orc-less asses home, clean up, and go to the conference room for a meeting with Lords Cadence and Kyrylo.

The lords, Victor, Rahim, and some of the elves from the tech department were sitting at the conference room table, drinking coffee and munching on a tray of sandwiches. Lord Cadence looked up when the Rangers walked in and smiled at each of them, and the relief on their faces was immediate. This was not furious Ice Queen Lord Cadence but Ms Caddy, their beloved boss. She was back to normal, too.

Kyrylo started. "Gentlemen, take your seats, have a sandwich, and I'll get started."

"So Lord Cadence and I have decided to send you three on a mission, and today we're starting the prep for it. One of the purposes of becoming a Ranger is to do independent special operation missions out of range of elf help. So now we're going to do one."

The three Rangers leaned forward, eyes laser-focused on Lord Kyrylo. Even Tuân put down his sandwich. This is what they were training for.

"When we were in New York, we met a woman who told us about an isolated lord living in the Banff Mountains. Since then, we've talked to this woman several times and have made extensive satellite recon of the area, and while we have generally narrowed down the area the lord might be living in, it's still a big, wild wilderness, and the lord is living deep underground and only surfaces occasionally.

"What we want is for the Ranger group to go in, find the lord, and make contact. This lord has been hiding and surviving for 3,500 years and is surely terrified of being found by humans and orcs. Her name is Lord Ratna. If you can convince her, at the least, to engage with us, that will be mission success. If you can convince her to leave her safe home and become a part of our lord clan, that would be a triumph.

Lord Cadence is pregnant, and we don't think it's wise for her to be running out mountain climbing and waking up elves in western Canada at this point. But if this mission is successful, we'll expand our foothold to North America and maybe go to Banff after the baby is born. If the lord can't be contacted or if she wants to stay where she is, maybe we can give her some elves to live with – if they are there at all."

He paused – and then he grinned. "So, men. A road trip! Are you up for it?"

And of course they were. Excited and fired up over the prospect of finding a lost lord, all three started peppering Kyrylo with questions, and he put his hand up. "We've been thinking about this for weeks now. Now the real work will start."

Then he and the other seniors methodically laid out the goals, tactics, training, and logistics of the mission. The meeting took all afternoon.

The Rangers

The Elf Nation was in the process of purchasing an embassy in Ottawa, and once that was done, there would be an official state visit there to open it and establish relations with the Canadian government. While no one on the lords' side had made any promises, in secret channels, the Canadians frequently mentioned their openness and desire for elves to be established there. They had no idea how the lords managed that, but there were rumours, and their intelligence networks had a very good idea that Lord Cadence was the person they needed to convince. Too many humans had been involved in waking up the elves to keep the process entirely secret anymore, no matter how strict the vows of silence.

It was late autumn, and winter came early to the Banff Mountains. So the actual mission date was set for spring with the hope that they would be successful before the autumn rolled around again. This gave the Rangers some months to train in tracking, mountaineering, and wilderness skills as well as cold weather survival in case they had to go up high or were trapped in a freak storm.

They studied the satellite photos and memorised every existing mapped trail and a few that only showed up by satellite. Training expanded to longer mountaineering practice exercises away from Lowestoft, first with day trips to Wales and Scotland, and then longer excursions to the Alps.

Tuân loved the Alps, which were as opposite to the steamy jungle deltas of Vietnam as they could be. He spent every waking minute free-climbing on the huge artificial rock wall the elves installed in Lowestoft, but that was nothing compared to the rush he got from hugging the side of real rock and feeling the grinding power of continental drift as it vibrated up from deep inside the Earth's core.

Kyrylo was forced to pull him aside and specifically order his step-great-grandson to use ropes and safety gear, and when Tuân baulked, he pointed out that if he didn't use the gear, his brother Rangers might not either. If they fell, they would die, and he had to lead by example. Put that way, Tuân readily agreed. No free-climbing in the wild, and he would get used to abseiling by the book and using all of the safety gear.

The Rangers had long talks with Martha, the Stoney Nakota woman who first spoke to Lords Cadence and Kyrylo. She told them every detail she could remember of the week she had spent with her father and Ratna. Most of the time, she had been inside Ratna's home, so she couldn't describe the entrance or the trail leading up to it. She did remember that the doorway was hidden deep inside a very narrow, doorway-width cleft in the wall of the mountain, but if you stood in the doorway and looked up, you could see a narrow slit of sky.

She remembered hiking home and seeing the pyramidal peak of a huge mountain in the distance. Later, in her school-issued Canadian History book, she saw a picture of it from a slightly different angle, and there it was called Mt. Forbes. The Stoney had no name for the Minihapa mountain that they shared with outsiders, so she used Mt. Forbes, too. It was easier.

The plan was for the Rangers to fly to Banff, stay with Martha for a couple of days, and RumLot Security would arrange a couple of local guides to get them started on their way. They would establish a base camp as close to where Martha saw Mt. Forbes as they could guess and spread out from there, methodically searching sectors of the mountains and hoping they would stumble on the lord, or better yet, she would come to them. Kyrylo was sure that once they started looking, she would know they were there. She didn't survive 3,500 years in those mountains without knowing what was going on with the humans around her.

Lester and Meecham

The Tsar Lester of Russia directed his ambassador to the US to make a new push to normalise relations between the US and Russia and explore the easing of sanctions. Hadn't enough time passed for that happy day to come? After all, the war with Ukraine was history, and Russia now had a new leader. Surely it was time for a fresh start.

Russia, the ambassadors and envoys said to whoever would listen, had suffered terribly as a result of the war (conveniently forgetting that they had started the bloody conflict in the first place). The long-suffering Russians lost almost ten per cent of their population due to war deaths and emigration, and lost Crimea (illegally annexed), parts of Ukraine (illegally occupied), Kaliningrad, and (illegally occupied) parts of Georgia. The Russian economy was in shambles, and the flirtation with a centralised Soviet style economy really didn't work out the way they hoped it would. It was time to move on and invite the West to re-enter the Russian World. All Russia wanted was to live in peace and harmony with everyone. Its days of wanting world domination were over.

President Meecham thought this was eminently sensible and so agreed to arrange a few exploratory meetings. At least, he thought to himself, I won't be meeting with damnable demons with pointy ears. When an aide mentioned that the Tsar was a Lord, too, Meecham replied it wasn't the same. For one thing, Tsar Lester had never used his power to kill anyone, and there were now verifiable instances where both Cadence and Kyrylo had used their power that way. Obviously, the warmonger wasn't the Russian.

There were still issues with the US's European allies, who still held bad feelings over Russia's destruction of an entire country on their doorstep and the attempted genocide of its people. Meecham wasn't ready to stand against the Europeans – yet. But his responsibility to US interests meant that he couldn't ignore the Russian overtures.

Tsar Lester was eager to meet with President Meecham in person, if only for a few minutes, so the US arranged a short, private, exploratory meeting in Dubai while the President was on his way to a state visit in Saudi Arabia.

Meecham thought it all went very well.

"The Tsar is charming! A truly wonderful, humble man who wants to bring Russia back to normalcy!" Meecham enthusiastically told his wife after the meeting. "I looked into his eyes and thought, here is a man I can do business with."

"If you bring Russia back into the world, that will cement your legacy. It would be as good as Nixon in China!" She was thrilled, too. Something about Russia always appealed to her. Maybe it was the romance.

Meecham leaned back in his chair and tented his fingers, well pleased. "Yes, it would, wouldn't it?"

Lester

During his visit with Meecham in Dubai, Lester heard an interesting piece of gossip. It seemed the President's wife had gotten violently ill when she met Lords Cadence and Kyrylo. Some of Meecham's staff wondered if the lords had cast a spell on her. The rumour led the Tsar to wonder if she was an orc.

So he spent an hour looking at dozens of photographs and videos of the FLOTUS posted on the internet and soon concluded that she was indeed an orc. She had the look and the walk, even if he couldn't tell from the photos if she had the purple cast to her eyes.

Maybe, Lester thought, President Meecham needed a little history lesson to learn about the natural affinity between orcs and humans. Maybe here was a person who would steer his country away from elf worship and who didn't want to have an infestation of imps. Lester would have to be careful how this was all phrased so that he didn't get lumped in with the bad lords, but it could be done if he could position himself as the one on the side of the Christian God. He'd walked this fine line before during the witch-burning years and had been pretty successful overall.

When Meecham was back home and not distracted by his travels, Lester would call him and have a chat. He was looking forward to it.

Caddy

Caddy	Alizah
Jack	Tuân
Neptune	House
Kyrylo	Sam
Conary	Ratna (if she exists)
One in the oven.	Lester (can't forget about him!)

Caddy looked over the list scribbled in the margins of her Fiendish Sudoku and took a sip of her tea. A puzzle in a puzzle.

In all the world, hidden among billions of humans and orcs, there were a dozen lords. There were hundreds of thousands of elves in Europe and every day elves recovered more of their kind. As they burst from the ground and shook off their 3,500-year sleep, they integrated into humankind. The little guys worked hard, with desperate efficiency, and they were constantly looking for more lords. They couldn't help it; they couldn't stop if they wanted to. Without lords, they would die.

They hadn't found any.

Lords found elves, not the other way around.

Now, twelve lords were roaming the Earth, protected and nurtured by a ring of grim, determined elves. Only three were adult women who could make the pheromones and the lord babies the elves so desperately needed. If Ratna really existed, and if she were still sane, maybe she'd join them. Caddy included her, anyway.

Lords were functionally extinct.

How was Caddy going to bring back Balance if she didn't have lords to weigh the scales?

Caddy put her hand on her belly; she could feel a roundness now. The baby was growing, and at her next doctor's visit, she'd have an ultrasound. If the baby was turned the right way, she and Kyrylo might learn its gender.

She didn't know what she wanted more, a boy or a girl. She didn't know what would terrify her more. All she knew was that one fertile female lord wasn't going to solve the elves' problems. Caddy wasn't an Eve.

Would a girl baby grow up with her choice of Sam, Neptune, or Lester as a bond-man? Conary shouldn't even be considered; he was her brother! Tuan wasn't much better – he was her nephew. Oh, it was physically possible, but they'd end up like the ancient Egyptians – inbred and dying. Out of the unbonded men they had now, Sam was the only real possibility.

If she and Kyrylo had a boy, there wouldn't be any unbonded female lords at all by the time he was old enough to go hunting one. He'd have to find a human to love and live with. Ratna would be bonded to one of their men inside of a year, Caddy knew that in her heart. The twin pull of hormones and loneliness would ensure that.

But a mate for her child was a future problem that would need to be solved twenty years down the road.

Lester, a lord himself, wanted to kill them all. The entire tribe of orcs wanted to kill them all. Both were leading easily swayed, easily wooed humans in their quest to kill them all.

If she didn't find more lords – and soon – Lester and his orcs would succeed.

They had to be out there, hiding, afraid, watching. Lester had told her himself that lords popped up regularly, and he murdered them. It was her job now to find them before he did.

They were out there. She knew it. She could feel it the way she could feel the elves under her feet when she went to an awakening.

Lords were out there; they had to be. Would the gods have allowed her to come this far just to slap down two complete tribes? Caddy didn't think so. That the gods were rooting for her didn't mean they'd make it easy.

She sighed and finished the last of her tea, and put the puzzle away.

Cadence Aeldor, The Queen of the Fairies, had work to do.

End of Book Three

Book 4

A Ventureous Fairy That Shall Seek

Continue the adventure!

This and all books in

The Return of the Tribes Series

are available for download on

Amazon Kindle
or
The Rum Lot Publishing

www.rumlot.com

E-Publishing, Hardback and Paperback versions of all
books are available on amazon.com

Donate to the Excelsior Trust

If you enjoyed this book (and we hope you did!), please consider a small donation to The Excelsior Trust, a registered charity that is dedicated to preserving heritage fishing boats, in particular The Excelsior, LT 472.   As part of the trust's mission to preserve Britain's maritime heritage they also subsidise unique training and sailing experiences for young people.

https://www.theexcelsiortrust.co.uk/

https://www.theexcelsiortrust.co.uk/donate

Registered Charity Number 285899